VIBEKE HIATT

# The Forgotten King

*For Sandy*

# Acknowledgement

To Alexis Sollami and Kelly Martinez, my earliest supporters and mentors. Your valuable feedback helped me to build this story.

To Deidre Logan and Vivien K. Wilk, my awesome beta readers. Thank you for bringing clarity and sense to my words (and Vivien in your non-native language!).

To Kyle T. Davis and Laura Detering for answering my unending questions.

To the online writing community for the support, insights, and good conversation.

To my children for sharing me with my stories.

To my husband, Brett, for providing constant encouragement, for taking on more than your fair share, and for being my partner every step of the journey.

And to God, who gave me this story and any talent I have to see it through.

# Chapter 1

A sudden difference shivered through the air. An unsettled and discordant current moved through it, though the wind didn't blow. The moment between stillness and action froze and stretched, as though the world had stopped. Helen stood still and looked around, unsure of what she was looking for. Her heart beat faster, stealing her breath. Thoughts crowded her mind. Disquiet gripped her like steel fists. She had the impression that someone else was in this clearing—someone who didn't belong there.

Large boulders and sparse clumps of trees littered the wide meadow. Anyone, large or small, could hide behind the boulders or in the trees without being visible. Fear ran beneath her skin at the thought of being caught. The hills around the meadow were covered with aspens, their white trunks like beacons and their leaves hanging like silent bells from the branches. If she could just make it to the hill, she could rely on the protection of the trees.

Since leaving home, the landscape had shown little variation. It was hard to tell where she was. Helen could only measure the distance traveled in days, as well as by those landmarks she could remember from journeying this way before. She hadn't been in this place since she was a child and she was farther from home than she had ever been alone. For the first time on this journey, she wished she knew there was a farmhouse or cottage just over the next hill. The feeling wouldn't escape her that the threat she had left behind in her city had followed her and was now not far away. Ahead of her, though, were the familiar, snow enveloped mountains—one feature she remembered well—just south of Camdor. She didn't have much farther to go.

Softly, the chilly wind began to blow, not unlike any other breeze that blew as winter passed and spring came to life. Only it wasn't quite normal. The unsettled feeling grew stronger. Helen focused her mind on listening, straining her mind to catch every sound. Her ears were now filled with the papery sound of fluttering leaves, a distant river running, birds and animals in the trees, the whistling of the wind. Nothing sounded out of place. Yet the uneasy feeling remained of unwanted eyes upon her.

A movement and the snapping of a twig startled her, and she spun to see a figure darting among a large cluster of rocks. She turned her body as she peered through the large gaps between the stones, slowly stepping backward. It was hard to tell if it was animal or human, where it had come from, and where it had gone. The late-afternoon sun cast unusual shadows. It made the rocks and trees look much larger than they were and almost alive. Helen started walking again, quickening her pace, focusing her attention much more than before, listening for the slightest sound.

She hadn't gone far before the soft sound of pebbles and cloth sliding against a rock, accompanied by the muffled crunching of dry leaves, forced her to stop again. She turned to see a man standing not twenty feet away, at the edge of the clearing, his appearance a sharp contrast with the natural landscape around him. His clothes were very fine—not like those of the farmers who lived in this part of the country—but they were sullied by travel, stained by leaves and grass and dirt. He stared at Helen, wearing a casual smile like it was a part of his attire. She wasn't sure if she should run or smile in return.

"Where are you going?" the man asked, walking toward her.

Helen hesitated. An odd, empty feeling sprouted inside of her, like a bubble in her chest. She couldn't understand why. His white smile, set into a handsome, sculpted, perfectly tanned face, invited her to trust him. Light-colored eyes opened wide to add to the invitation. It was only the dark, heavy feeling—which drifted off of him like a strange haze—that made her distrust him.

"Where are you going?" he repeated, the corners of his mouth twitching as he tried to adopt an air of friendliness.

"I'm just taking an afternoon walk," she answered, knowing as soon as she said it that her answer was too weak for anyone to believe. He looked her over, making her feel horribly vulnerable. She hoped that the shaking she felt in her bones was only on the inside.

"So far from any city or village?" he questioned.

"It's a very long afternoon walk," she shrugged.

He continued to stare with concerned eyes, but they didn't match the feeling he gave off. Helen tried to release the emptiness with her breath, but it wouldn't shift. "It's not safe to go through an empty land," he said in a cool tone. "You never know who you might meet. There's a path not far from here. I can take you to it. It would be safer to follow the path."

"I know where I'm going," Helen answered, clasping her hands together behind her back to hide how they shook. "This is the route I need to take."

There was a pause. The man stared at Helen and the more he stared, the more vulnerable she felt. His eyes were searching hers and she didn't like it. She took a chance and turned away, walking again, keeping her eyes and ears alert.

"Tell me," the man called after her, "what do you expect to find out here? Why is a girl like you traveling so far on her own?"

"I'm sorry," Helen replied over her shoulder, "but like you said, you never know who you might meet. Thank you for your offer, but I don't need help and I'd rather not answer any more questions."

She heard the man running up to her, but she tried not to visibly react, keeping her chin up and her pace steady. Helen's hand moved to the opening of her bag, where she could easily reach the small crossbow she had brought with her. Soon, he stood next to her and placed a hand on her shoulder. A jolt ran through her entire body, stopping her strides, as though all of the warmth and air were being sucked out of her.

"Listen," the man said with lightness in his voice, after a lengthy pause. "I have a house not far from here, and I have a carriage. I can take you wherever you need to go. It would be much safer."

Helen looked at the man, trying not to let him see how afraid she was. Over his shoulder, she saw a phantom-like movement again, in the trees. This man was not alone, she realized. Someone else was there, but she couldn't tell for certain how many more intruders were lurking just beyond the clearing.

"I must seem very impolite," the man continued. "I should have introduced myself. My name is Ian."

She smiled only with her lips and took a step back. "Thank you, Ian, but no," she told him, sure to put a hint of finality in her voice. It was becoming increasingly hard for her to mask her panic and think of a way to get herself out of this situation. "I know where I'm going, and I like the solitude. I feel safer on my own. Please, excuse me."

"There's nothing to be afraid of," he said softly, his words pulling on the bubble in her chest. "You can trust me."

The tone of his voice and the expression in his eyes caused the empty darkness inside of Helen to grow stronger. Her heart beat faster as she tried to fight it. His presence was like an intoxicating fume, a strange power that drained her of hope. She was beginning to believe that, even if she could move forward, she wouldn't want to. When Ian looked at her, her journey became a futile and distant dream, fading on the horizon of her memory. She felt the urge to sit down where she stood, to not continue walking toward the hills. In desperation, a faint glimmer of light inside her mind fought this urge—a light that was fading with each passing moment.

Ian let go of Helen's shoulder and took a couple of steps backward. Helen knew that she should try to walk away again, but she couldn't make her feet move. All she could do was stare at Ian and fight the conflicting ideas circulating in her head.

"Come with me, Helen," he said. "I'll take you where you need to go."

"I never told you my name," she found herself saying, and the sound of her own voice brought the warmth back into her body and the life back into her eyes. Fear gave way to hope as she considered Ian, a thought coming to her. "Have you ever heard the name 'Zaric'?" she asked, and Ian's face froze.

His reaction drew out a new confidence in Helen. It was a confidence that felt foreign to her, rising up to stand alongside her fear. Ideas filled her mind that were not her own. As though she followed directions whispered into her ear, she held out her hands. Her fingers tingled. Although it wasn't cold enough, a dark grey fog gathered in the meadow, spreading unnaturally outward and upward from where Ian and Helen stood. In only a few seconds, the fog filled the meadow, obscuring their vision. Frustration marred Ian's face and he lunged toward Helen.

Without hesitation, Helen turned and ran toward the trees, Ian's arms missing her by inches. She wasn't able to see more than a foot ahead and she hoped the same was true for Ian. The fog made it difficult to tell in which direction she was running and she had to rely on an instinct that came with this unfamiliar confidence, leading her like a rope. She heard indistinguishable, frantic shouting behind her, mingled with the sound of footsteps, but she forced herself to focus forward, willing herself to run faster. As long as she didn't trip over a rock or a log, she was sure she would be safe.

Once she reached the trees, the wall of fog ended, as though it were a boundary between the forest and the clearing. Helen continued to run between the trees, her lungs aching, her body straining against the gradual incline of the ground beneath her as she tried to avoid protruding roots and fallen branches. Within a few minutes, she reached a small leveling of the hill, where she could look down above the trees and survey the meadow. The fog was contained to the small area where she had stood. It still laid there in a dense sheet. Helen saw shadowy movement in the fog–two shapes–circling aimlessly. Taking a deep, staccatoed breath, she cast her eyes over the hills, wondering if there were more people hiding in the surrounding trees. After one more searching look into the fog, filled with uneasiness, she turned and continued to climb.

* * *

The longer he walked through the village, the more uncomfortable Neil grew. He walked with as much speed as possible without drawing too much attention to himself, knowing that most of the eyes in the village were already focused on him. It was like this whenever he came to this place, since his visits were rare. He wouldn't have come today if his blanket wasn't so threadbare. It was a miracle it had lasted the winter. After the day's necessary chores, with his mind in complete and not-so-quiet rebellion, he had gathered a couple of coins along with a dozen eggs and headed to the nearest shop in the village that would allow him to trade his goods for a good quilt. No one spoke to or even acknowledged Neil as they watched him walk past. He attempted to show indifference by not looking at them at all, although he kept a tight grip on his new quilt. He tried not to notice the whispers, but the more he tried to keep them out the more his ears heard. It annoyed him to hear one young woman say, "It's the recluse," before laughing quietly with the friend who stood next to her, thinking that her words were clever and original. His tension alleviated when he reached the edge of the village, but he tried not to let his posture show it. Away from it, he didn't worry so much that he had just given its inhabitants something different to talk about at dinner that night.

Neil crossed his field without haste, shoulders weighed down with prolonged apathy, as he wiped the sweat from his face with his sleeve. He looked forward to a good dinner and an evening rereading an old book. He swept his eyes over the small fields as he breathed in the landscape around him. The sun hung heavily in the west, where the wooded hills cast long shadows over the valley. In the bowl of the valley rested the village of Camdor—more comforting when seen from the isolated distance of his own farm. A slight shiver ran through him as he looked at the land, as though a breeze was blowing over his fields. When he looked at the grass, though, it sat motionless. Cautious and puzzled, he glanced around, then walked a little faster, deciding it must be an early spring chill.

Reaching the low gate blocking him from the path to his front door, he stopped again. The feeling that passed over him felt like it was inside of his body, not coming over the fields. It was an unfamiliar feeling and the thought came into his head that something was changing. He breathed in again and wondered if he should go to bed right after dinner, instead of going through the books. He decided he must be more exhausted than he realized. Still, he scanned his surroundings with careful attention, hoping to find a visible source of his uneasiness.

He was surprised now to see a figure—a woman—walking at a purposeful pace down the hill, her long cloak billowing as she walked. He wanted to think that she was making her way to the village, but no one ever came over this particular hill. There was a road farther down in the valley, emerging from a pass in the mountain, but there was no path over the hill. Neil hated to think that she was coming to his cottage. His first thought was to ignore her and go inside, but she would only come to the door and knock. Neil sighed and tapped out his impatience on the gate with his fingertips, waiting for the woman to come within hearing so that he could send her away. As he looked at her, the thoughts in his head swirled in a rush of words and images, though he couldn't quite see or hear what they were, which merely frustrated him more.

"I don't want wanderers here," he called to the woman once she was near enough. "Turn around and go back where you came from."

She stopped, about twenty feet away, relief spreading across her face. "But I'm not a wanderer, Neil," she called back. "I know exactly where I'm going."

# Chapter 2

eil stared at the woman standing before him. Thoughts swirled through his mind, asking him how she knew him, where he had seen her before, why she was here. The recognition came from the back of his mind and he heard himself say, "Helen."

It was her. Somewhere in the face of this young woman was the little girl who had meant so much to him as a boy. As his parents' closest friends, Helen's parents brought her to visit two or three times a year, staying for two weeks at a time. But the visits stopped without explanation—or at least none that he heard—more than seven years ago. He thought they would come when his grandfather was sick, but they didn't. He thought they would come when his parents fell ill, but they didn't. He thought they would come when his parents died and take him to live in their home. No one came.

And now, four years too late, stood a woman with the face of the girl and her mother and her father, all combined into one person. She had her father's water-drop nose, pointing to a full-lipped mouth, and her mother's green eyes, like the trees of a midday forest. Freckles dotted her ivory cheeks and nose. The daughter of a governor stood before him with her brown hair woven into a messy braid, her simple travel dress—a basic tan shift covered by a dark brown overdress, like a common villager—and hooded dark blue cloak streaked with dirt and dust. Gone were the fine fabrics she had always worn before. A leather strap crossed her body, ending in a nondescript travel bag at her hip. Studying her, conflicting emotions and thoughts fought for Neil's attention. He wondered what she was doing here, in this state. He wanted to tell her to go away, angry that she hadn't come years before. He felt compassion for her, especially when the sound of rustling leaves and the sight of a flock of blackbirds caused her to jump and tremble.

"What are you doing here?" he asked, in an attempt to mute his contradicting thoughts.

Helen opened her mouth to respond, but yet another sound from the woods stole her attention and she spun to search for its source. She gave Neil a shaky smile as she turned back around and asked, "May I come in?"

"Is there something wrong, Helen?"

"Let me come in and we can talk. It's been years since I saw you."

"I know." Neil kept his hand on the wooden gate, reluctant to open it. He hadn't decided yet what he wanted to do.

Helen pushed a lock of hair behind her ear, her fingers trembling. For a fraction of a second, Neil saw a ten-year-old girl, begging his grandfather to tell her scary stories, then sleeping with the blanket over her head to protect her from the monsters. Without another thought, he swung open the gate, motioned her forward, and led the way to the cottage's front door.

With the door closed and bolted, Neil stared at Helen for half-a-minute, not sure what to say. His gaze embarrassed Helen. She felt that she offended him simply by being there. Pulling her eyes away from his gaze, she glanced around the once-familiar cottage. The table where the family once ate, two chairs next to the fireplace—which also served as the cooking fire. A shelf for pots, pans, plates, and utensils. The ladder leading to the loft where Neil slept as a child—and Helen and her parents during their visits. The bed in the corner beneath the loft where his grandfather had slept. The door leading to the only other room—the bedroom Neil's parents had shared. Nothing had changed. It was all as she remembered it.

"Are you hungry?" Neil asked. "What have you eaten since leaving home?"

"Bread," she answered with a sigh. "Bread and water. I had some cheese, but it ran out a week ago."

"Your parents aren't with you?"

A pang pinched Helen's heart. "No," she answered with no desire to elaborate.

Neil nodded, then set about preparing a meal, cutting up vegetables and dropping them in a pot. Helen crossed to the chairs by the fire, closing the curtains over the window as she passed. Settling into a chair, she let its softness envelope her, resting her head as she watched Neil prepare the fire. The boy she once knew had changed more than she imagined he would. His round face had become squared at the jawline, clean-shaven from ears to chin. Brown hair swept just over the tops of his ears—the same shade as his eyes. The corners of his mouth turned up in a perpetual smirk. His familiar olive skin was weathered by too much time outdoors at the height of many summers.

In an automatic motion, Helen's hand reached for a small necklace she kept beneath the neckline of her dress, rolling it between her thumb and forefinger, comforted by the feel of its intricately-carved silver.

A sadness filled the cottage—the sadness of a place that had once witnessed so much life, but now knew only loneliness. Helen half-expected Neil's mother to burst into the room and pull her into a warm embrace. Knowing that it wouldn't happen made the expectation more painful.

"I was broken when I heard about your parents," Helen said, her gaze fixed on the closed bedroom door. She hoped that the words would ease the ache in her heart. No reprieve came.

Neil said nothing.

Helen tried to swallow the growing lump in her throat. "My parents wanted to come for you—"

"Then why didn't they?" Neil snapped. Helen flinched and held her breath. Tension hung in the air like an invisible fog. Setting down the knife he was using, Neil held the edge of the table, shaking his head. When he spoke again, his tone was calmer and more measured. "I waited for you, after I wrote the letters and sent them off with the courier. I knew how long it would take him to ride there and back. I counted the days. I thought your parents would come and take me to Veren. Or at least send someone to get me."

"They would have returned with the courier if they could have come," Helen answered, trying to suppress the irritation she felt, wanting to protect her parents. "At least they wrote to you. I know they did."

"I never got any letters."

"That doesn't mean they didn't send them." Realizing she was starting to argue, Helen decided to change her approach. "What do you know about the political situation in Camdor?"

Neil laughed without mirth, confused at the turn of the conversation. "I don't care much about the governor or the political situation he's created. We haven't seen him in years because he's set himself up comfortably in a fortified residence far from all the towns and villages. His tax collectors come once every season, take half of what we have 'for the good of the region,' and we never see the goods or money again. I live alone and have what I need, so it makes no difference to me."

"And the rest of the people of the village?"

Neil shrugged.

"Five years ago," Helen went on, "my father went to a meeting with the governors of most of the land's regions. They were unhappy with the division of the lands. They wanted to renegotiate borders, but everyone felt that he had too little and no one was willing to give up the smallest fraction to appease the rest. My father's was the only voice of reason. Being the man he is, he tried to settle the argument, but all he managed to do was draw more attention to Veren. His efforts were fruitless. The rest of the governors nullified every treaty binding the regions together."

"I've heard rumors of skirmishes between border cities," Neil put in.

"That's why we couldn't come for you. We would have had to pass through two other regions between Veren and Camdor. My father's status as a governor made no difference. Once outside of our own region, his position would not be recognized or acknowledged. Robbers, guards, bandits, scavengers… anyone could have captured us, putting not only our family but all of Veren's citizens in danger."

A retort rose in Neil's throat—an argument that a thirteen-year-old boy on his own was worth the risk—but he swallowed it down when he saw Helen brush at her eyes. The ten-year-old girl resurfaced.

Bringing the pot to the fire, he put the handle over the hook. With trepidation, he turned to Helen, took her hand in his, and pressed it. "I wanted to come myself," she said, quieter than before. "I planned it out in my mind. How I would leave the city at night and steal my way to Camdor. But the way would have been more dangerous for a thirteen-year-old girl on her own than for a governor without a treaty. A governor's daughter would demand a large ransom. Slave traders care nothing about status. So many things could have happened. Even at that age I understood that."

"Just as dangerous now for a seventeen-year-old by herself," Neil stated, sitting down in the chair opposite Helen. "Why would you risk it?"

Helen stared into the fire, but she didn't notice the flames. Instead, her vision filled with memories: her mother's panicked, grief-stricken face; the sound of soldiers marching through Veren's streets; her father being dragged away. She closed her eyes to hold back the tears.

"Do you remember the stories your grandfather used to tell us?" she asked, avoiding Neil's question.

"Which ones? He told so many. I still remember how the ghost stories scared you—the restless dead walking through the land at night."

"No, not those," Helen shuddered. "The real world is enough to scare me without adding ghosts, too. I mean the stories about Zaric."

"Zaric." Neil flinched. "I haven't heard that name in years. Now *you're* the one talking about ghosts. Why are you interested in those stories?"

"Did your grandfather write them down?"

Neil considered the question with a sigh. He went to the corner of the room where the simple bed stood and pulled a box out from underneath it. Shifting the books inside, he found the one he wanted and brought it to Helen. She held it between her hands like it was a holy relic, running her index finger over the edges of the cover and weighing it between her palms.

"They're just stories," Neil said dismissively. "There's no way to know which of Grandfather's stories were real and which were make believe, especially those he wrote at the end."

"Zaric is real," Helen said, lifting the cover and tracing the handwriting on the first page.

Neil chuckled and shook his head, plopping back down in his chair.

"He is," Helen snapped. "I know it. Your grandfather wasn't the only one who believed the stories. My parents did, your parents did, you and I did...."

"We were children. We believed everything. Why is it so important to you?"

Fear constricted Helen's throat as her mind brought up the image of her mother's face. She wasn't ready to tell Neil what she had left behind. "Is the food ready?" she asked instead, not lifting her eyes from the book.

Neil knelt by the fire, stirring the food in the pot, sneaking glances at Helen. Pulling a piece of paper from her pocket, she compared it to a page in the book.

"What did you find?" Neil asked.

"These maps," Helen answered, "the one my mother gave me to find you and the one in the book, they were made by the same person."

"It's not a secret that my grandfather traveled. He made maps, too."

"But it's the map that I need." She held the book out to him, holding her map against the page. "It's the continuation of the one my mother gave me. Don't you see?"

"See what? I don't know what you're looking for. All I see is a map of all of the land's regions. Did you only come for this book?"

"No," Helen contended, unable to keep the sharpness out of her tone, "I came for you."

Neil scoffed. It had been years since he expected anyone to include him in anything. "Why, Helen? You talk like I should understand, but I can't when you won't give me a direct answer to my questions. What is going on?"

"The stories, Neil. The stories are coming true."

A laugh escaped Neil's lips. "Sure, the stories might *resemble* reality, but that doesn't mean they're coming true."

"But I've seen it, Neil," Helen insisted, unable to hold back the stinging tears that leaked from the corners of her eyes.

Neil swallowed back his frustration as he looked at his old friend. She had seen something, experienced something, that he couldn't brush aside or ignore. "What's going on, Helen?" he pressed, softening his tone.

Helen thought for a minute, trying to decide how to put her swirling thoughts and memories into words. Out of habit, she again reached for her necklace.

"What is that?" Neil asked, nodding at the necklace.

"A gift," Helen answered with sadness in her voice. "From my mother." She took a deep breath and slowly released it. Thinking about her mother, she found the courage to begin her story. "Mered is real. I don't just believe that, I know it. A few weeks ago, an army came to Veren. We tried to fight them back, but we weren't prepared, or even completely united. They drove us back like we were nothing more than a swarm of insects. Many of our young men died."

Helen stopped, trying to swallow down the lump of memory and emotion forming in her throat. Neil didn't try to fill the pause. She went on, "They occupied our city in the name of Mered. My father was accused of conspiring against his fellow governors—an obvious lie that carried no weight—and was taken prisoner. When it was announced that my father would be taken to Mered's stronghold, my mother and the others who are loyal to him planned a revolt."

"It failed," Neil guessed, fear written on his face.

"I don't know. My mother sent me away before it took place."

"To find me?"

"To fulfill the prophecy. To find Zaric."

Heavy silence filled the air between them. Then, Neil smirked. "There is no prophecy," he said, "only a fairy tale."

Helen sighed and thumbed through the book in her lap, searching for the words she remembered. She stopped, went back a couple of pages, and read aloud, "'When Mered rises again, a young woman and young man will make their way through the Old Kingdom, following the Path of the Ancients to the remnants of Camelora and the faithful King Zaric.'"

"You're risking the lives of the people of your region based on the words of an old book?" Neil scoffed.

"My parents believe these words," Helen shot back. "So do I. So did your parents and grandfather."

"My parents and grandfather aren't here anymore. All of their beliefs did nothing to save them."

A chill passed between them, despite the steady flames of the fire. Neil bent down again to stir the food in the pot, his face set like ice. Without a word, he stood and went to the shelf, took down a couple of bowls and spoons, then went back to the fire. Even without words, his message to Helen was clear: any faith he once had in Zaric was gone and he refused to be moved by Helen's story.

Dishing out some food, Neil handed a bowl and spoon to Helen, then served himself. He settled back in his chair, eyes fixed on the hearth. They ate without speaking. With each spoonful, the tension dissipated bit by bit.

"The fact that Mered exists," Helen ventured when the atmosphere had cleared, "that supports the idea that Zaric is still alive, too. After all, they lived and fought each other hundreds of years ago."

"Mered could be a common name. Perhaps it's a coincidence."

"And the fact that he attacked a governor who believes in and supports Zaric, is that a coincidence, too? What about the man I met on my way here, just two days ago?"

"What man?" Neil snapped, obvious concern tinting his words.

"The man who gave off a dark feeling and knew my name."

"Could he have followed you from Veren?"

"And waited three weeks to approach me?"

"Why would you travel all this way alone, Helen? He could have killed you in your sleep or abducted you or—"

"I had no other choice, Neil. More than one person would never have been able to slip out of Veren without being caught. I needed to make my way to you, and then to Zaric. Mered has returned and Zaric is the only one who can stop him."

"That's the worst part of it all, that you could have died for a fairy tale!"

Helen sat back in her chair, stunned. Their conversation had turned into an argument without her realizing it. She stopped herself before responding with a biting remark. In the lonely days since leaving Veren, she had played their conversation out in her mind, but in none of the various iterations had she imagined this. She felt stupid for not considering how hurt, angry, and bitter Neil might have become.

"I didn't come here to fight you," she said, measuring her words before saying them. "I came because I need your help. Not a day has gone by when I haven't thought of you. Through the years of not seeing you, I still thought of you as my best friend."

"I don't know how I can help you," Neil responded, calming himself down. "I can give you a place to stay while we wait for news from Veren."

"There is something else you can do for me: you can go with me. Help me find Zaric and Camelora."

Neil laughed and shook his head.

"No, listen to me," Helen pleaded, dropping to her knees before his chair, her bowl clattering to the floor as she took his hand between hers. "What do you have to lose? Help me to follow the course on the map. If it really is a fairy tale and we find nothing at the end, we can come back. You can go back to living as you do now. It isn't going to hurt you to try."

Silence fell. The only sound was the crackling of the fire. Neil's eyes were fixed on the flames while Helen's were fixed on him. He took a deep breath and said as he exhaled, "No, Helen. I'm not going to risk my life chasing a myth. I know I can't force you to listen, but I'm begging you not to go, either."

"I need to see this through," Helen said, gulping back her disappointment, her resolve like iron. "The only hope for my parents and my city is to find Zaric. Only he can stop Mered. Please, Neil, come with me."

"Ask for anything else and I will give it to you."

Their eyes locked, each one determined not to give an inch of ground, their strong wills warring in the quiet. Helen tried not to show the panic she felt, wanting to respect Neil's choice, hoping he would change his mind without her saying another word. The prophecy ran through her head, along with the scenes her imagination had composed to accompany it. She knew she couldn't—and wasn't meant to—do this without Neil.

"Can I take the book?" she asked, finally relenting. "And stay here tonight. Sleep in a real bed. Eat good food."

"You can stay as long as you want," Neil answered, knowing it was what his parents would do for her. "But, Helen, please, don't do this. You owe it to your parents to survive."

"What I owe to my parents—and what you owe to yours—is to fight for the cause they believe in. I owe it to them to find Zaric."

This was the last effort she could make, but Neil sat unmoved. With a sigh, Helen got to her feet and picked up her bowl from where it fell. Setting it on the table, she said, "I really am tired. Can I sleep in the loft?"

"No, you can have my parents' room. It's what they would have wanted. And you can take the book. I have no use for it."

Helen nodded once, lacking the energy to argue anymore. She picked up her bag and the book, wished Neil a good night, then went into the cottage's second room and closed the door. Neil stayed in his chair, staring at the door long after it had closed, resolve and guilt fighting for dominance in his mind. He knew that he was right, that Helen's belief in the stories would only end in disappointment.

So why did the guilt tug so strongly on his heart?

# Chapter 3

As night faded to dawn, Neil sat next to the window, a candle burning on the table. He stared out through a narrow part in the curtains at the waning moonlit sky, patched with iridescent clouds, edged in yellow and white. After a fitful night and very little sleep, he had decided that there wasn't much use in trying to rest. He replayed everything that had happened the night before—Helen's sudden appearance, the gamut of emotions it awoke inside of him, the stories she told, her plan to find the long-forgotten king. His mind drifted to his parents and their avid belief in all of the stories his grandfather told. He could picture their faces beaming, as they spoke in excited whispers when they thought Neil wasn't listening. As a child, he had believed because they believed.

But when he was twelve, Neil's grandfather went away for a few months and came back feverishly ill. He came home to be treated by Neil's mother, his face pale and sweaty and his eyes darting as though they couldn't be controlled. He died within days. For weeks Neil escaped to the woods every morning before his parents awoke, closing his eyes and wishing for Zaric to come and bring his grandfather back to life. One of the legends told about a man who died and came back. Neil knew his grandfather was just the sort of man who deserved this. His grandfather often spoke about Zaric as though he knew him, as though they had always been close friends. How could Zaric not come to the aid of his old friend? When Zaric didn't come, Neil wondered if he should be angry with the king, or simply stop believing that he existed. In the end, he chose to do both.

A couple of years after his grandfather's death, Neil's parents fell ill in the same unexplainable way. Part of him waited for Zaric to come, while the other saw it as a reason not to place faith in the man. In his mind, Zaric had become nothing more than a man whose accomplishments turned him into a legend. To Neil, the kingdom of Camelora was a place that had died years before, along with Zaric. If by chance he was still alive, he believed Zaric was living very happily in exile, and that he had no need for Neil, or Helen, or anyone else in this part of the kingdom.

Neil's parents died within two days of each other. The funeral in the village was small. At first, it hurt Neil, but he soon saw it as a good excuse to keep his distance from the people of the community. He didn't feel obligated to show friendship toward them, allowing him to live as though he had no need for anyone besides himself, centering his life around his cottage and his fields, only going into the village when he needed to sell his crops at the market or when he needed something he couldn't produce himself. No one thought much of him. He lived without interruption. And although he lived a life of indifference at best, at least he didn't have to live with any new pain. A couple of years ago he had thought of running away and never coming back, but there was security in his cottage and fields, knowing where he belonged.

Although his eyes were fixed on the woods as he wandered through his memories, it took some time for Neil to realize he was seeing movement in the trees. Startled, he peered out. In the distance, he thought he saw figures weaving through the trunks and branches. An uneasy vibration filled him from his toes to the top of his head and he got to his feet. The villagers went into the woods only when traveling to trade with other villages, and then only when they were desperate.

They never went into the woods near Neil's farm. Remembering the anxiety in Helen's face when she had heard noises the evening before, Neil rushed to the door to check that it was bolted, but stopped himself halfway there. Of course it was locked. He had locked it before going to bed, just as he did every night.

Neil walked to the table and blew out the candle, hoping to see better without its interference—as well as to avoid being seen. The blue-tinged moonlight mingled with the rising morning glow cast him into shadow. From this place in the middle of the room, he looked out again at the trees.

His breath caught in his throat. He dropped to his knees and knelt on the floor, trying to get a better look while not being seen. Standing at the edge of the trees, illuminated by the pale light, stood a man, staring at the cottage. He appeared ghostly in this light, standing very still, with his arms folded. It was impossible for Neil to see anything about the man in great detail from this distance. His mind went back to Helen's story from the night before, to when she mentioned being approached by someone in the woods. Could this be the same man? Why was he so interested in Neil's cottage?

Neil looked around the room, wondering what would happen if the man outside were to suddenly burst through the door. Even if he left through the back door, how far would he get before the man followed? The people of his own village would likely not protect him, and certainly wouldn't protect a stranger like Helen, if it meant endangering themselves. In fact, they would probably waste no time in giving them away.

Neil's mind then focused on Helen. If all she had told Neil was true, this man was probably looking for her. He didn't want to admit that she might be right, but he couldn't deny that she was terrified of this man and Neil didn't want her harmed in any way. He remembered her as the little girl who had once been so much a part of his life, who had shared his dreams and imaginings. She was stubborn enough to search for Zaric, whether Neil went with her or not, and she would be followed every mile, maybe even overtaken.

Neil had changed over the past few years, become a harder person. But Helen's appearance broke through that, awakening the boy he had once been—the boy who loved her like family. His parents and grandfather were no longer here to care for, but suddenly Helen was, and she was asking for his help. Someone needed him.

He crossed again to look out the window, just in time to see the man retreating into the trees. In half a second, Neil made up his mind. He looked around his little cottage, but tried not to think too much about it, or what it meant to him. Briefly, he looked out at what he could see of his land and farm and inhaled deeply, then turned his back to the window. In long strides, he crossed to the door of the bedroom where Helen slept and knocked, surprising himself with the sudden disturbance of the silence. For a few seconds, he heard nothing, but soon the sound of bare feet on the hard floor came through the door. Helen opened the door just wide enough to look at Neil with half-opened eyes.

"We need to leave, Helen," he stated in a casual tone. "I don't think we should lose any more time."

"We?" Helen asked, confused.

"And we'll lose even more time if you ask questions. Get your things together. I'll wait, but don't be too long."

Helen wanted to argue, but only shook her head and closed the door again. Neil moved around the cottage, filling a bag not much larger than Helen's with all of the things he thought would be necessary. He was sorry that he didn't have more food in the cottage for a long journey, but of what he did have, he took as much as he could carry, along with a change of clothes, a small knife, and a few other items. He stood and walked halfway across the room, then stopped again, casting his eyes toward the cot in the corner. For a few moments he thought, then went to the cot and knelt beside it. Hesitating, he reached underneath and pulled out a heavy sword in a worn leather sheath. His grandfather's sword, the one he had taken with him on all of his travels—the sword Neil had always imagined using. Now, he wasn't certain he wanted to. But if the dangers were as real as Helen said, it could be useful. Standing again, Neil fastened it around his waist, finishing just as Helen came out of the bedroom, fully dressed with her bag slung across her chest.

With an emotionless smile, Neil handed Helen a piece of bread, then opened the back door. After casting his eyes around the clearing ahead of them to see if anyone was there, he stepped aside to let Helen pass through the doorway, then followed close behind, closing and locking the door.

Once outside, Neil walked directly to a small enclosure, divided into two spaces. A cow stood in one and chicken coops occupied the other. Acting before he could think twice about it, Neil opened the pen to the cow and urged the animal out, then pointed it in the direction of the village. He then went to the coops, opening each one and removing the chickens, setting them free as well.

"We should have left an hour or two ago," Neil said. "It's getting too light. Someone might see us."

"And did you know you were coming with me an hour or two ago?" Helen asked astutely. Neil looked at her out of the corner of his eye, but said nothing. With caution, he took her hand and pulled her toward the trees, hoping he wasn't pulling her directly into the path of the strange man he had seen before.

They walked along the forest, about fifteen feet away from the treeline, hoping that the distance would give them enough time to see anyone coming out of the trees, but close enough to be protected by the shadows. Below them, the village was starting to awaken and move, its sounds drifting dully up to Helen and Neil. Helen looked down at it with curiosity, but Neil hardly seemed to notice the sounds. When his eyes strayed from looking straight ahead, it was either to glance at Helen or peer into the forest. Without comment, Helen followed his gaze each time, but saw nothing there. They had nearly reached the opposite edge of the village before either of them attempted to say anything.

"Yesterday," Neil said quietly, "you spoke of someone who approached you on your way to me. Who was it, Helen?"

"I think you already know what I'm going to say," she replied, "even if you don't believe they're real."

"I don't have to believe the stories to believe that you saw someone—someone very real, and maybe even someone dangerous. If there is someone following you—us—I think you should tell me."

Helen thought before answering Neil's question. Even before leaving Veren she knew that she could trust him, that her confidence in their friendship was strong enough, even after all the years that had passed. It had never occurred to her that *he* would doubt *her*, but his reluctance to accept what she had said made her hesitant to confide in him in return. She carefully sifted through the words she wanted to say, trying to find the ones that would answer his question without making herself vulnerable.

"I saw a man three days ago," she stated. "As I was walking through a clearing, he approached me. He called himself Ian. He spoke the right words, but something about him made me uncomfortable. I ran from him."

"Is that all? A man gave you a bad feeling and you believe he's one of Mered's men? He could have been a slave trader or an entitled nobleman hoping to lure you back to his home. Either of those would be just as dangerous as the enemy you imagine."

"I've been part of this longer than you have, Neil. Have you forgotten why I left home? Don't discredit what I feel just because you haven't felt it yourself."

Helen said this with more bitterness than she intended and wished that she could erase the words as soon as they were out of her mouth. She tried to formulate a less accusing follow-up, but she could only imagine how everything she said would be taken the wrong way.

Neil remained silent for a minute or two, and when he spoke again, it was with less compassion than before. "There was a man outside my cottage this morning," he said, "and I felt more curious than uncomfortable."

"And you waited until now to tell me?"

"I wanted to be sure," Neil stated.

"It's hard to be sure of anything," she said, stopping. "Not until it's too late, in most cases."

Neil opened his mouth, but closed it again with a shake of his head. His thoughts were broken by a loud commotion in the village below. For the first time, he looked down at it in confusion. They were too far away to see anything clearly, but the sound of people shouting rose up the hill. As Helen and Neil listened, bells started to ring all over the village. Certain she knew what it meant, yet not wanting to believe it, Helen raised her eyes to the opposite hill, toward Neil's farm. The spot where the cottage stood glowed with dancing orange flames, with smaller spots of orange scattered in the fields around it.

"We need to go," she said, unable to disguise or repress her fear. "We can't let them find us."

Following the line of Helen's gaze, Neil looked over. Once his mind accepted what his eyes saw, he began to walk toward the village. "My farm," he whispered in shock. "They've… All of the fields… And my cottage…"

Helen lunged forward and caught his arm. "Please," she pleaded. "It's not safe for us here."

"It was safe enough before!" he shouted, turning his wet eyes toward Helen, then back to the fire. "I was going to go back. My life is in that cottage. My life…"

Helen pulled on Neil, trying to drag him into the safety of the trees. At least, she thought it was safer than being out in the open, staring at the fire. If they didn't move, she was afraid it was only a matter of time before the people who started the blaze were able to track them.

"We need to move!" she exclaimed, tugging hard enough to pull Neil off-balance.

When he steadied himself, he caught Helen's gaze, his jaw clamped shut as anger flared in his eyes. Helen was afraid, but didn't let go. "They see you as just as much of a threat as they see me," she said, nodding toward the opposite hill. "Do you believe that now?"

Neil's eyes returned to the burning cottage and fields. He muttered something Helen couldn't hear and his body relaxed. This time when she pulled, he didn't resist.

# Chapter 4

They ran until the air burned their lungs and their legs tightened, threatening to drop them to the ground. Gradually, they slowed down before stopping in a small clearing. The noises from the village rang in their ears, but the actual sound had vanished not long after they descended the northern side of the hill. Helen tried to hide the new anxiety that flowed beneath her skin. When she left home, Helen wanted to believe that she would be able to stay ahead of Mered's men—that they wouldn't notice she had gone—and reach Camelora before there was any real danger. But the events of three days ago, and now those of today, proved that Mered's men were right alongside them, toying with them, and she couldn't imagine what their plans were. They weren't simply trying to stop Helen and Neil.

Helen stood panting in the middle of the clearing. She spun in a slow circle, peering into the woods, feeling that there were a thousand eyes focused on her. Then she looked at Neil, who leaned against a trunk, trying to take deep breaths, absently casting his eyes at the tops of the trees as the lines of a frown framed his mouth and eyes. Helen's guilt tugged at her heart and mind, but she didn't know what to say or do. The state Neil was in, she was bound to anger or irritate him if she chose the wrong words. So she waited for Neil to speak instead.

"What sort of men are you dealing with, Helen?" he finally asked, fear and incredulity tinting his voice.

"I'm not 'dealing with' anyone," Helen defended before she could stop herself. "I didn't ask for them to follow me. I didn't ask for them to take over my city."

"I won't be able to go back," Neil continued, his eyes darting around the clearing, unable to focus on any one object until they settled on Helen, flashing with anger. "I thought that I could take you to Camelora, and then go home, but now I can't go back. You led them to me."

"It's not my fault!" Helen shot, folding her arms and trying to look strong, though she felt so small.

"It's *all* your fault!" he returned, taking a few steps toward her, face twisted in rage. "Why didn't you just leave me alone? I hadn't heard from or seen you in years. You could have kept it that way."

They stood staring at each other as long moments passed. The longer they stood, the more the tension eased. His face softening, Neil pulled back from his attacking posture and Helen dropped her arms to her side. "I'm sorry, Neil," she stammered. "I never realized... I had no idea what they would do. Nothing they've done has been consistent or logical since I left home. I don't think they want us dead, at least. Otherwise, they would have stormed the cottage instead of waiting until after we had gone."

"Well, that's a grace, I guess."

Sounds of men shouting in the corridors of her father's house filled Helen's memory and she turned away from Neil as she tried to shut it out. She remembered her mother's face and wished that she could remember it with an expression of joy instead of such intense fear. Closing her eyes, Helen tried to picture Zaric instead. If she could just remember the kind face she had constructed over the years—the face of a wise, compassionate, and noble monarch—it might break her fears and replace them with hope.

"Do you believe now what I was telling you yesterday?" Helen asked after some time passed.

"I believe that we live in a very dangerous world," Neil stated. "There could be many reasons why those men want to hurt us, but I still can't believe it has anything to do with a few old fairy tales. Maybe they're bandits and you have something they want."

"Like what?"

"That necklace, perhaps?" Neil shrugged.

Helen reached up her hand and fiddled with the silver around her neck. "But to target me *and* you—"

"Maybe I didn't pay the tax collectors enough," Neil cut in. "The way the laws change, that's always possible. I told you that they tax us 'for the good of the region.' Well, the common people in the region never see a single coin from what's collected. The rumors say that the governor and his friends use the money for grand parties and lavish homes, while the people barely have enough food to survive. I wouldn't be surprised if the governor attacked me because one of his spies saw the daughter of a rival governor come to my cottage."

"Do you honestly think that's why?" Helen questioned.

"I don't know, Helen. They don't seem to mind destroying things, at least, and I don't want to be next. We need to keep moving."

They walked for as long as they had light, stopping only one time near a stream to fill their water bags and eat some bread. Helen carried the book in her hand, checking the map every few minutes, trying to decide if they were moving in the right direction. The woods led them northward, over ground that sloped steadily upward, and it was filled with unrecognizable sounds and flickering images that flashed in the corners of their eyes. With apprehension, they pushed themselves deeper into the forest, afraid at every moment that someone would step into their path. When it was too dark to move anymore, they stopped in a tiny opening and risked lighting a fire to warm themselves.

Without a word, they both settled on opposite sides of the fire. Most of the day had been spent in this same silence. Helen watched Neil, who didn't seem to be paying much attention to the woods around them. His mind was lost in thought. The more Helen watched him, the more she wished she had something to say. It felt strange to talk about everyday things, but it felt even more uncomfortable not to talk at all. As children, he had been much the same way, not inclined to speak unless it was important. Helen wished she could be like Neil, not always needing to fill the silence. She tried to hold back the words now, afraid of angering Neil even more.

Helen turned again to his grandfather's book. Reading would be more useful than sitting in idle silence. The day had felt directionless, as though they were trying to remain hidden rather than trying to find their way. She pushed back the thought that told her if she hadn't needed this book, she could have moved on alone, without Neil's help. A knot of frustration swelled in Helen's chest as she thought of how far they needed to go. Another knot formed as she looked at the map, noting its lack of detail. There was a clear line from Neil's village to Camelora, showing the hills and valleys they needed to pass over and through. But the scale wasn't right to show them all the setbacks they might face. Becoming lost wouldn't help them in any way. Helen hoped that the stories in the book would provide more direction. She wanted to know everything it contained.

The book's outer appearance was worn and discolored, just as Helen remembered it, only older. It was more used than any book Helen had seen before, not like the books most people in Veren kept, giving the appearance of intelligence, though they never really opened them. The edges of the pages showed signs of frequent openings and thumbings. But inside, the pages were only slightly yellowed, and remarkably intact. As a child, she had only seen the book in Neil's grandfather's hands, and he had always held it so that she couldn't see inside. She wondered who the handwriting belonged to. Turning the pages with care, she scanned the writing with meticulous attention. She only remembered a few of the stories Neil's grandfather told from it and she had never realized how many more there must be. Everything she knew about the king was so small compared to what this book held.

The stories—written in the same way Neil's grandfather had told them to Helen and Neil when they were children—were arranged in chronological order, beginning with Zaric's early reign and the peace the land enjoyed. But Mered, unhappy with the role he played in the government, made promises to the governors who would support him in his bid to take the kingdom from Zaric. The book wasn't very clear on how, but Mered disappeared in battle. Still, the governors were discontented and exiled their king, sending him to the northern edge of the kingdom. After that, the stories jumped ahead through the centuries, telling of the time when Mered would come back, the young woman and young man would go out in search of Zaric, and the supporters of Zaric would defend the kingdom, reinstating it to its former prosperity. These last stories were the most familiar to Helen, and she only allowed herself to focus on a few words on each page as she moved through the book.

When Helen's eyes passed over an unusual passage toward the end of the book, her hand stopped. She had never heard these words before. With curiosity, she studied them, only running her eyes over them at first, then going back and reading again from the beginning. She realized that it must have been written after her family had visited Neil's family for the last time. The handwriting told her how hurried Neil's grandfather had been as he wrote the final story in the book, though it wasn't much of a story at all. It was difficult to decipher and the ink was smudged in many places. She had a hard time figuring out what it was trying to say. But as she read over it a few times, most of it became easier to understand, though there were still parts where she had to guess at the meaning. Reaching the end for the fifth time, she realized that this journey she had decided to take was nothing she had expected it to be. A quarter of an hour had changed the appearance of everything. They weren't simply walking to Camelora anymore.

"What answers has the book given you?" Neil broke into the silence, making Helen jump. She didn't know how to answer the question. "Will we be at Camelora soon?" he continued.

"It doesn't look like it," Helen responded, pensive. "Neil, did your grandfather ever mention keys? Or did you read about them?"

"Keys? Keys to what?"

"Never mind," Helen said, shaking her head. With a soft clap, she closed the book and slipped it back into her bag. "I'll have to keep reading to find out exactly how to get to Camelora."

She drummed her fingers on the bag. In her mind, judging by his reaction to her request the previous night, Helen could see how Neil would react to this new idea that their course to Camelora might not be a direct one. She wanted to be sure before she told him too much. Trying to disguise her unease, she looked at Neil. "Have you ever read this book?"

"Please, Helen. I'm not in the mood to argue about the stories tonight. Isn't it enough that I agreed to come? I only want to know how long it will take to get to Camelora."

"I don't know. A few days, maybe, or a week or two. You must remember that I've never been there before. Have you read the book?"

Neil looked down at his hands, showing no interest in answering the question.

"I think there's one thing you're not considering, Helen," he said instead.

"And what's that?"

"Zaric might not even be at Camelora anymore. He might have moved on a long time ago. And that's only if he's still alive. If he's as old as the stories, he would probably be hundreds of years old by now."

"I've considered that," she said. "It doesn't change what I believe."

Neil studied Helen's manners with a mingled expression of annoyance and reluctant admiration. She looked away and hoped that he would stop looking at her.

"We'll take turns sleeping tonight," Neil stated with a large intake of breath. "I don't want to be taken by surprise. At least the woods are too large to make it likely that we will run into anyone else. Let's just hope they aren't tracking us or following the same map we are. I won't feel safe until there are four walls around me and a roof over my head. You sleep first, and I'll wake you in a couple of hours. I'm not very good at telling time without a clock, though, so we'll have to see how fair I can be. Hopefully, no one will surprise us."

Helen didn't argue, but she found it hard to fall asleep, just as she had every night since leaving Veren. She wanted soft, rhythmic sounds to soothe her, but there was nothing soft, rhythmic, or soothing here. Her ears strained for the sound of a brook or a bird singing. And her mind was restless. Events hadn't been so against her before and she hadn't realized that when she stopped for Neil she was making the situation more dangerous for them both. Mered's plans were too erratic for her to understand and she didn't like not understanding. Sighing, she realized that it wasn't the woods that lacked softness, but her own mind.

Neil really was a poor judge of time, but it benefited Helen more than it harmed her. When she was able to sleep, she slept for a long stretch of time, and the things that had disturbed her early in the night didn't seem as bad when she awoke again. She felt hopeful while taking her own turn to watch. Still, when the sun came up, Helen was ready to move and find a way out of the forest. She was glad that Neil felt the same way, and they were soon walking again through the trees.

As the morning wore on, Helen again felt compelled to fill the silence between them, but didn't know how. Her attempts at conversation before had all failed. She tested words in her mind, but didn't like where any of them led. It was unusual for her, considering so carefully what she wanted to say. She wished the two children who could talk about anything with absolute freedom hadn't become these two near-strangers.

Beside her, Neil chuckled. Occupied by her thoughts, Helen was at first offended, then embarrassed by her own offense. Neil had no idea what she was thinking; he wasn't laughing at the thoughts running through her mind.

"What's so funny?" she asked.

Neil reached out. She flinched and leaned back as his hand came toward her. But, he only pulled a twig out of her hair and tossed it to the ground. Helen's cheeks burned, but she chuckled, too, feeling an ease in the tension between them.

"The girl I knew would have felt that in her hair," Neil said.

Helen reached up to smooth her braid and felt the locks that had come loose. "My mother never liked it when I came back messy. Not fitting for the daughter of a governor, even in another region."

"I remember. I've never met anyone else like you, wanting to be rebellious and adventurous while trying to stay clean. The children of my own village weren't like that, anyway. Do you remember the day we tried to cross that stream? You with your skirt pulled to your knees... I still remember the look of concentration on your face."

"I'm still convinced you pushed me, *pretending* to help."

"Would I really do something like that?" He placed a hand on his chest, his face covered with mock-indignation.

"Yes," Helen frowned, but she couldn't disguise the twinkle in her eye. The boy she once knew was showing through.

"I admit nothing," Neil protested with a touch of drama.

"My mother was *not* happy."

"She was too polite to show it in front of my parents. Anyway, I think she was laughing inside. My father told me she was the same way as a girl."

There was a brief pause, then Neil continued, "Have fashions changed so much in Veren? I remember your clothes always being much finer that this, even when you were traveling."

"With all of our trading options closed, we've had to adapt, trading finery for convenience.  Even trying to trade outside of the Old Kingdom hasn't been an option, since there are two regions between Veren and the southern border."

"Well, to be honest, I think it's an improvement."

"Oh, do you?"

"Yes.  It looks much more durable and you don't stick out like a diplomat. Plus, I have no intention of sacrificing myself for a dress."

The sun didn't shine down on them for long. Thin, wide grey clouds covered the sky, rolling toward each other until every blue crack was filled. Once they had accomplished that, the clouds began to thicken, growing darker as the day passed. A chill filled the atmosphere. The emerging leaves on the trees enhanced the darkness, making the woods appear thicker and more menacing. Helen hoped it was late enough in the year to only rain. Being soaked by rain was a more welcomed thought than finding their way through snow.

"I wish we could get out of this forest," Helen stated in frustration.

"Well, yes," Neil said, "but that's really hard to do when you don't know where the forest ends. Anyway, I think you were the one who led us into the trees in the first place."

"It's too dark. I don't like not being able to see what's around me. I don't even know if we're still going north."

"How did you make it this far, Helen?"

"There aren't many forests in the southern lands," she replied. "Didn't you ever learn the basic geography of the regions?"

"We'll be out soon enough, I think. The trees are getting thinner."

Helen looked around, but she couldn't see any change. The clouds were still dark, the forest was still dark, and the entire atmosphere was still uninviting. "How do you know?" she asked.

"I come from a *central* land. I grew up next to a forest."

It was still a few minutes before Helen herself could tell, but she soon realized that it wasn't quite as dark and her line of vision broadened. She didn't feel stifled by the closeness of the vegetation. Her mood lightened along with the forest and, just as Neil had guessed, it wasn't much longer before they were able to see that the line of trees stopped a few yards ahead of them. They stepped out of the shelter of the woods into lightly falling rain.

"I think I would have preferred if the forest reached a little farther," Neil said, pulling his traveling mantel over his head. Helen pulled on the hood of her own cloak.

Before them lay a valley, much larger and far different from the one Neil's village rested in, or any that Helen had passed through. Less than a mile from the hill where they stood, the grey stone ruins of an old abbey sat nestled among a sparse grove of trees. A river ran through the valley between the hill and the abbey, running across the wide space ahead—the only sign of movement in this empty place. Tree-covered hills bordered the valley on three sides. The ones to the left and right were not too far away, but on the opposite edge of the valley, a mountain reached much higher than any Helen had had to pass before. From where they stood, it looked as though it must be at least a day's journey away, though Helen was sure it would look farther once they were in the valley. Hoping that wasn't the way they were meant to go, Helen stepped back beneath the canopy of the trees to look at the map in the book.

"That's where we're heading, isn't it?" Neil asked, seeing the look on her face. Helen didn't think it was possible for him to sound any more disheartened, but his tone somehow managed it.

"We had better get moving," Helen replied, trying to show more confidence than she felt.

"Well, yes, I agree that we don't want to waste any time, but with this rain and dusk coming on, I think we need to find shelter."

"There could be shelter farther along the valley," Helen argued, wanting to cover as much distance as possible.

"Helen," Neil stated, fixing her with a firm gaze, "we can't pass up convenient shelter when it's *right there.* Maybe Zaric himself left it there for us."

"Do you think so?" The words were out of her mouth before she could stop herself from saying them. One look at Neil told her that he was toying with her. "You make a good point," she went on, standing a little straighter, "even if you think you're only teasing. Fine. We can see if those ruins will offer shelter for the night."

The thought of stepping out into the open made Helen nervous. In the forest she couldn't know if someone was hiding in the trees, but in the valley there was nowhere for her and Neil to hide if someone approached. She suppressed her fears, though. They needed to move forward, even if it put them in danger. They began their descent down the hill. Rain fell harder. Neil and Helen increased their pace while carefully making their way through the wet grass and over the slickening mud. It took longer than Helen wanted to reach the valley. She didn't feel very glad when they did. Once there, they still needed to make their way to the ruins, which appeared much farther away from this point.

Neil continued to walk at a steady pace and Helen had to swallow back her disappointment and try to keep up. The ground clung to their boots as they walked, trying to hold them down. The tall, wet grass dampened their legs and the water made Helen's skirt heavy. Neil looked back and gave Helen a half-smile, but she wasn't sure if he was attempting to encourage her forward or simply aggravate her. Her boots had stopped keeping the dampness out and a chill ran from her feet to the top of her head. She shivered.

They finally reached the river and stopped. From this angle, the ruins were obscured by the trees and bushes growing around it, grey stone showing through at irregular intervals. Helen scanned the surface of the water for large stones to walk across, or even a footbridge they had failed to notice, but found none. Annoyance and irritability rose within, but she pushed it down, willing herself to stay calm.

"I hope you don't mind getting a little wet," Neil remarked.

Helen laughed, not trying to conceal her lack of amusement. She had already pulled her cloak together as tight as she could, but it hadn't prevented the rain from soaking through. "Does it look deep to you?" she asked. "I'm afraid it will be deeper than it looks."

"Not too deep, but I guess we'll just have to find out. Try not to lose your balance."

"I guess I'll need you to show me," Helen countered.

Neil shrugged and waded into the water. Helen followed.

The water reached their waists at its deepest and it wasn't moving with enough force to push them downstream. Still, Helen nearly lost her footing a couple of times and had trouble regaining control of her feet. Neil didn't turn around until he had reached the other side, climbed out of the river, and offered his hand to help her onto the bank. She smiled her thanks, but was too cold to open her mouth and speak. Shivering, she hugged herself in an effort to keep her teeth from chattering.

They fixed their eyes on the stone structure ahead of them. The sky had yet to change its mind about drenching them with rain. A loud, lingering crack of thunder reverberated through the valley. "Come on," Neil commanded, taking Helen's hand and running, nearly slipping on the wet grass.

The ruins were even more desolate now that they were so close. Helen doubted that they would find any part preserved enough to provide them with shelter from the rain. Long, green arms of ivy grew up the walls and around what was left of the narrow, ornate windows. Most of the walls had fallen down, large rocks littering the ground that had once been a stone floor. Grass grew up through the cracks.

"There!" Neil exclaimed, pointing toward the most interior part of the old abbey, where a steep roof appeared among the ruins, still intact. Helen sighed with relief.

Shelter.

# Chapter 5

Neil pulled Helen around a corner, through the tall grass and past stray seedlings. Rounding the corner of another crumbling wall, they saw the double wooden doors leading into the only preserved part of the old structure.

They had to work together to push one heavy door open, their feet sliding on the wet ground, yet the hinges didn't creak as it swung inward. Its weight was its only resistance. Helen was hesitant to step inside, afraid that they had found one of Mered's secret refuges in the northern lands. Neil didn't notice her reluctance, walking over the threshold without a second thought. Suppressing a sigh, she followed. They found themselves in a room almost black with darkness. There was a strangeness to this place that defied description—coldness that wasn't cold, shadows that didn't forbid, echoes that didn't feel empty.

Once they were inside, another boom of thunder sounded from the sky and a flash of lightning illuminated the room through long, narrow windows. The wind blew and unleashed rain poured through the open door. Neither of them was sure which made them most uncomfortable: the darkness of the room or the coldness of the rain.

"Close the door," Neil instructed, beginning the effort of moving the solid wood.

"But how will we see anything?" Helen argued. "We should try to find a candle first."

"The wind is too strong to light a candle. I'd rather close the door and sit without light until the morning than freeze to death because of the draft. There's no point in finding shelter if we let the outside in."

"We might freeze to death, anyway," Helen muttered. Her clothes were as wet as the river they had crossed and she felt they would never dry.

Still, she positioned herself next to Neil and helped him shut out the rain and wind. The bang of the door echoed through the room, which was now deeply enveloped in blackness.

"You might not mind sitting in the dark," Helen stated, startled by the echo of her own voice, "but I need light."

After blinking a few times, though, she realized the room wasn't as dark as she thought. Dim light came through the narrow windows in the walls on either side of the room, casting strips of bluish-grey across the floor. Neil felt his way along the wall, with Helen at his elbow, until he bumped into a small table. Something rattled when he disturbed it and he reached out his hand to catch it before it fell to the floor. He ran his fingers over it and realized that he was holding a candlestick.

"Light," he said, tapping Helen's shoulder with the metal rod.

Before he had time to wonder how he was going to light it, something high up on the wall flickered. They both looked above them and saw that the candles of a large candelabra over their heads had burst alight. Then, in a great rush, the rest of the candles in the hall lit themselves, the light rippling from one candle to the next. Neil dropped the candlestick onto the table with a loud clang.

"What is this place?" Helen asked in awe. The walls to their left and right were covered with candelabras, mounted at regular intervals. There was a large fireplace set in the farthest wall, with a door on either side of it. Aside from these and the table Neil was standing next to, the room was empty. Neil noticed, too, that there was no dust, even though the abbey must have been abandoned centuries before. The flames from the candelabras reflected brilliantly on the polished stone floor. There was no visible purpose to the room, yet its air was welcoming and comforting. Helen's eyes shone brightly, excitedly, in the flickering light, relieving Neil of some of the uneasiness he felt.

"I don't like it," he said, not quite sure he meant what he was saying. "It must be some sort of trick."

"You think everything is a trick, Neil," Helen answered.

"Is it mentioned in the book?" he asked, though it surprised him that those words came out of his mouth.

Helen shook her head thoughtfully. She lifted the strap of her bag over her head and dropped it on the floor. Filled with wonder, she focused on the fireplace across the room and began to walk toward it. Neil took a step behind her.

Then, without warning, the silence was broken by a sound like shattering glass. The next second, a cylinder of shimmering green light sprang out of the floor, engulfing Helen. Neil couldn't see her inside of it. It was as though she was standing in a whirlwind as fierce as the wind outside. Her hair whipped around her face as she tried to turn to Neil, her eyes panicked and pleading. Calling her name, Neil rushed forward, but just as suddenly as it had appeared, the light dissolved, replaced with emptiness.

Neil ran to the spot where the cylinder had been, his gaze focused on the floor, but all traces of Helen had disappeared with the cylinder. Dropping to his knees, he pressed his hands against the glistening stone. It was solid. There was no sign of a loose block or a trapdoor. As disbelief and numbness flooded his mind, he got to his feet and turned in circles, trying to find a door that he had missed the first time he surveyed the room. Trying to take everything in, Neil put his hands to his temples. He blinked his eyes over and over, hoping that he would open them and find himself standing back by the table, watching

Helen—or, better yet, find himself lying in his own bed, waking up from a nightmare. But each time he opened his eyes, the scene remained the same. Helen was gone and this shining room remained.

"Helen!" Neil called frantically, but only the echo, then silence, of the room answered. He called again, but he knew it was pointless. He went back to where Helen had been standing and retraced her steps, stopping at the point where she disappeared, and closed his eyes. The green light didn't come back.

The air in the room changed. It was soft, almost imperceptible, like a current passed through the hall on a slight breeze, yet nothing moved with it—not even the flickering flames of the candles. Neil glanced behind at the door, but it was still fixed shut. It felt like someone moved behind him, yet when he looked over his shoulder, he only saw the empty room. He strained his ears for the sound of footsteps. He heard none. Still, he listened.

Then, out of the corner of his eye, he saw Helen's bag lying on the floor, a few feet away. He rushed, dropped to his knees, and slid on the floor until he was next to it, taking it in his hands. He cast his eyes around the room again, slowly standing. "Helen!" he called out, his voice shaking. "Helen, are you there?"

There was no answer, but Neil had hoped for rather than expected one. The scene of Helen removing the bag and dropping it played in his mind. The bag assured him that she had been there, but where was she now? Pulling his knees to his chest, he folded his arms around them and buried his face, dropping the bag. He thought back again, but this time to life in his cottage, before Helen had come. Life was simple, and that simplicity was comfortable. He understood the past two days as much as he understood what had happened just now. He was in a strange place, with no idea of what to do, and he was completely alone—again. How had he managed to get himself mixed up in this? He was on a journey to a place he didn't believe in, experiencing situations that couldn't possibly be real, with no home to go back to.

Again, the tingle of a breeze moved past him and Neil jerked his head up. This time, he was sure he had heard a voice whispering to him, but he couldn't tell what it said. Motionless, he sat on the floor, waiting for it to repeat itself. A huff of breath escaped his lips. Having spent the last four years mostly in silence, he couldn't understand why it bothered him so much now. He looked down at Helen's bag and remembered his grandfather's book. Feeling agitated, he opened the bag and searched through it.

Helen wasn't carrying much with her, but Neil was still surprised by what he found. On top was a small crossbow with a bundle of arrows, a sign that Helen really did believe herself to be in danger and that she was prepared to defend herself—something Neil hadn't considered before. Under this were her scant supply of food, a change of clothes, and, at the very bottom, the book Neil had given her the night she had come to him. Carefully, he took the book out and set the bag back on the floor.

Neil ran his hand over its cover, touching it with the tips of his fingers. Then, he opened it and hastily turned the pages. He skimmed through the stories, and his memory flooded with his grandfather's voice, like a forgotten, yet still comforting and warm, blanket. He passed through stories of war and stories of peace. He read words used to teach, to bring shame and regret, and then hope and joy. The memories of the Zaric he had always imagined were enlivened and Neil felt himself getting lost in the words of this book.

A sharp flash of lightning and crack of thunder brought him back to the reality he was facing. He glanced around the room again, then turned the pages a little more quickly.

As though they were jumping out of the page, Neil soon found himself looking at the words, "the light room," only a few pages from the end of the book. He stopped skimming and began to read. In great detail, the book described a long, empty chamber with a polished floor. On the walls of this chamber were many candelabras, which all looked exactly the same. The rest of the words on the page were smudged and nearly impossible to read. Neil squinted and pulled the book close to his face, but it was no use. There was only one sentence he could make out.

"Cast the true lights into the fire," Neil muttered softly to himself. He felt it shiver through him and he thought for a moment that he could hear the voice again. Over and over he read the words, trying to decipher what came before and after them, hoping to make sense of this sentence. What did it mean by "true lights"? What fire? He looked helplessly at the fireplace in the opposite wall, empty and cold.

"Cast the true lights into the fire," he read aloud again, realizing now that the voice he thought he had heard before was really his own—an echo heard before the sound that made it.

Neil peered around the room, his eyes pausing in turn at the table by the door, the fireplace in the farthest wall, and the candelabras on the walls. He set the book down and got to his feet, wondering if this puzzle was the way to make sense of this situation. In long strides, he walked back to the table and picked up the candlestick he had fumbled with before. He looked at it, but didn't see it, instead thinking about the strange sentence. None of the lights in this hall seemed like true lights. They had lit themselves, and the light they cast could very easily be just an illusion. And it was also possible that this sentence had nothing to do with his problem at all. Frustrated, he threw the candlestick into the middle of the room. It hit hard, bouncing, then rolling in a circle on its side, clanging and ringing. Neil walked to the middle of the room. Trying to slow his mind down and think clearly, he inhaled deeply and stared at one of the many candles as it flickered on the wall. He breathed out slowly, closed his eyes, and thought.

"Cast the true lights into the fire," he said out loud, almost shouting.

The reverberation of his voice was strong and encouraging, wiping away Neil's frustration.

The answer was impossible, brilliant, and simple. He smiled to himself. With firm steps, he walked to the first candelabra on the left wall, placed both hands around it, and pulled. The stone that held it crumbled, releasing the candelabra into Neil's hands. His confidence didn't waver as he walked to the fireplace, making sure none of the candles went out. He held the candelabra in the fireplace, dropped it among the few small logs littering the hearth, then pulled his hand away. A small flame grasped at the logs until they caught fire and the candelabra melted and dissolved. Neil waited.

Nothing happened. Turning on his heels, Neil looked at everything within sight, but the room remained the same. With a little less certainty, he walked to another candelabra, reached up, and tried to grasp it as before. This time, instead the feeling of metal beneath his fingers, his hand went through the stem as if it wasn't there. Neil's confidence drained away. A muffled roar of frustration escaped him. Hoping he had only imagined it, he reached up and tried again, and again his hand passed through the candelabra. He went to the next one and tried to grasp it, but it was just like the one before. Pressing his head with the palms of his hands, he turned and leaned against the wall. He wasn't prone to hallucinations. The candelabras on these walls were real—or at least they appeared to be. How could he not touch something that was so obviously real?

Closing his eyes, Neil emptied his mind and listened to the room. As he did, he felt himself relaxing and his frustration disappearing. Through his closed lids, he thought he could see the room growing brighter. Opening his eyes, he focused on each individual candelabra. They still looked the same. He focused deeper.

This time, he noticed a slight change, a difference so small, no one could have noticed it without paying close attention. Five candelabras held candles that burned with flames glowing whiter than the rest. This whiteness was merely an occasional flicker, but it occurred often enough for Neil to watch and see the pattern. As he focused on these, the rest faded back, until they were ghosts of themselves. His confidence returned and, one at a time, he went to each solid candelabra, pulled it from the wall, and took it to the fireplace, throwing it into the fire. With every candelabra the flames grew higher. After the last one melted away, Neil stood back and waited, staring into the flames.

For a few moments, the fire looked like any fire, its flames dancing like unpracticed feet around and across the logs. Soon, though, a pattern developed in its flicker and the fire began to change, turning from orange to yellow, from yellow to blue, and then from blue to green. A small speck of light appeared in the middle of the flame, spinning and growing into the shape of a sphere, light dancing over its surface. Then it stopped, hanging inside the flame. Curiosity compelled Neil to plunge his hand into the fire and touch this sphere. He followed his impulse, expecting the heat from the fire to singe his hand. But he felt no change in the temperature as his hand went into the flame and closed around the object. At that moment, the flames fell like water and the fire went out.

Neil pulled his hand out of the fireplace and opened it. The sphere was a perfectly round emerald, more beautiful than any stone he had ever seen. He wondered how something so small could matter so much.

Behind him, the remaining candelabras started to fade away. Afraid of being immersed in darkness again, Neil frantically looked for another source of light. Just as the last candle disappeared, he noticed the candlestick he had thrown before. A small flame rested on the wick where there had been none before, although the candle still lay on its side. Neil slipped the green stone into his pocket and rushed to the center of the room, not wanting the light to go out. Gingerly, he raised the candlestick and held it in both of his hands.

And then, a sudden flash of blinding light illuminated the room. Neil turned his head away, closing his eyes against the light, afraid of what might be happening. Blinking, he slowly turned his head. He relaxed and grinned, the tension dropping out of his shoulders. In the same spot where he had last seen her, Helen lay curled up on the floor.

"Helen!" he cried, dropping the candle and rushing to her. He gathered her in his arms. Dazed, she opened her eyes and stared up at him. At first, those fearful eyes set in her pale face widened and she pushed against Neil's chest. Once recognition arose, though, she smiled and let out a breath. He felt her face to make sure she was real, but she brushed his hands away.

"Don't be silly," she said, pulling herself up to a sitting position. With shaking hands, she held her head. Then, stuttering, she asked, "Did—did you find it?"

"Find what?" Neil questioned in return.

"The key," Helen stated.

# Chapter 6

"Helen!" Neil shouted, concealing his fear with anger. "You disappeared and I had—have—no idea where you went. And all you can think about is a key? Where were you?"

"I—I don't know," she faltered. "I don't really remember. But I'm here now. I'm fine."

"You don't look fine."

"Please, Neil. Did you find the key?"

Neil growled in annoyance, then sighed. He considered her for a few seconds before pulling the stone out of his pocket and turning it in his palm. "Is this what you mean?" he asked, a scornful bite to his words as he offered it to Helen.

As she took it and held it up between her thumb and forefinger, the weak candlelight danced through its transparent green body. Breathing out, her fear subsided. As a governor's daughter, Helen had seen many exquisite and beautiful jewels around the necks, on the fingers and wrists, and in the hair of many exquisite and beautiful women, but she had never seen a gem so perfectly round and smooth, beautiful in its simplicity. The wonder of it transfixed her. She wanted to study and learn this stone, playing with it in the light. With a sigh, she allowed the stone to slide into her palm and made a fist around it. It was unlike any key she would have imagined, and she wondered how it could ever possibly open a door, or a gateway. She handed it back to Neil, who put it back in his pocket.

"Are you all right?" he asked, concern written in his expression as he let go of his anger and gazed at Helen. She was relieved to hear the concern in his voice. He reached a hand toward her face, but pulled it back. "You look pale."

"How can you tell?" she answered, trying to make her voice as light as possible. "It's so dark in here. What happened to all the lights? And it's cold. Do you think we can build a fire?"

"If we can find some wood, we can build a fire."

Helen nodded and stood, while Neil continued to stare. She knew that he wanted a better answer than the one he had been given, but Helen wasn't sure what to say. Her head felt numb and muddled, like she had fallen down a long flight of stairs. She had no idea how to describe where she had been and she didn't want to think about what had happened when she stepped into the room. She didn't understand it. As her heart began to swell and race, cutting her breath short, she turned her face away.

Helen took the candle and they went through one of the doors next to the fireplace, hoping it didn't lead back outside. They were in luck. What they found was a small storage room, littered with the wooden remains of old furniture, the fabric long since rotted away. Helen loaded Neil's arms with bits of wood, then took what she could beneath one arm.

"Do you know about the keys, Neil?" Helen asked, once the fire had begun to burn and they sat eating some of the bread and fruit Neil had brought.

"I know that they're part of the story," he stated. "And I believe they're a myth."

"But you do know about them. You have one in your pocket."

"I have a small gemstone in my pocket. I wouldn't call it a key. Where did you hear about the keys, anyway, Helen?"

Helen considered her answer for a few seconds before she said anything. She was afraid that if she mentioned the stories again, he would dismiss anything else she had to say. Still, she wanted him to trust her, and the truth wouldn't change, no matter what he believed.

"I read about them last night, in your grandfather's book," she told him. The smirk Helen was expecting didn't appear on Neil's face. He stared at her with thoughtful eyes. She wondered what he had experienced when she disappeared because his manner was different than before. Realizing that he wasn't going to dismiss her story outright, she went on. "He didn't speak about them very much, so I didn't even remember the stories he told us about them, only that they exist. They seem to be the last things he wrote about and all his information is disjointed. I'm not asking you to believe the stories, Neil, but if you remember them, I would like you to tell me what you know. The keys might change everything."

Another minute went by. Neil alternated his gaze between Helen, the fire, and the empty room. "How long do you think it's been since anyone looked at that book?" he asked.

"Years, probably," she replied. She wanted to guess that Neil's father or mother were the last to read it, but stopped herself, worried that bringing them up would darken his face and stop his story. His demeanor was open and she didn't want to lose that openness.

"I know almost every word of that book, Helen," Neil said with carefully measured emotion. "Every word that hasn't been made illegible by the years. I know all the stories about Zaric and Mered, and I know about the keys. I could probably recite every story without lifting the cover. Those stories were the work of my grandfather's life. I think he lived a lot of them himself, or made himself believe he had. You never knew him the way I did. When you and your parents were visiting and he happened to be at our cottage, you heard his stories, but I was there when he came back from his travels. He told me every story before he recorded it in his book. After he was gone, I read the book every day, even when I stopped believing it. It helped me feel close to him."

"So you knew before we left your cottage that this wasn't just a matter of simply walking to Camelora," Helen said.

"The stories aren't necessarily real," Neil argued. "They're fairy tales. We don't have to do everything they tell us to do. Even if we tried, how much of it would even be possible? I knew about the keys, but they might have been added to make the whole thing seem more interesting. His mind wasn't exactly sound when he wrote that part."

"You think that anything that doesn't fit your definition of logic—"

"—can't possibly be true. Exactly."

"You only believe in what you can see."

"While you only believe in what you can't see. They're probably both impractical views, but there you have it. I'll tell you what I remember about the keys, but don't ask me to believe it."

Helen stared at Neil, realizing how little she understood him. The hardness in his voice was underlaid with something she couldn't recognize—something that hung on the edge of her mind. Both curious and nervous about what Neil would say, she nodded her assent.

"When he relocated himself and all of those who wanted to follow him, Zaric devised a way to protect his people. They moved to Camelora and he set up a barrier around it, which can only be opened when the keys are taken to the Gateway. To ensure that no ordinary person would find the keys and open the barrier, Zaric—with the help of my grandfather, if you believe the stories—scattered the keys, leaving cryptic clues to find them. I think they ended up more cryptic than they planned, since by the time my grandfather wrote them down, he was too sick and weak to make much sense. The end of the book is smudged and illegible, as you've seen."

"But it seems like a very plausible plan," Helen said with a light chuckle.

"The keys are named Happiness, Sincerity, Wisdom, and Hope. None of those things are tangible."

"Yet you have a very unusual stone in your pocket."

Neil pursed his lips as though he was trying to think of a smart reply, but instead stated simply, "Yes."

Helen sighed. She took a small pouch out of her bag and opened it, spilling the contents—a handful of gold and silver coins—into the palm of her hand. She handed these to Neil, who traded the green stone for the coins, putting them in his pocket as Helen dropped the stone in the pouch. Helen closed the pouch and returned it to her bag.

"If I had known you were carrying so much money," Neil stated, "I would have demanded we stay in an inn instead of a ruined abbey."

"We need to find the rest of the keys," Helen said, ignoring the remark. "I think that's what the map is directing us to do. We know what we're looking for now. I don't know if we can reach Camelora otherwise."

"You're going to assume this is a key, and that the rest all look the same?" Neil replied. "You expect too much of that book, Helen—and my grandfather. Not everything was planned in detail."

"But it was planned enough. We have the stories and we have the map. They tell us what we need to do."

Neil nodded, unconvinced, but said nothing in return. Helen was relieved, too tired to argue. They finished their food without speaking another word. They soon tried to sleep, each lying on one side of the fireplace, deciding to face the risk of intrusion and not keep watch. But Helen found it hard to sleep that night. At first, she was afraid to close her eyes because of the images she saw and the feeling of intense loneliness that deluged her when she did. The growing darkness frightened her, the fear made even worse when she closed her eyes. When sleep did come, she was haunted by scenes of emptiness, a thick black space she could feel against her skin with occasional flashes of strange colors, lights, and shadows—greens, blues, yellows, and purples that she could never quite focus on. In the silence, it was hard to push away the fear of the place she had gone to when she had been pulled from the light room, and the most frightening thing was that she hadn't been taken to any place at all. She hung suspended in a void that felt like it was outside of time with nothing solid to hold onto, apart from the world and afraid that at any moment she would fall into complete and irreversible oblivion. And yet, she knew that oblivion wouldn't come. Her greatest fear was that she was not afraid at all. It wasn't until the first tinges of morning light flitted through the windows that her mind was able to relax.

They left the ruins before dawn. Too little sleep made Helen's head and eyes ache and she had trouble making her feet move as she wanted them to. The rain from the day before covered the long grass and dampened their clothes and legs as they followed the path cut through the valley by the river. Yet, the valley ahead of them was no longer as imposing as it had the day before. The clouds that littered the sky were a soft shade of pink, gradually turning to pale yellow and then white as the sun came up behind the hills, and the cold left behind by the wind and the rain was soon dispelled by the sun's warmth. Helen was amazed by how immense the sky looked from where they stood. It was as though no other place existed in the world. She tried to share this observation with Neil, but he only responded with an automatic, "Yes." They again lapsed into silence. The quiet minutes made Helen anxious.

"You really don't say much, do you?" she finally stated.

"I do when I have something to say," Neil answered.

"Have you spoken to anyone since your parents died?"

Neil appeared a little bit stung by this question, though it was simple and natural. "I go to market sometimes," he said shortly.

"Did you ever have any visitors?"

"I tend to hide in the fields when they come. No one in my village really cares, anyway. Is there a point to these questions?"

"I'm only trying not to feel uncomfortable and alone."

"You don't need to talk to not feel uncomfortable and alone."

Helen wished she could agree with this. She couldn't quite understand Neil's moods—the mask that he wore and removed without any regularity. The openness from the night before had closed while Neil slept. It aggravated her, though she wasn't sure if it was a problem without a solution, or even a problem at all. She only wanted to be talking. Neil did not. Helen wondered how anyone could be comfortable with such silence. In the quiet, it was hard to prevent her mind from dwelling on the thoughts that came without invitation.

"Don't you ever feel like just saying *something?*"

"Like you do? Not usually."

"Will you tell me about your parents?" she asked, a little more exasperated than she intended, as though she were clutching at the last thing she could see.

"No, Helen. I don't really want to. Why don't you tell me about yours?"

He said it sharply to make her stop—and she did stop, but not because she was offended. Her mind didn't have the space to be. Helen couldn't stop the memories from filling her head. The noises and voices wouldn't go away. She tried to see her mother's bright, smiling eyes, calm and relaxed features, unhurried movements—instead of her eyes wide and glistening with tears, face tightened in failing self-restraint, bustling Helen out of the governor's palace through a narrow, secret passageway. If she had only left before her mother had discovered what danger Helen was in. If only Helen herself had realized the danger at that time, and not so much later. And if only she had seen her father before they took him, perhaps she would feel stronger now.

Unable to remember her parents without remembering the fear and danger, Helen realized why Neil was unwilling to talk about his own parents. For the first time, the thought hit her that he had not only seen them in all the happy moments, but also during their last moments, when they were ill and weak and dying. Caring for them, how could he not be plagued with memories of their final days? Helen had the hope that her parents were still alive and that she could save them. Neil had only loneliness.

Folding her arms as if holding her chest in place, Helen tried to smile at Neil but knew that it was only a faint imitation of one, then turned away from him. She quickened her pace until she was a few yards ahead, wishing she had thought about Neil and his feelings before he had hurt her own.

A sudden, low, and humming breeze drew Helen's mind away from her thoughts and she stopped. She turned around and saw that Neil had stopped, too. Moving down the southern hill and through the tall grass was a coil of wind, concentrated to two narrow paths which passed them on the left and right, pushing the grass in a spiraling motion. Everything else in the valley was still.

"Have you ever seen this before?" Neil asked. Helen shook her head, continuing to watch the trail of the wind.

With an unexpected flash of violet light, a deafening crack resonated through the valley. Helen's hands flew to cover her ears as she spun around, but she saw nothing and no one besides Neil and herself. Again, the sound split the air, and then again a third time. Helen's ears rang. Neil searched the valley as well, but he looked just as perplexed as Helen. Then a flash to her left caught her eye and Helen shifted her gaze to the edge of the valley. A pillar of violet light rushed toward her. Neil took a few steps forward, but the light moved too fast. As it reached the point where Helen stood, it violently threw them both to the ground. They landed hard on their backs, yards away from each other. Gasping to fill her lungs, Helen raised herself and watched as the light moved around them. A transparent wall of violet, about three times as tall as Helen, formed in the wake of the pillar, splitting itself into two when it reached the river. The two walls wound around Helen and Neil, ending where the pillar had begun. The pillar vanished, but two transparent boxes were left behind, enclosing Helen and Neil separately.

They both sat for a few seconds without moving, the ringing in their ears dying down, then Neil stood and walked toward the wall that separated him from Helen. Within a foot of it, the wall resisted his approach, pushing him backwards. The harder he tried, the more forceful the resistance became, until his feet slid on the grass and he fell to the ground. Helen's heart pounded as she noticed that the box around her was shrinking.

As they stood in their strange cages—Helen feeling helpless and puzzled and Neil's face growing more and more bewildered—the faint sound of a horse's hooves filled the valley. It reverberated in the silence that was left when the pillar disappeared. Helen spun in a circle, trying to locate the intruder. Looking through the walls around her was like trying to look through a thick veil. It was hard for her even to see Neil. The horse was only a few yards away before she saw a man in dark clothes on its back, coming toward them at a moderate pace. As he moved closer, Helen thought she recognized his face, though it was hard to tell. An uncomfortable emptiness formed in her chest. It was this feeling more than what she saw that made her realize that the man was Ian.

He stopped his horse at the point where the two boxes joined and dismounted. "Helen," he said with mock concern, "what happened? You seem to be trapped."

Helen said nothing and only watched as Ian paced along the wall, back and forth, his head moving up and down, side to side as he studied it. Ian put out his hand and touched the wall as he walked, moving closer. His fingers went through it without any trouble, the light dancing around them like lightning. Soon his hand came through, then his entire arm. The cloudiness of the light dissipated until the walls were more like tinted windows. Helen's fear grew faster than she could control. Fumbling, she pulled the small crossbow from her bag and stepped backward until the resistance of the wall stopped her. She set an arrow in place and pointed it at him, though her hand shook noticeably.

Unaffected, Ian smiled, continuing to pace until he again reached Neil's portion of the box. In a deliberate and exaggerated way, he walked straight forward, stepping through the wall like he was crossing a line on the ground.

"Are you going to introduce me to your friend?" he asked. Confused by Ian's demeanor, but not willing to show it, Neil stood without saying a word, his cautious gaze fixed on Ian. Ian waited for a reply, but when he didn't receive one, he took a deep breath and went on. "Helen and I met before. She was on her way to meet a friend. I assume that *you* are the friend she was going to meet."

Helen was irritated by the way he said this, knowing that she hadn't told him about Neil before. But, she was sure he only said it in this way to bait her, to make her argue with him. Fighting the irritation, she remained quiet while her mind worked on the puzzle of how to get out of this box.

*So this is the man Helen has been running from,* Neil thought to himself, trying to suppress his feelings of panic with curiosity. He hadn't expected such an ordinary person. Short blond hair complemented Ian's hard blue eyes. Every feature in his face was strong. The cut and style of his dark leather clothing brought to Neil's mind a man always prepared to fight, but in a position higher than a common foot soldier. A general, perhaps. Certainly someone in a position of great trust.

"Why are you both so quiet?" Ian asked after another pause. "It seems to me you're in trouble and I may be able to help you. Let's just try to think up a solution to this problem."

"You're willing to help us?" Neil stated.

"Of course," replied Ian. "After all, I didn't have any trouble crossing that line, so it looks like *I'm* the one who can help *you*."

Trying to force herself to be confident, Helen rushed forward, but the wall pushed her back. As Ian spoke, the darkness she felt intensified. She was desperate to find a way to dispel it. Picking up a small stone, she threw it at the wall. She cast her arms over her face as it bounced back at her. A growl of frustration rose through Helen's chest and it took a great effort to push it back down. Not far from her feet she saw a long, thick stick lying on the ground. She took it up, held it with both of her hands, and swung it at the wall like a hammer, sparks flying with each hit. When she ran out of breath and strength, there was still no change to the light. It was just as it had been before. Ian's only reaction was a chuckle.

"We don't need any help," Helen said. "Not from you."

"This seems a little familiar to me, Helen. You really need to learn to trust me. This is a dangerous place and I'm afraid you're going to get hurt. Just look at what's happened to you now."

"You did this!" she exclaimed. Her mind raced to find a solution, but it only made her feel more helpless than before. She didn't remember any stories from the book about boxes of light that might trap them.

"Really, Helen, you should be more careful. You don't have many chances left. You're lucky I'm feeling merciful today. Choose to come with me or I might be forced to do something you won't like."

"No," Helen replied.

"Such a brave little fool," Ian jeered, "and so determined. But it won't do you much good. I'm beginning to think you'd rather destroy yourself—and Neil—than accept help from anyone. Are you really that arrogant?" He turned his attention to Neil. "Listen, Neil. I know this place and I know how to get around it. The people of this region don't like trespassers and create these traps to capture new slaves. It's against their laws to travel this way without permission and your enslavement would be well within their rights. But the design of the trap is flawed. If you let me assist you, I can help you find what you're looking for and you can help me find what *I'm* looking for."

Neil stood still, his expression unreadable. It was impossible to tell if he was considering what Ian said or if he was only trying to compose his own response. Holding her breath, Helen looked on, hoping Neil would choose not to listen to Ian, but knowing her own position was vulnerable no matter what he chose.

"Somehow," Neil said so quietly Helen had to strain to hear, "I don't think a man who's generous enough to save my life would try to make a bargain."

Ian's pleasant, helpful expression melted into one of disappointed anger. Deftly, he pulled a small dagger from his belt and pointed it at Neil. "Your chances are slimming, too, Neil," he stated. "I'll have to kill you if you don't come with me. You're too much of a threat to our plan."

The three of them stood motionless for just a few seconds and a gentle breeze began to blow. It vibrated through Helen, filling her entire body with a strange lightness. Not really knowing where it came from, a sudden idea formed in her mind and she knew what to do.

Lifting her crossbow again, she pointed it at Ian. Her fear replaced now by confidence, Helen raised her free hand. Ian's hand began to shake, only slightly at first, but gradually the shaking became more violent. His grip on his dagger eased and it fell to the ground. Surprised, he cuffed his wrist with his other hand. Then Helen looked up into the sky. The white clouds that streaked it thickened and turned dark grey, building on themselves, filling the expanse in a matter of seconds.

Heavy rain poured down like the emptying of a bucket.

Helen again turned her eyes to Ian, who stared back with unmasked malice, holding his wrist and trying to stop the shaking. With determination, she shot the arrow in her crossbow. Shards of violet light flew out and fell to the ground like pieces of glass as the arrow penetrated the wall, then continued on and pierced Ian's shoulder. He screamed and fell to his knees as the rest of the walls shattered and fell to the ground before dissolving.

Without a word, Neil ran to Helen and took her hand. He pulled her toward the nearest hill and the trees that covered it. Though she didn't take a chance to look, Helen could hear Ian shout in pain, then the swishing of the grass around his legs. She hoped they could reach the trees and disappear before he managed to follow. A few more seconds went by, then just as they entered the trees, she heard the horse's hooves. Ducking behind a trunk, she looked at the clearing. Instead of riding toward them, Ian rode away.

# Chapter 7

Confused and nervous, they watched as Ian grew smaller and smaller, ascending the hill he had descended not long before. "Do you think there may be more men on the other side of that hill?" Helen whispered.

Neil fixed his gaze on the opposite end of the valley. "Were there men with him before?" he asked.

"I'm not sure. I thought I saw someone else, but it was only a shadow in the trees. Neil, I'm sorry for that." Helen nodded her head toward the clearing, where rain was still falling heavily from the low-lying, dark clouds, blurring the scene before them.

Neil shrugged off her remark, his expression softening. "What, the trap? It caught me, too, so there's nothing to apologize for. You got us out of it, anyway, so if there really was a reason to apologize, you've already made up for it."

Helen appreciated the compliment, but tried not to let Neil see it. "I meant I was sorry for saying the wrong things."

The rain in the valley came to an abrupt stop and the clouds split apart, drifting idly, exposing the rich blue sky. The sunlight came down in warm beams, just as it had done before. Aside from what they remembered and the moisture coating the valley below, no one could know that anything unusual had happened here.

"You don't need the sound of my voice to reassure you," Neil said, walking further into the trees. "I'm not going to leave you if I can help it. I made my choice. And if anyone tries to take me away, I'll make enough noise to keep you from wondering."

Helen tried not to doubt his words. In her mind, it was hard not to admit that she was afraid his indifference to Zaric would make him choose to go with Ian, if another opportunity came. It troubled her that Neil didn't seem to sense the danger like she did.

"Wait!" she called after him, fumbling to open her bag. "Is this the way we're supposed to be going?"

Neil didn't stop. Flipping as fast as she could, Helen checked the map, making sure he was moving in the right direction before following after him.

The forest floor was dry and packed, preventing them from leaving footprints and allowing them to move easily. It wouldn't be too difficult for them to make progress before anyone tried to follow them. The dreaded sound of horses didn't come, but Helen still focused her attention on the sounds around them, in anticipation. When Neil slowed down, she looked up in surprise and confusion. Not far ahead of them, the trees ended and, a few yards beyond that, the wall of a cliff rose. At the top of the cliff was another portion of the forest. Helen felt foolish for not noticing the break in the trees before. She stepped forward, hoping, but not expecting, to see that it was only a large rock. Instead, she found that it stretched farther than she could see from east to west, wrapping out of sight as it hugged the mountain.

"Is this on the map?" Neil asked, a touch of sarcasm peppering his voice.

"The map isn't that detailed," Helen responded. She wanted to add that Neil already knew that, but the trap they had only just escaped was too fresh on her mind for her to tamper with their fragile peace. "When I checked, though, it *did* show that we were moving in the right direction, so there must be a way past this."

"I don't think the trees will be much help," Neil remarked, surveying the distance between the trees and the cliff. "No way to climb it…. I guess we just walk along until we find a way around."

Helen sighed and nodded in resignation. "I hope we find it soon. If we stay too long in one place, someone might catch up to us."

She examined the cliff in one direction, then the other, her hands resting on her hips. "West," she said, pointing that way. Neil fell in line with her as she went in that direction.

Helen put out her hand, running her fingertips along the face of the rock. It was smoother than she had anticipated, more like finished granite than weathered stone, with not many jagged edges. Neil stayed next to her, helping her to keep a steady pace.

It felt like an hour had passed. Helen's hand now traced absently along the rock and she stumbled when it unexpectedly slid away from the cliff. She looked up to see a narrow pass in the rock and she stood still. "Here it is," she said, beaming with the knowledge that she had been right.

The pass was cut so cleanly into the cliff, they couldn't see it until they were standing directly in front of it. Ahead of them, it reached up too far to see the end, appearing to climb up into the sky. The floor of the pass rose in broken stone steps, littered with tufts of grass. Helen realized they must once have been set into the path with great attention and care, but time and erosion had crumbled them until it was hard to see that they were man-made. The contrast of the smooth cliff and broken steps amazed Helen. She stepped onto the path without hesitation, but Neil put his hand on her arm to hold her back.

"We don't have time to explore, Helen," he said with pointed force. "Let's keep moving."

"I am moving. A staircase cut in the mountain must lead somewhere."

"Does it lead to the right place? Are you sure it's safe?" he asked.

"Are you sure it's not?" she replied, freeing herself and continuing on. "A path of some kind is better than none, and it looks forgotten. Who else do you think will use it? And, this is still the way the map tells us to go."

Hesitating for only a brief moment, Neil followed, knowing he wouldn't be able to change Helen's mind when she believed she was doing as the book instructed.

The staircase went into the mountain for a few yards before turning into an overgrown path, winding around and through a narrow pass. The path was only just too narrow for them to walk side by side. Neil stayed a step behind Helen, the mountain to one side and a steep drop on the other. Unlike the forest, there weren't many trees to protect them from the heat of the sun, only an occasional turn into shadow from the mountain that offered very little relief. They stopped every few minutes to rest from the exertion of climbing the slope, leaning against the wall of rock and sipping sparing amounts of water from their pouches. The last of their fruit was refreshing, making them wish they had tried to fill their bags a little more.

"What if we don't reach the top before the sun sets?" Neil asked during one of these breaks.

"We'll keep walking," Helen said. "Hope for a moon tonight."

"We still don't know who or what might meet us at the top," Neil retorted.

"A spot on the map," Helen responded without much thought.

Exhaustion pressed on them much faster than any they had suffered yet. Helen felt like the path narrowed. She stopped to catch her breath, forcing Neil to stop, too. A few deep breaths calmed her mind. She saw that the narrowing sensation was just her imagination. The realization of this, though, only made it worse.

"Are you all right?" Neil asked, placing his hands on her shoulders.

"It's getting hard to breath," Helen answered with a shake of her head.

"Let's rest a minute. Like you said, no one else is likely to find this path. We don't need to push ourselves so hard."

He handed her a waterskin and she took a grateful gulp.

But being found by Ian or anyone else wasn't her primary concern. If the pathway did narrow as they reached the top and they found that it led to nothing at all, they would have to climb back down with the knowledge that they had wasted all that time. Her tired mind began to think that Neil could be right. It was absurd to think that someone would build a path that led nowhere, but she didn't know this land and it was very possible that the people who had once lived here had built the staircase as a trap. Her next fear was, even if the staircase had been built for a reason, that reason might no longer exist. So much of the land from Zaric's reign had changed.

And the sun was getting hotter. Helen reached back and took Neil's hand to steady herself.

Only a few minutes later, the steep drop next to the path began to shorten. A field came into view. The mountain wall became shorter and shorter, too. They pushed themselves forward, emerging onto a lush green hill that stretched out for miles, dotted with large, leafy trees. Helen moved forward a few yards before turning around to look at the path from this perspective. The distance to the valley below made her dizzy. She was terrified by the awareness that if she or Neil had lost their balance, it would have meant a painful—perhaps deadly—tumble down the mountain. As though he read her thoughts, Neil walked to her and took her by the arm, pulling her to the shade of a nearby tree.

"We can rest for a few minutes, but I don't think we should stop tonight," said Neil as they sat on the cool grass. The sun was close to setting and the air moved around them in a cool breeze. "Not until we find a place that's safe and secure, anyway. We might as well get as much of a lead as possible. Which way do we go?"

Helen answered by pointing to the hill ahead of them.

A full moon rose that night, its light enwrapping the hill and trees in various shades of blue and white. Helen felt comforted by the moonlight. Although she was certain she should feel some uneasiness, it never came. Instead, the moonlight awoke in her a sense of life and hope with no hint of danger. But if Neil felt the same, he didn't show it.

By midnight they reached the top of the next hill. What lay ahead of them rooted their feet to the ground. It was too unexpected. Sprawling below them and covering most of this next glen was a small, white city. It was like nothing either of them had seen before and the pale white light cast down from the sky only enhanced its magnificence, contrasting against the darkness of the landscape.

"I think we might be safe here," Helen stated as a wave of comfort washed over her.

"How can you be sure it's safe?" Neil asked. "Is it Camelora?"

"I don't think when you see Camelora you will need to ask that question," she answered softly.

"What does the map say? You said there was a dot on the map."

Helen pulled out the book and opened to the map, tilting it to catch the moonlight to read what was scrawled on the page. "Ven," she read. The simple grey dot didn't do the city justice.

Behind the city was another mountain, adding to the sense of shelter Helen felt looking at the city. If only time would stand still and she could stay in this spot—all she wanted was to hold onto this peace she felt for the first time in years. The slight pressure of Neil's hand pulled her out of this thought and forced her forward.

"We'll have to be careful, though," Neil whispered, afraid someone might be close enough to hear. "This may be one of Mered's cities. I hate to think we're walking into danger just because the city is beautiful."

As they walked toward the city, they were impressed by an odd sense of silence. The ground underneath them soon turned into a path, appearing more and more visible the closer they came to the city walls. Helen soon realized that all along, the path had been wide enough for cart wheels to pass along it; it was only when three or four different paths converged that the ruts were made clear. Fresh tracks were visible in the soft dirt—a strange contrast to the silence hanging in the air.

"Do we go in or around?" Neil asked.

"In," Helen said without much thought.

"*Carefully*," Neil reiterated.

They were close enough now to see the detail of the arched gate set into the wall around the city. Surely they were near enough to see the signs of life that any city would show. Yet no lights appeared from the towering structures within the walls. It didn't have the same feeling of emptiness as the abbey, yet there seemed to be no one there—no voices or laughter, no footsteps, no flickers of life. Neil slowed his pace as they walked through the open gateway.

"Do you think there's anyone in this place?" he asked.

Helen shrugged her shoulders, baffled. "Maybe they have no reason to be out of bed," she said. "Or it's abandoned, like the abbey. Let's just see what we can find."

"It doesn't feel like anyone's here."

They walked through blocks and blocks of streets, all of them empty. No sounds came from the houses lining them. Many of the doors of these houses stood open, as though their inhabitants didn't care whether anyone went inside. To add to the eery silence, everything looked identical: stone houses with flat roofs built three stories high, with green vines growing from planter boxes at the windows. None of it was overgrown. If the city had been abandoned, it wasn't long ago. Helen worried as they walked that it was cursed and they would never be able to find their way out again. Seeing this beautiful place in this way gave Helen a feeling of uncomfortable sadness. She imagined

Veren looking like this, its citizens killed or carried away as prisoners and she regretted the decision to come inside.

"I don't think there *is* anyone here," she said, stopping in the middle of the street.

"Let's try one of these doors, then," Neil suggested. "Even if there's no one to help us, we can at least have shelter for the night."

The sound of crunching gravel made them both jump. A chill ran down Helen's spine and she held her breath, as though she had been drenched in icy water. They turned to see a man holding out a long sword. His tall stature made Neil feel vulnerable in a way he wasn't used to. Instinctively, he stepped in front of Helen. Annoyed, she touched his shoulder and pushed until he moved out of the way.

"Who are you?" the man asked. The moonlight was at his back and his face was distorted by shadows, preventing Helen from judging his expression.

"You can put down your sword," Neil said. "We're only looking for help."

The man stood frozen, considering them, then lowered his arm. "I'm afraid we aren't really in a position to help anyone," he said.

"We don't need much," Helen spoke up, stepping out from behind Neil. The man had a kind voice, despite his cold attitude. He didn't give her the same feeling of emptiness she felt when Ian was around. She didn't doubt he would be willing to at least give them shelter and point them in the right direction, assuming the people of the north knew anything about their destination. She hesitated, not knowing what reaction to expect, before adding, "We only need help finding our way to Camelora."

He showed no reaction to this statement. There was no disbelieving laughter, no twitch in his posture, just the same unwavering, appraising stare. "What are your names?" he asked.

"Helen and Neil," Neil replied.

It was then his reaction showed. "Well, Helen and Neil, come with me."

"You can help us?" Neil asked, incredulous.

"We'll see."

"Who are you?"

"Stephen," he answered simply as he sheathed his sword and turned around. Neil and Helen exchanged glances, then walked side by side a few paces behind Stephen as he wove in long strides through a short series of streets, then turned onto one that was wider than the rest. Growing steadier into view, at the end of this street, was a large white building, grander and more beautiful than any governor's palace Helen had ever seen. It was the center of the city, the place around which everything else was built and revolved. A five-foot wall enclosed it and they entered by an arched gate, which looked like a miniature of the one they had passed through into the city, into a manicured garden—an orderly arrangement of blossoming trees and grass and colorful spring flowers. White stone steps rose to the door of the palace, which was surrounded by large stone pillars encircling a wide terrace. The façade of the palace was all stone, carved with images they couldn't distinguish in the moonlight.

"Have you ever seen anything more beautiful than this?" Helen whispered.

"Not many things, no," Neil answered.

The doors opened into an entryway made of polished yellow and white marble, lit by many small oil lamps. Blue and white tiles in the floor formed an exquisite mosaic that Helen wished she didn't have to walk on. The polished walls gleamed around them and there were many clay vases resting on pedestals resembling the pillars outside the palace. But the entryway was appealing in a simple way, without excess ornamentation—lacking the finery Helen would have imagined.

Stephen led them through a set of doors. A woman stood in the middle of the floor, lit by the lamplight, her back to the door, dressed as though she, like Helen, was about to leave on a long journey. Her head was bent over a scroll, which she rolled up as she turned at the sound of the closing doors.

"I thought everyone was gone," she stated with surprise. Then, after a pause, she continued, "I've never seen these two before."

The amount of unconcern she showed made Helen wonder how often strangers appeared in the middle of the night. That wasn't the only thought the woman drew from Helen, for Helen had never seen any woman like her before. Her beauty was stunning. Though she had seen dark-skinned people from the south when they came to meet with her father, the men were the only ones she had seen up close, and their visits were rare. The woman she saw now had the same wide nose, the same full mouth, the same dark eyes. Her brown skin radiated light and kindness. A mane of curls framed her face. Like the palace that surrounded her, the woman evinced simplicity—in her dress, in the expressiveness of her face, and in the graceful way she carried herself. Helen was embarrassed by her own inadequacies in manner and appearance.

In the clear light of this room, Stephen's features were more visible, and, as he stood next to the woman, their similarities in manner stood out, but manner and posture were all they had in common physically. Stephen stood tall and thin, the lightness of his skin contrasting the woman's darkness. He looked to be about thirty years old—perhaps a couple of years younger than the woman—with short reddish-brown hair and blue eyes, like the color of a sun-filled summer sky. In the street, he had used the trick of the moonlight to his advantage, because any amount of light would have betrayed his own look of kindness. His face was more serious than the woman's, but it was constantly expressive. That expressiveness was gentle.

"Meira," Stephen said to the woman, though his eyes were fixed on

Helen and Neil, "this is Helen, and this is Neil. They would like our help finding Camelora."

At this last word, Meira's eyes brightened more than Helen thought possible, darting between Helen and Neil and Stephen, before finally locking on Stephen. Then, they both smiled.

"Helen and Neil," Meira exclaimed, "trying to find Camelora."

She looked the two of them over, making Helen more self-conscious than before. Trying not to let the trembling of her fingers show, she reached up a hand and tried to straighten her hair the best she could. She also attempted to dust off her tattered gown, but knew that it was no use. The woman laughed quietly, taking a few steps forward.

The more Helen watched Meira and Stephen, the more confused, then worried, she became. She wondered if she was just too tired. This situation was very much like a curious dream. A heavy doubt began to take hold of her. "Is this Camelora?" she asked, thinking of the empty city outside, which was nothing like she had imagined, and thinking she was wrong to believe she would know Camelora when she saw it. "I didn't believe it was...."

"No, it's not Camelora," Meira answered, shaking her head. "It's only a pale vestige of Zaric's kingdom. Have you come far?"

"I come from Veren," Helen replied, "and Neil comes from Camdor."

Neil placed a hand on Helen's arm, wishing he had done so before she blurted out the information.

"You aren't sure you can trust us," Meira stated with admiration in her voice. "I'm glad. You can't be too careful. But we aren't trying to deceive you. Helen senses that."

"We've never been so far south," Stephen put in, "but we knew someone from Camdor once. A wonderful man. He traveled throughout every region and told the most impossible stories. They were all true, of course. No friend of Zaric could tell a story that isn't true."

"That sounds like my grandfather," Neil said, his own expression softening.

"Can you help us?" Helen asked, feeling more comfortable knowing that these people were friends of Neil's grandfather. "We only need shelter for the night and help finding our way in the morning."

"We can show you which way to go," Meira replied, "but we can't give you shelter for the night."

"But, from what we saw outside, you have plenty of room."

"It isn't a question of hospitality," Stephen said, his eyes apologetic. "It's a question of safety. No one should be here in the morning. We shouldn't even be here tonight. Mered's men are coming."

# Chapter 8

"I thought this place would be safe," Helen said, unable to disguise her disappointment.

"It's safer than most," Meira reassured her. "But every city falls in the end—except Camelora. We've received reports from our watchers that a group of Mered's men aren't far from here. They haven't found us yet, but they probably will by dawn. All our people left this morning. I wanted to go, too, but Stephen wanted to wait a little longer. He was sure you would come."

Helen didn't immediately understand what Meira said. When she did, surprise swirled through her mind and she couldn't find the words to respond. How many people knew what Helen and Neil were doing, while they were only finding it out for themselves? Finally, Helen simply repeated, "He was sure we would come."

Stephen blushed. Then, his eyes widened as though he were remembering something. "I prepared a couple of bags with food for you, just in case," he said, rushing to the corner of the room to retrieve the bags for them.

"I'm sorry now that I doubted you," Meira went on. "I've lived long enough to know that people always come when you stop expecting them to."

"How did you know we would come?" Neil asked, suspicious. "Have you been following us?"

"No," Meira chuckled. "The man Stephen mentioned, the man from Camdor, he told us you would. Long ago. He didn't say when. I thought he must have been wrong. But he was never wrong. Your coming tonight proves that."

"Won't they notice so many people leaving?" Neil asked in a very practical tone. "This is a large city. If everyone left at once, they won't be able to move discreetly."

"They'll disperse before they get too far," Stephen answered. "It's part of the plan. By tomorrow night, our city will be scattered over the land until each family group is swallowed up into the cities on the outer borders of the kingdom. Have you ever been to the outer borders of the kingdom?" Helen and Neil shook their heads and Stephen continued, "There are only two regions between Camdor and the northern frontier, and they are much less populated than the coastal and southern regions. If our people spread out enough, no one will notice them relocating. Speaking of spreading out, we need to get moving ourselves."

He placed his hand on Meira's back and the two started for the door, but Helen reached out and grabbed Meira's arm, stopping them both.

"I thought they would have gone to Camelora," Helen stated. "Why aren't they?"

There was a strange pause, and Meira was visibly confused by the question. "No one can go to Camelora," she stated in a measured voice. "Not yet."

"But we're going to Camelora," Helen argued. "If no one can go yet—"

"You're different," Meira replied simply.

"The Gateway," Helen stated, and Meira nodded. "I didn't realize no one can go beyond it."

"That's why it needs to be opened," Meira kindly pointed out.

Stephen's manner became impatient. "I wish we didn't have to leave, and I wish we could do more to help you, but it isn't safe for any of us to stay here. I'm glad you came when you did and not a few hours later. If we can get out of the city now, we might still be able to disappear."

"Disappear?" Helen repeated, eyes widening in disbelief, picturing Meira and Stephen dissolving into a cloud of dust.

"He means, use our superior intellect to evade them," Meira said, "which is easily said and even more easily done. But we don't have much time. As we walk, you can tell us what you would like to know. If you don't ask questions, we'll most likely give you the wrong answers."

As she and Stephen crossed to the door, Meira glanced at them. Her face was so full of hope, Helen felt herself relax. "Meira," she said, quickening her pace to walk alongside the woman, "do you know Zaric?"

Meira's eyes flashed with bright memory, adding to the effect of her beauty. "Of course," she answered with reverence in her voice.

"What's he like?"

"My words could never convey all that he is. You will know for yourself when you meet him."

Stephen looked at the sky, then walked faster. Helen and Neil struggled to keep up as their guides led the way through the city they knew so well. Helen fought to push back the haunting memory of leaving her own city and wondered how Meira and Stephen could leave theirs with so little regret. Shaking those thoughts aside, Helen searched for the right questions to ask, afraid they would run out of streets before she and Neil learned anything useful. "Please don't be surprised if we know less than you think we should," Helen began. "What do the keys do?"

"There is a barrier," Stephen replied, "that separates Camelora from the rest of the world. A physical barrier. The keys must be taken to the Gateway, which opens this barrier. No one can pass through it until all of the keys have been found and the Gateway is opened. Well, besides Zaric himself, but he doesn't count."

"Can Zaric leave Camelora?" Neil asked.

"Of course," Meira said. "He created the barrier, after all."

"I thought he went to Camelora to seal himself off from the rest of the world," Neil expressed.

"He isn't trying to protect himself, but the people inside of Camelora," Stephen said. "Mered has managed to persuade many regions to follow him, but Zaric's people are too loyal to ever turn against him and Mered knows it. If he could get to them, he would kill them all. Camelora is also a symbol for anyone who still remembers the stories about Zaric. If Mered can destroy it, he can destroy the idea of Zaric. Power like that would earn him the fear and devotion he so desperately wants."

"Then why do we want to open the barrier?"

"Because the Camelorans are also the *strongest* people in the kingdom. They have been taught by Zaric himself. With enough support, they can defeat Mered. Being closed off for so long has only made them stronger. In most respects, anyway. For generations their families have been prepared for the coming battle by Zaric, who knows Mered better than anyone else alive."

"Zaric is also protecting the *idea* of Camelora," Meira added. "As long as a part of the kingdom is set apart from the rest, there is a hope to hold onto and spread."

"We found a green stone a couple of days ago, in an abandoned abbey," Helen told them. "It's small and round and unlike any gem I've ever seen. Is it one of the keys?"

"Yes, that sounds right," Meira nodded. "Though I've never seen the keys myself. How did you find it?"

"That's a long story," Helen said.

"Another time, then."

"Do you know where we can find the rest of them?" Neil asked. "The keys?"

"Their locations aren't marked on our map," Helen explained.

"I'm afraid we don't, but I can't imagine it will be too hard. Did you have any trouble finding the first one?"

Neil wanted to say yes, but decided it would sound as sarcastic as he felt.

They turned a corner and found themselves facing the eastern wall of the city. They made their way to the gate leading to the field outside, which looked like the one Helen and Neil had passed through not long before. It was a secluded place to build a city and Helen now understood why. "Perhaps when we open the barrier to Camelora," she said to Meira, "you and your people will be able to come back here."

"It's only a city," Meira said. "Stones and mortar. What matters is that our people are safe, even if it means never seeing this place again. Stephen and I are the protectors of the people, not the buildings in the city. We'll work to strengthen Zaric and Camelora, defeat Mered, then return to our region to make it stronger than it was before. Opening the Gateway won't instantly solve the kingdom's problems. Stephen and I have work to do."

"We need to leave you now," Stephen apologized. "It would be dangerous to stay together, with an army coming this way. Meira and I are going to the western trees, but I think the two of you should go east."

"But the path on the map goes—" Helen began, but Stephen held up a hand to cut her off.

"Go east. You will find a place to rest there."

"Can't you come with us?" Helen asked, the fear of yet another threat overwhelming her.

"Our purpose is different than yours," Meira stated, laying a gentle hand on the young woman's arm.

"You can take refuge in a garden about two miles from here," Stephen went on, "and wait for the men to pass."

"Won't they find us in a garden?" Neil asked, not worried about revealing his derision this time.

"Not this garden."

Meira stepped forward and embraced Helen and Neil in turn. "I wish we had more time. You're coming has confirmed all of our hopes, and it allows us to hope for even more."

She gave one last reassuring smile, then turned and walked toward the trees. Stephen stepped forward and shook Neil's hand, clapping the opposite hand on the young man's shoulder, and then pressed Helen's hands between both of his. "Take care of each other," he instructed. "We'll see you again."

"And I thought we were going to have a comfortable night's sleep," Neil said as they watched Meira and Stephen disappear into the forest. "I'm tired, I don't want to move anymore, and now we need to find a garden for protection. Flowers, probably, and maybe a few trees and bushes. Though, to be fair, there are probably some rocks, too."

"Please, Neil, stop," Helen said, exasperated. It was difficult to keep her mind from thinking of the empty beds in the city they had just left, her feelings torn between pity for the people who had left them, and pity for herself and Neil, who so desperately needed to rest. She also tried to breathe away her disappointment at not being able to ask Meira and Stephen more questions. She still had no idea who they really were, besides friends of Zaric and Neil's grandfather. Her tired mind almost believed that the last half-hour had been nothing more than an illusion, a drama played out in her own exhausted imagination.

But they had said there was a garden where they could find protection and Helen believed them.

Helen almost wished for an omen of danger, some sign to propel them forward and keep their pace from slackening. Yet the moon still shined down in bright beams, a few birds sang songs of encouragement, even a warm breeze wound across the landscape. There was no hint that some menace was threatening to overtake them.

"It would have been easier to do this if we had to cover ten miles," Neil said, "instead of just two."

"Then maybe we should pretend it's ten," Helen retorted.

"Do you remember," he went on conversationally, though Helen suspected it was only to prevent himself from collapsing from fatigue, "the balls you used to tell me about when we were children?"

"I used to hide on a balcony above the ballroom in the governor's palace, watching the people laugh and dance and flirt and talk. My mother knew I was there—I remember her sometimes looking up at me and smiling. I always imagined what it would be like when I was old enough to actually go downstairs."

"You used to promise me that, when we were older, you would send a carriage to pick me up and bring me to one of your balls. I dreamed so many times about what it would be like, seeing all of those important people in their finest clothes. Yours was a life so different from mine in our little cottage."

"I never forgot those promises, even if they seemed a little too childish as I got older. When we heard that your parents had died, my father wanted to send for you and bring you to live with us. But we were under suspicion by then. It wasn't safe for you to come. By the time I was old enough to go to the balls myself, we had stopped having so many of them. When the other governors turned against my father and we closed ourselves off, there was no one to invite. Well, we did have some with the people of our city, but the finery wasn't there."

"As I got older," Neil said in a rare understanding tone, "I realized I would never enjoy those balls as much as I wanted to, anyway. So many people! I would have missed life in my cottage."

"We didn't forget you," Helen reiterated.

"I know," Neil said. "I'm starting to see that. I've been so focused on my little life in Camdor, I had no idea what was happening in the other regions."

They pushed themselves forward as the ground flattened and cleared around them. Ahead of them, like a mirage in the desert at midday, the moonlight played with their vision, dancing for a few moments before finally stabilizing, reflecting off a short wall of white stone—no more than six feet high—broken by an arch in the same pattern as the ones in the city they had just left. Shadowy trees stood at regular intervals inside the garden. It was in no way unusual.

"I don't see how this garden is safer than the city," Neil stated in a flat tone.

Helen ignored him and walked with heavy feet and stiff joints to the archway. She silently agreed with Neil, but didn't want to satisfy him by expressing her own opinion. Stephen said the garden was safe and Helen trusted him. This land was new to her, but familiar to Stephen. Despite the doubts he expressed, Neil followed Helen in.

In the half-light, they were only able to distinguish the outlines of the objects in the garden, caught up in shadows. Helen stifled a scream when she thought she saw a man standing a few feet away, before realizing it was only a shadow. Flowers and bushes, benches and statues, along with the tall trees they saw before: their dark silhouettes created an eerie landscape where nothing felt quite real. Yet the air soothed Helen in a way she hadn't anticipated. The contrast between what she saw and what she felt struck her.

"I don't think we'll find anywhere safer tonight," she said. "And I'm too tired to try. We'll sleep here and hope Stephen and Meira were right."

She found a patch of grass beneath a tree and laid down, taking her blanket from where it was tied to her bag. Neil watched her—unable to set aside his uneasiness as well as Helen did—then glanced around again before finally walking over to the grass and sitting down.

"If you believe we're safe," he stated, "I really don't have the energy to think you're wrong."

* * *

The heavy tramp of horses awoke Helen in the morning. Her eyes fluttered at the first sound, and at the second, sleep dissipated. Her body lay still and stiff. She had turned in the night and was now facing the outer wall of the garden. A group of mounted men were visible above it, bringing their horses to a stop as they cast their eyes around. Helen moved her eyes as far as they would go without moving her head. At least twenty men were within her line of vision; it wouldn't be long before they looked toward the tree she was under and spotted her. And as she became more aware of where she was and how she had arrived there, her hope fell. Stephen and Meira must have been wrong.

"The marks end here," one man called out, his voice coming clearly over the wall. But his next statement was confusing. "I don't understand it."

Still afraid to move, Helen wondered why the men hadn't noticed her or Neil yet. There were a few bushes between them, but nothing large enough to shield them from view. She could see the men clearly. Carefully, she pulled her knees to her chest and used her arm and shoulder to spin herself on the grass, until she was facing Neil. He looked back at her with confusion that matched what she felt herself. Not far away was the archway they had come through into the garden. Another group of men had stopped beyond it, yet none of them looked through it. Helen waited another minute or two, then raised herself up with caution, first sitting low, then kneeling, and finally standing. The wall was too low for this to go unnoticed. But it did.

"I don't understand it," the same man repeated. "They couldn't have disappeared. That's impossible."

"Maybe they covered their tracks," another man suggested.

"We would be able to see that. The tracks just—stop."

Feeling a little more confident, Helen moved to find an unobstructed view and study the men a little more thoroughly. They were a band of about one hundred, dressed in identical dark blue uniforms, carrying swords and shields, though they wore no armor. Many of them swept their eyes over her as they glanced around the clearing, but no one fixed his eyes upon her. Her fear of them melted away. She smiled down at Neil, who got to his feet and stood next to her.

"What are they doing?" he whispered. Helen put up her hand to silence him, noticing that one man reacted, his head snapping up when Neil spoke. He looked in their direction, but said nothing.

"They must have gone into the woods," the apparent leader said. "Maybe they retraced their steps somehow. Let's split into groups and scour the trees. We'll merge again five miles to the east. We might at least drive them to a place where we can overtake them."

The men hung back uncertainly. The leader continued with impatience, "They can't hide in the middle of an empty field. The grass isn't long enough, and we've been over the entire place."

He issued a few commands and the men dispersed in small groups, riding toward the trees. Helen and Neil stood still for a few minutes, even after the sound of the horses stopped ringing in their ears. They were afraid to speak until they knew the men weren't coming back. If they believed this was only a field, there wasn't much chance of them returning. At last they sighed in respite and wonder as they took this first opportunity to examine the garden in the morning light.

The colors that met their eyes were vibrant, almost alive. Flowers of every shade and kind covered the ground. There were no seasons in this garden. Spring flowers and summer flowers and autumn flowers grew side by side, complementing each other in an unusual way. Some trees were only blossoming, while others bore ripe fruit. Still others were shedding their leaves. There were weathered marble pedestals and benches, gravel walks and a large, dry, marble fountain. Great archways, some intact and others collapsed, stood outside the garden at regular intervals. It was like they were looking at the remains of a ruined temple, though it couldn't have been more beautiful if it was restored. The garden appeared to be carefully tended, with cut grass and flowerbeds clear of weeds.

"What is this place?" Neil asked as Helen sifted through her memories. This was all somehow familiar. It was strange that she hadn't thought that before. She sat again on the grass and pulled the book from her bag. She scanned the pages, her fingers finding it difficult to keep up with her mind. Toward the middle of the book, she found the page she was looking for and stopped to read it to herself.

With a bright, clear look, she fixed her gaze on Neil. "It's the Sanctuary," she told him.

# Chapter 9

"And what is the Sanctuary?" Neil asked.

"It's a place untouched by malevolence," Helen answered, allowing her feet to move her, taking in the beauty and color of the garden as though she were quenching her thirst at a mountain brook. "Most travelers can't see it. According to your grandfather, anyway. Zaric is rumored to have built it."

"How can one man in one lifetime do all the things Zaric is said to have done?" Neil stated wryly, following Helen.

"Who says it was one lifetime?" Helen reached down and ran her fingers across the petals of a cream-colored rose. Its scent grew and filled the air around them for a few seconds.

"Do you honestly think it's impossible for evil to come in here?" Neil asked.

"You saw what happened just now," Helen said emphatically. "I wouldn't be surprised if Zaric built hundreds of sanctuaries that we just don't know about. He really does want everyone to be safe, and he would want places for the people to be safe in."

"And Camelora would be the ultimate sanctuary." Neil sat down on a stone bench not far from where Helen stood. With deep breaths he tried to soak in the stillness of this place. The early morning sun shone across the garden and only a few wispy clouds rested suspended in the sky. The more he sat still, the more Neil felt the easiness of safety, but still he thought of the imminent danger that waited outside. He looked back at the wonders of this garden and thought of the city not far away, so easily abandoned by its people in favor of a nomadic life, despite the city's solitude and apparent comforts. He thought of Ian and the army outside the walls and wondered how safe he and Helen would be once they left this sanctuary. A sliver of his heart hoped Camelora was real, and he thought he understood why Helen felt the same way. There had to be something to look forward to, or they might as well let Ian or the army kill them now.

"But why would Zaric need a garden?" asked Neil, just loud enough for Helen to hear. "A fortress would have been much safer. A hundred fortresses would have been safer."

"A garden is where things grow," Helen answered, basking in the tingle of her skin as she breathed in the fragrant and clean air. "You can't help feeling alive when you're surrounded by life. I can't speak for Zaric, though. That's just how I feel. Fortresses are stone—hardness—and they feel like war. They're only safe when there are people to guard and defend them."

"My mother loved flowers. I'm sure you remember the flower gardens we used to have around our cottage. I've never been very good with them. I prefer to grow plants that are useful."

"Flowers are useful, in their own way," Helen argued.

"Not as useful as vegetables and fruit trees. My mother would be disappointed if she saw what happened to her flowers after she died. At first, I was doing all I could to get by. By the time I thought of them as a way to remember her, most of them had died."

"I always dreamed of having a garden like the ones I saw in other regions or the illustrated books we had in our library. But we never had the right kind of soil for a garden. There were a few plants and flowers suited to the climate, but not many. A few of the rich people in our city had gardens that would sometimes peek over their walls, but never anything as beautiful as this."

"You speak about the rich as though your family wasn't."

"We weren't—not really. My father didn't believe that a governor should have more than he could earn. He was too busy looking after the people of the region to take the time to make himself rich—and I admire him for it. What money we had wasn't spent on importing soil and bulbs and seeds to make an exotic garden, only to hide behind a wall for no one but our family to enjoy."

"Daffodils were my mother's favorite," Neil said, standing up and walking to a cluster growing a few feet away. "She was tall and blonde, too, so I guess that was why. Nothing like me. I looked forward to seeing them in the spring because they reminded me of her. They were one flower that thrived after she was gone."

Smiling to himself, he took one of the flowers at the bottom of its stem, twisted it slightly, and pulled. The stem snapped. He held the flower out and studied it, then turned and held it out to Helen.

She reached out to accept it, smiling in return, but froze when she noticed the ground at Neil's feet. Confused and horrified, covering her mouth with her hand, she slowly walked to it and knelt on the gravel. Neil looked down, too, and the daffodil in his hand fell to the ground.

The patch of yellow and white and orange flowers withered in only a few seconds, leaving behind a cluster of brown. Not only the daffodils were affected, but a few smaller flowers near them withered as well. The dirt in that part of the flowerbed became parched and dry. The flower lying at Neil's feet was now dry and withered as well.

"What did you do?" Helen asked.

"I only picked one," Neil defended. "People do that all the time. You saw me do it."

"But what happened to the flowers?"

"I don't know. If I did, I wouldn't have done it."

Getting to her feet, Helen walked down the path, sweeping her eyes over the flowers and other plants. A dread came over her that the Sanctuary's powers were fading, and it was losing its ability to protect them. Somehow, she thought, its safety had been compromised, and anyone would be able to enter it. She examined the ground for more dry patches but found none. She stopped in front of a cluster of rose bushes, scanning the plants and trees. Her initial panic subsided.

After standing still for a moment, thinking, she stooped down, picking a small red rose from one of the bushes. Then, she waited over it, until, like the daffodils, the flowers withered before her eyes and the leaves of the bush turned brown.

"Don't kill any more of them!" Neil exclaimed, rushing to her. "What if Zaric comes and sees that we've destroyed his entire sanctuary? I'm sure he would understand one or two dead patches, but not the whole garden. Let's just try not to touch anything. We should probably get out of here."

"It's just strange, though," Helen said. "Picking one flower shouldn't do so much harm."

"If there really is some sort of power in this garden, maybe the flowers aren't meant to be picked. It might weaken the whole place. Pretty soon, those men will come back and find that we aren't invisible after all."

Helen considered this theory again, but she wasn't sure she could really accept it now. It made sense, protecting the garden's power, but if only good was allowed to enter the garden in the first place, the walls wouldn't allow someone to pass through who could possibly destroy it. If anything, the flowers themselves would have a protective power for anyone who picked them. The strangest explanation was the most probable one.

"The next key is in here," Helen stated firmly.

"In this garden?"

"Yes."

Neil stared at her and thought about it for a minute. "In one of the flowers?" he finally asked.

"It makes sense, doesn't it?" Helen said, glad Neil had caught on to her thought.

"No," Neil said, shaking his head. "Most things haven't made sense so far. In a flower and not in a crevice somewhere."

"In a flower," Helen answered, growing more confident in the idea.

"But it might not be here at all. You might be wrong."

"It won't hurt us to try, Neil."

"It might hurt the garden," Neil stated, unable to stifle the bite in his voice.

"What if we don't look, and it really is here? I don't really think we can change our minds later and come back. Anyway, Stephen was adamant that we come this way, even though the map pointed us in a different direction. That fact must be important."

"Wait, are you saying you might think the map was wrong?"

Helen ignored this remark, turning her attention instead back to the garden.

Neil sighed and nodded. "All right," he said. "We'll look. But what exactly are we looking for?"

"I don't know, Neil," Helen answered, exasperated. "Just trust your instincts."

"Are you sure *you* trust my instincts?"

"Just try not to pick anything unless you're pretty sure it's the right flower."

With a sigh of frustration, Neil rubbed his brow and turned away from Helen, walking down the gravel path, studying the flowers with meticulous attention as he went.

Helen looked around at the acres of park-like land surrounding them. It was like a painter's palette, a sea of every color imaginable. The flowers varied in size, from bigger than Helen's head to the size of her smallest fingernail. She stooped down to look at some, stood on the tips of her toes to look at others. She studied every flower as thoroughly as possible, examining them inside and outside, turning them as much as she could without breaking the stems.

Time passed. The lack of progress frustrated her. Many times, she reached out her hand to pick a flower, then pulled it back, not sure if she was acting out of a desire to move on or because she really thought it was the right flower. From time to time she looked across the flowerbeds to where Neil was standing—his hair rumpled from repeatedly running his hands through it in frustration—as he stared at another cluster, then she turned and went in the opposite direction. Frustrated as well, Helen looked down at the ground. She took a deep breath and picked a small blue flower before she could think twice, only to watch its cluster and the yellow cluster next to it wither beneath her eyes. She had thought this would be easier, that she would see one flower among the rest that would be obviously different and that she would know without a doubt that it was the right one.

"It's no good," Neil called from a few yards away. "It wouldn't be so hard if only the ones we pick die, instead of all those around it. We just can't know for sure which one it is without picking every flower here, and then we might lose it. And we still don't know what we're looking for."

Helen tried not to believe that he was right, but she couldn't see any other way herself. None of these flowers looked special in any way. They were simply ordinary, common flowers, like those she could see anywhere in the land at any time, only they all existed at once in the same place.

"We need to look deeper," Helen said in return, trying not to sound discouraged. "Please, Neil, just try a little harder."

"A little harder?" he exclaimed with stinging bitterness. "Helen, this is impossible. It's like trying to find one special grain of sand on a beach, and I'm not going to look anymore. Not until I've had half an hour to close my eyes and pretend someone isn't trying to kill me and someone else doesn't want me to walk to a place I can't even be sure exists!"

With that, Neil plopped down on the ground and looked at Helen like a defiant child. Stunned, Helen could only stand with her mouth half open and her eyes wide. She dropped the withered flower she still held in her hand and marched to Neil, not bothering to stay on the path. Careful not to step on any plants, she crossed over the flowerbeds that separated them.

"*You're* impossible, Neil," she said as emphatically as she could, though she knew it sounded weak. "You want everything to be easy, and when it's not, all you do is complain. I have to do a lot of hard things, too, and I think you don't realize that I was alone for three weeks before I came to you. I'm not doing this because I want to or because I like it, but because thousands of people don't know that their lives are being taken away and we're the only ones with the knowledge that can save them. If I have to look at every single flower in the garden to do it, even if it takes a month, I will. You don't have to help, but you do have to shut up and stop criticizing me."

Neil flinched, and looked down at his hands. "*You* baited me," he said.

Helen didn't reply. Instead, she sat down on the ground next to Neil, relieving her annoyance with a sigh.

"If this is a sanctuary," Neil went on in a calmer way, "I want to let it be one, just for a little while. I don't want to worry about finding the key or running from a small army. I wasn't made for this kind of life."

Helen sat quietly, growing embarrassed for allowing herself to snap at Neil. "No one else would have come with me," she said, taking off her shoes and letting her feet rest on the soft grass. "It's hard to convince people that Zaric can help them when he isn't even much of a legend anymore. He's only the smallest whisper and there's too much noise in the world for anyone to hear."

Neil rested on his heels, rocking back and forth, then stood and began to walk around the garden again. Helen watched him for a minute, then closed her eyes, though she didn't try to clear her mind. There was one flower in this garden that was different from the rest. It would have to be the sort of flower Zaric would choose to place his key in. Not a flower set on a pedestal or in the most visible spot of land, but one that would be growing among other flowers, the last one anyone would really think to look at. It wouldn't be as grand as a rose or plain as a poppy. It would blend in by being not too common and just common enough.

Taking a deep breath, Helen opened her eyes again. This time, she looked at the garden and not the flowers or trees or bushes inside it. Her eyes swept over all of them, taking in the peace and serenity of the place. The bright morning sunlight poured down, making the colors around her more brilliant and vivid. A few yards across the pond of flowers and plants, Helen's gaze was attracted by the glint of something in the light.

She got to her feet and moved to a flowerbed near the base of a flowering apple tree, where the flowers were spaced out evenly, a palette of cream, white, yellow, blue, and violet. It was the tallest of the violet flowers—an iris—that glimmered. Helen bent closer to it. This flower was familiar to her, like a detail in a half-forgotten dream. On the most inside part of one of the petals was a simple drop of dew.

"Only one flower in this garden has dew on it," she observed out loud. Neil turned toward her, then crossed the garden to where she was kneeling.

"Only this flower has dew on it," she reiterated now that Neil stood next to her. Her nerves and hands shaking, Helen reached out, paused for a moment, then took the stem in her hand and picked the flower.

She looked at it intently, wondering if something fantastic would happen to it. She didn't at first notice that none of the flowers around it withered. When she did notice, her tension eased. She held out her hand and tilted the flower over it. At first, the dew drop clung stubbornly to the petal, but it soon began to roll toward the outer edge, where it hung for a moment, then fell into Helen's hand. She looked at her cupped palm and found that she wasn't holding a drop of dew, but a perfectly round amethyst. Triumphant, she stood up straight and held her hand out to Neil.

# Chapter 10

Neil looked down at the two stones sitting side by side in his palm. He ran his finger across their smooth surfaces. "Keys," he said. "They're so small."

Helen only nodded as she gathered up their bags. Finding another key was exhilarating and her mind was anxious to find the next two. A task that before seemed daunting, even after one key was found, now seemed possible, almost easy. With a sense of purpose, she was able to keep off the constant and draining weariness and insecurity that threatened to overtake her.

Yet she was fighting a different threat now. The peace she had felt when they first entered the garden had grown almost tangible, surrounding her like a fog she couldn't see. It would be easy to stay here, where it was safe, and stop moving. She held out the small drawstring bag for Neil to drop the keys in, but he only stood still, staring at her.

"It really is quiet here," Neil said. "Would it hurt us to stay a little longer?"

"Yes," Helen replied, masking her emotions, not wanting to admit her own similar thoughts.

"It's not like we're in a rush, is it?"

"Well, there's no point in staying here. And we don't know where Ian is. Even if he can't come in, he can wait outside."

"But if he can't see this place—"

"I don't want to take a risk. Plus, we don't know what Mered is doing out there in the kingdom. How many more cities can he overtake while we're avoiding our responsibility?"

There was an uncomfortable silence. It wasn't hard to imagine Ian standing outside the Sanctuary, staring at what he couldn't see and waiting until they needed to come out. Neil seemed unwilling to relent, but Helen didn't want to, either, so she stood with shoulders back and head held high, daring Neil to drop his gaze first. He did.

"If we don't move at a steady pace," she said, "we might find it hard to move at all."

Neil continued to look determined, but soon nodded his acquiescence. He let the keys roll out of his palm and into the purse. Helen closed it and put it away in the bag slung across her chest.

"I think we should make our way northwest," Helen stated, casting her eyes in that direction, "find our way back to the path on the map. We need to get back on course."

They gathered their things and headed to the northern archway of the garden. When she was sure Neil wasn't watching her, Helen glanced back through the archway at the beauty they were leaving. She wondered if they would ever be able to come back, or if other sanctuaries dotted the path, offering respite for the worn-out travelers trying to find Camelora.

"When my parents were ill," Neil said after a time of silent walking, "I didn't believe they would die. A boy of fourteen doesn't want to believe that it's possible to lose everything. I understood that my grandfather was old when he died and had lived a full life—even if I was reluctant to accept it—but my parents were too young. So I waited for Zaric. They believed Grandfather's stories and trusted in Zaric so much, I was sure he would come to heal them. Grandfather always told me that Zaric could heal the people. I hoped and waited… and they died.

I stopped hoping after that."

Helen opened her mouth to reply, but closed it again. Throughout her life, she had heard the same things about Zaric, from her own parents and Neil's grandfather. As an adult, she understood what it meant. Zaric was not the Eternal One. She wanted to point out the fact that Zaric had lived much longer than them and he was so much wiser, but it wasn't up to him if someone lived or died. Helen had her own growing doubts—not about Zaric's abilities, but about her own. To this point, her words had made no impact on Neil. If she didn't have his complete support, nothing else she accomplished would really matter. Having lost his confidence in Zaric, Helen wished that *she* could be worthy of his trust instead. It seemed like an impossible hope.

Not wanting to dwell on this thought, she turned instead to a different subject. "I was supposed to be married a year ago," she said. "He was the son of a wealthy landowner in our city. Philip. He was a good man. But we heard that Mered was mobilizing an army not far to the south. Veren was the last strong outpost in the southern region. A group of young men—Philip included—decided to attack Mered's army, hoping more than believing that he hadn't built it up strongly enough. They were wrong. Most people don't realize Mered has been moving for hundreds of years, planning and organizing, because his name only entered our history a few years ago. It's easy to see now how foolish this plan was, but at the time I admired our men for their courage. Mered's men killed all but one of those who went to fight, and the last was only spared to come back and tell us what had happened. These men were good, young, and strong. They would have been an ideal addition to Zaric's army. But Zaric didn't save them, either. Whatever his reasons, they must be good ones."

"Do you miss him?" Neil asked. "Philip."

"Yes," Helen replied after some thought.

"Did you love him?"

"In a way. I admired him, respected him. Yes, I think I did love him. Mostly, I try not to think about any of it. Philip is gone now. As a governor's daughter, love wasn't the most important qualification for marriage. My parents wanted me to think about the people I could influence more than I did about myself, which is always a good ambition. Philip and I would have made a good co-governors, once life calmed down. You, at least, would have had a choice."

Neil let out an abbreviated chuckle. "But now, you're hundreds of miles away from that future. Do you think you'll ever find it again?"

Helen didn't want to find the words to reply. Instead, she said, "Just listen to you. Before, I couldn't get you to tell me anything. Now, you won't stop."

Neil was self-conscious at having this pointed out, but didn't let that stop him from continuing with a subject of his own. "My parents weren't exactly popular in our village. They told such strange stories and believed odd things. The sort of things *you* tell and believe. The chances of finding a girl willing to marry their son weren't great. I never could have been interested in the daughters of any of the men in the village, anyway. Such empty-headed brats. They only cared about how much money a man could make at market or in trading with other villages and how profitable his land was. And since there has never really been anything interesting about me, I didn't have much of a chance."

"What makes you say you aren't interesting?"

"I like to be left alone. Having a wife and family would have complicated that. Ambition isn't my strength, either. If I have enough, I'm satisfied. In the end, I couldn't leave what my parents had worked so hard to build."

"You left with me," Helen pointed out. Neil didn't answer.

"If I told you that I'm afraid we won't find Camelora in time," Helen stated, measuring her words, "that my parents will be dead by the time we reach Zaric, you would understand how I feel."

"Yes, Helen, I understand, but you're not supposed to be like me."

This brought a smile to Helen's face, which soon turned into a soft chuckle. "Frightening," she said with a mock shudder. "Thank you for putting it all into perspective. I will do everything I can to avoid being like you."

Neil smiled himself. He liked to see that expression on Helen's face and was glad he had put it there. "After seeing that garden," he said, "I almost believe Zaric knows what he's doing."

"You will have to do better than 'almost believe' if you expect him to help you."

They laughed, but Helen stopped abruptly. She stood in the middle of the path and put out her arm to stop Neil. Though it was hard to tell, she thought she heard a horse's hooves in the distance behind them. From the look on Neil's face, even though the sound was so faint, she could tell that he heard it, too. Without saying any more, they ran.

Soon they reached the trees, moving together as much as the trees would allow. The sound behind them was growing louder. It only occurred to Helen for a brief moment that whoever was following them might not want to harm them. She discarded the thought. There were more dangers than friends on this path. The sound was of only one horse and Helen had a good idea who the rider would be. It wasn't worth taking a chance.

As the sound came closer, it was obvious they wouldn't be able to outrun their pursuer. The horse didn't have any trouble keeping a fast, steady pace through the trees, and Helen and Neil couldn't run fast enough to outrun him. The impulse to get away gave way to the simple desire to find a place to hide. Neil found a tree with a branch hanging low enough to reach and stopped, pulling himself up onto it with more skill than Helen realized he had. He reached down and grasped Helen's hand, helping her to climb and swing herself up. They climbed up a little bit further, until they were well hidden by the branches and leaves below them. With their backs against the trunk, they tried to breathe without a sound, waiting for the rider to appear.

The horse slowed down as it tried to make its way through the thickening trees, the sound of its approach winding and filling the air, coming from every direction. All they could tell for certain was that the horse was coming closer to where they were hiding. Helen pressed herself harder against the trunk of the tree, hoping that somehow this would make her even less visible. At the same time, she was trying to think of a plan in case they were caught.

There was no mistaking that the horse was following their path. The horse's black head came into view and Ian soon passed directly under them. Neil gripped the branch he was sitting on until his knuckles were white, but didn't make any of the sounds Helen expected him to make—no gasp, no sharp intake of breath. Ian cast his eyes around the forest, peering through the leaves and branches and trunks. He went past the tree a few yards, then stopped and circled back. Though Helen was sure he couldn't see them, she wasn't sure that he couldn't sense them. She held her breath. From a distant corner of the woods, something heavy fell to the ground, its sound echoing through the trees. In a swift motion, Ian urged his horse in the direction of that sound. Helen relaxed.

They waited until the clatter of the horse's hooves died down, then waited a few minutes longer before lowering themselves from the tree. A comforting breeze took Helen by surprise as it moved through the woods. Still, every sound made her uneasy, the tingle of fear swelling beneath her skin. Neil tried to reassure her with a smile, but she saw the uneasiness in his eyes, too. Once again, they turned north.

"We're getting close to the lake country, aren't we?" Neil asked in a muted tone, hoping to lighten the fear in the air.

"I believe so," Helen answered. "I've always wanted to see it."

The gaps between the trees became wider. The sunlight spilled down more brightly now. There was an unnerving blindness in the depths of the trees, and the leaves and branches made her feel as if eyes were constantly watching her, though always hidden. The increased visibility now relieved Helen. The path was almost clear ahead of them. With this balance of security and visibility, she hoped they would make good progress.

Neil's foot came down a little too heavily on a twig, and he grimaced as it snapped loudly. "Don't come any closer," a sharp voice said. They stopped as a woman stepped out of the trees, holding a bow with an arrow ready to spring.

# Chapter 11

They stared at the woman, unsure what to do. She didn't try to hide her fear, but she looked ready to fight them if they stepped closer. Helen darted her eyes within her frame of vision, wanting to be sure that the woman was at least alone. The trail was empty of everything else except the woman, who carried a bag across her body much like Helen's, besides the bow and quiver. Helen subdued her concern in order to study her, trying to decide what to say and how to say it. Feelings of inadequacy and insignificance rushed over Helen. Everything about the woman's features was perfect. Her face was not too round and not too square. A small nose sat above a delicate mouth, while vibrant amber eyes held her and Neil in their stare. Her brown hair was pulled back in a coil of braids, set much more carefully than Helen's own braid, though a few stray strands were left to frame her face. She was the same height as Helen, but her back was straighter—she carried herself with more confidence. Only a few smudges of dirt around the hem of her dress marred her appearance. Helen assumed she was simply lost, though something about this assumption didn't seem quite true.

"You can put your bow down," Neil said in a calm tone. "We aren't going to hurt you."

"That's what you say," the woman replied, "but how do I know I can believe you? Just go back. Find a different way."

"It isn't that simple," Helen said.

"I don't want that man to find me."

Helen glanced up at Neil, who asked, "What man?"

"Don't think you can trick me! The man on the black horse. I know he's here somewhere and I won't let him find me. And since I don't know whether you work for him or not, I suggest you turn around and go back. I'll kill you before I'll let you kill me."

"If we worked for Ian," Neil stated, "you wouldn't have lived long enough to say that."

He wasn't sure this statement was true, but it made the woman hesitate, considering them once more. "You know his name?"

"We're running from him ourselves."

The woman stared at them a minute longer, looking from one face to the other as the fear dissipated in her own. She relaxed her bow and dropped her hands.

"What's your name?" Neil asked, stepping closer.

"Siri," she replied simply.

"My name is Neil, and this is Helen. Can we help you, Siri?"

"We'll see." She considered them as she said this, scanning their faces and clothing. "Where do you come from?"

"South," Helen answered. "Veren and Camdor."

"I've never heard of them before. We don't hear about the southern lands in the west."

"By the sea?" Neil asked cautiously.

"Yes."

"That's hundreds of miles away. Have you walked all this way?"

"It's no farther than Veren," Helen said quietly to Neil.

"Don't whisper!" Siri ordered, raising the bow again. "What are you doing here? Where are you going?"

Both Helen and Neil hesitated. Helen wasn't sure what reaction Siri would have to her naming Camelora. If she, like most people, had never heard of it, she might laugh or ask for an explanation Helen didn't want to give. It had been hard enough to convince Neil to come with her—Helen knew it would be impossible to convince a total stranger. And her readiness with the arrow made Helen nervous.

"North," Helen replied without elaborating. "Will you put the bow down?"

"There is nothing north of here," Siri said, frowning as she again lowered her arms. "Everyone says it's a dead land, a land of ghosts."

"Where are you going?" Helen asked in return.

"Anywhere safe."

Helen and Neil both knew what the other was thinking. Suppressing a sigh as she made up her mind, Helen didn't turn to Neil to see him look at her for approval; instead, she nodded, trying not to show any doubts. She again considered Siri's clothes and felt a rush of pity toward her, not sure if this strange girl was merely impractical, or if she had been forced out of her home without time to prepare herself. This pity overshadowed Helen's reservations. After all, seeing Ian in the woods made her suspicious of almost everyone. Neil's sudden manner of concern showed Helen that he didn't doubt this girl, anyway, and Helen trusted Neil. She wouldn't allow herself to distrust Siri without reason.

"Have you ever heard of Camelora?" Neil asked cautiously. Siri gave him a baffled look and shook her head. "If you come with us, we'll help you find somewhere safe. We haven't tried to hurt you," Neil reiterated, sensing her reluctance. "We haven't even drawn our weapons—not even when you raised yours. I'm sure you can see by now that you can trust us."

She stood in thought for a minute before nodding her assent. "I'll let you come with me to the next safe village," she stipulated, "as long as you make sure that man doesn't come near me. And this doesn't mean I trust you."

"Hopefully, you will," Neil responded, sounding unconcerned.

Siri scanned Neil up and down, her arms folded across her chest, as they fell into stride together. Helen noticed that the woman held back half-a-step, keeping Neil in front of her. Falling into line behind them, Helen followed.

A shiver ran down her spine and Helen stopped, rooted to the ground. She thought she heard someone whisper her name. She looked at Neil, who was in the middle of asking Siri a question. Siri walked silently, listening to him. It couldn't have been either of them.

Allowing them to move on without her, Helen opened her senses to the forest. A breeze wound through the leaves of the trees, the sunlight filtered down in patches, birds sang as small animals scurried among the twigs on the ground and branches above. *It must have been the wind,* Helen tried to convince herself. The shiver came again. Closing her eyes to focus her hearing, Helen listened again. The whisper didn't return. She jogged to catch up with the others.

Dark clouds rolled above them and it rained throughout the morning. Soon, they found themselves in a part of the land that alternated between clusters of trees and large clearings. Wildflowers of all colors grew around them, sheets of snow covered the tops of the mountains, and the air was refreshing and sweet. With Siri, the silence Neil and Helen had borne lessened, though most of their conversations were initiated by Neil. He showed a concern for Siri's comfort that he had never seemed to consider when he and Helen were alone. Helen tried not to feel slighted or offended, but her trying only made those feelings stronger. A fragility hung about Siri, as though she were made of porcelain, Helen realized—a fragility that Helen herself felt but made a great effort not to show.

"You're sure you've never heard of Camelora," Neil said after a while. Siri shook her head. "Have you heard of Zaric?" he continued.

A flash of recognition crossed Siri's eyes and her eyebrows furrowed.

"Is he part of a legend?" she asked measuredly. "One of the ghosts?"

"Something like that," Neil answered.

Helen felt a twinge of irritation at this statement. "He isn't a ghost," she stated with more sharpness than she intended. "He was once the king of all this land, until the people pushed him away. He lives in Camelora, and Neil and I are trying to find him. He's the only one who can fix what is happening to our world. Trust me; Zaric is very real."

"Wasn't the kingdom divided hundreds of years ago?" asked Siri. "The people decided such a large kingdom wasn't to our best advantage. That's what I've always heard, and if Zaric was the king at that time, he would be dead by now."

Helen opened her mouth to reply, but Neil placed a firm hand on her arm. With bitterness and anger uniting in her head, she pulled her arm away and fell back a few paces, allowing Siri and Neil to walk ahead of her. Reaching for the necklace at her throat, she rubbed it between her thumb and finger to ground herself.

"I'm only concerned with getting away from Ian," Siri went on. "I don't care if we find a king or not. I'll feel safe if we can find a town large enough to disappear in, as long as you are correct in assuming anyone lives in the north."

"How do you know Ian?" Neil asked, changing the subject.

"He came through my village a few weeks ago," she answered, after considering Neil again for a moment. "I think he was building up his army. I took something from him."

"So you're a thief," Helen said.

"No," Siri said, snickering at Helen's abruptness. "It never belonged to him to begin with. He took it from *us* first. I'm sure you know enough about Ian now to believe that. It was a small stone, passed from governor to governor for generations. If Ian had gone off with it, I'm afraid we would never have seen it again. It's the only thing protecting my people. You see, my father was the governor of our land."

Siri's statement struck Helen like a blow to the chest. Siri's story was improbably like her own. The daughter of a governor running from Mered's men, carrying a stone. Perhaps a key? It shouldn't be such a common occurrence. The difference was in the fact that Siri was only trying to make her way to safety and didn't seem at all concerned about Camelora or Zaric. It was also hard for Helen to imagine Ian building an army, when she and Neil had always seen him alone. True, they had seen Mered's soldiers while they were in the Sanctuary, but Ian hadn't been with them. He came later and alone.

"What's Mered planning?" Neil asked.

"Who?" Siri queried in return.

Neil looked at Helen, but she kept her mouth shut, unwilling to answer the question, so he answered instead. "According to the stories, he's Zaric's enemy. If you believe them, his goal is to unite the regions so that he can rule over them all."

"I really don't care about anything like that," Siri stated. "I only want to get away from Ian and find safety for my village."

"I would think that knowing what he's planning and stopping him would be the only way to find safety," Helen put in.

"If I can take the stone to the next village we find," Siri continued, as though she hadn't heard Helen, "I may find someone who can help my people."

Trying to stifle a sigh, Helen resolved that it would be better to stay quiet and let Siri and Neil talk to each other. They stopped talking about Zaric and Mered and allowed their conversation to turn to everyday things. Allowing her mind to wander was the best way for Helen to quell her frustration. Although she was annoyed with herself for feeling it, Helen hoped they would find the next village soon—though the map showed none.

As she tried to ignore the conversation ahead of her, another sound pricked Helen's ears. "What's that?" she asked, reaching out to put a hand on Neil's shoulder, cutting him off mid-sentence.

The three of them stood still and listened. Neil shook his head, only hearing the sounds of the forest at first, but soon the corners of his mouth turned down into a frown. "Let's get off the path," he said, herding Helen and Siri ahead of him as he pushed into the trees as far as the thick underbrush would allow. When they stopped, they listened again.

Voices. Shouts. Laughter. The ringing of metal against metal. Helen felt the drumming of her heart against her chest as she realized they were hearing the echoes of a camp. Instinctively, she dropped to the ground, crawling to the crest of the nearby hill. A wide dell came into view and Helen's drumming heart dropped. Spread out below was a small army. One man walked among the rest, inspecting everything he saw, and Helen realized it was the same army they had seen from the Sanctuary. She motioned to Neil and Siri, who came forward and fell to the ground next to her.

It was then that a familiar foe caught Helen's eye.

"Ian," Siri whispered next to her, seeing him, too.

"They can't be here," Helen muttered, fumbling with her bag and dragging out the book. "This is the way we need to go."

Landing on the map, she traced the line of their path with her forefinger. It went straight through this little dell.

"We'll need to go a different way," Neil stated.

"I don't want to take that chance," Helen argued. "Maybe we can sneak around them somehow."

"But *I* don't want to take *that* chance. Remember: going to the Sanctuary took us off the path on the map, and we still found what we were looking for."

Helen held her breath, trying to look at Siri through the corner of her eye. She was sure they hadn't mentioned the keys to her yet and

Helen hoped she wouldn't ask what Neil meant.

"But there was still a way to get back on track," Helen returned. "If we skirt this valley, there's no way of knowing if we'll be able to make our way back. Look at the terrain. We could be adding days to our journey and we might miss something."

"What other choice do we have? Are you suggesting we attack this camp—the three of us against all of them?"

"Of course not."

"I don't think they're just going to let us pass through. There are too many of them. How many more can we *not* see? I don't doubt you can get us past Ian, but I don't think you're strong enough to get us past an entire army."

Helen studied the camp again. She looked at the map. Her mind swirled, but more with fear than ideas.

"Maybe the map isn't what you think it is," Neil went on. "Do you really know for sure that it's leading us to the keys?"

Helen's eyes snapped to Siri, knowing that she must have caught Neil's words this time. But if she was curious, the woman didn't show it.

"It led us to the abbey. And Meira and Stephen."

"It didn't lead us to the Sanctuary. Isn't it possible that the map shows us where my grandfather thought we could find shelter? Or places that meant something to him? Don't be so stubborn, Helen. Are you really willing to risk our lives to follow a line in an old book?"

Helen's face burned with embarrassment. Neil's reprimand stung, made worse by the feeling of Siri's eyes upon her. She managed to push back the tears that rose in her eyes, though. She was strong enough not to cry.

"We'll just have to take a chance," Neil continued, oblivious to the awkwardness he had caused. "Which way should we go?"

"West," Siri blurted, as though she had been waiting for a chance to say it.

"Have you been this way before?" Helen questioned.

"No, but many people from my city have. This area is a common hunting ground—the nearest to our village. I've seen my father's maps."

"See, Helen? Siri has seen maps of this area, too."

Helen quashed the anger that rose in her chest and throat, threatening to come out as words she didn't mean. Instead, she gripped her hands into fists until her fingernails dug into her palms.

"Let's go before someone finds us." Neil led the way, staying low as he backed away from the top of the hill. Siri went with him and the two of them started to make a path through the brush, but Helen hung behind. Neil's cynicism was nothing new, but his words since meeting Siri were more biting. Much of it was directed at Helen. It baffled her. He was changing in a way she didn't understand. So suddenly, too. Once again, Helen felt alone.

* * *

The sky cleared just before the sun set that evening. The weather was more unpredictable the farther north they moved, alternating between clouds and sun, moon and rain. They found a small cluster of trees that had managed to stay dry through the day's showers. It was surprising how much distance they had covered that day and they were exhausted. They ate a monotonous supper of bread and apples, then debated whether to organize a watch-cycle. Siri was uncertain about the idea and Helen doubted to herself that Siri would warn them of danger. In the end, they hoped the sound of anyone approaching would wake them—Ian was on a horse, after all—and they went to sleep.

The moonlight fell on the clearing unfiltered when Helen awoke. Someone had spoken her name. She couldn't be sure if it was a voice in her dream pushing her or a person in waking pulling her from sleep. Looking toward the dwindling fire, she saw Neil and Siri still sleeping on their respective sides of it. Rolling onto her back, Helen looked up at the moon as she listened for anything out of the ordinary.

The sounds of the night forest enveloped the woods around her: an owl calling, animal feet scurrying, leaves rustling. Helen rolled again and knelt on her pallet with a sigh. She watched Siri for a minute, making sure her sleep was genuine.

A tiny flash of light in the corner of her eye made Helen snap her head around. There was another, then another, as though stars twinkled among the trees. The flashes clustered at the edge of the clearing. Helen got up and approached them with care, not wanting them to disappear before she could discover what they were. Her mind told her that it was dangerous to explore something so unusual in the middle of the night, but a deeper feeling told her that it was harmless. In an irregular wave, they moved into the trees, blinking yellow, scarlet, orange, and violet, their flashes appearing unpredictably. Led by her curiosity, Helen continued to follow. Her fear of wandering through the forest alone was overshadowed by a sense of wonder.

Helen found herself on a narrow path created by the animals of the forest, making it easier to move through the undergrowth without watching her feet. Her eyes focused on the lights. She reached out, trying to close her fingers around one as it flashed, but it continued to drift just out of reach. Ahead of her, Helen saw a shaft of moonlight washing the trees and forest floor. She was coming to a new clearing. A nagging thought pointed out how far she had wandered from the little camp, but she ignored it.

The lights stopped in the clearing, suspended in the air. Without hesitation, Helen stepped in among them, feeling like a child again. They surrounded and circled her, a swirling cloud of light. This time when Helen held out her hand, the lights didn't try to move away.

One settled on her open palm. When she looked at it closely, she saw that it was a bug—one Helen had never seen before—its little body illuminating in sporadic flashes. Helen's spirit swelled as she let it go. She turned around in the cylinder of glowing bugs, marveling at their beauty.

Pulling away from her, the lights went a little farther into the trees. Helen again followed. They settled around three trees in the next clearing, circling their trunks and drifting among the branches, casting their light over the area. The trees were unlike any Helen had ever seen before. The branches were covered in what she first thought were vine-like leaves, but soon discerned were streams of water. The water reflected the moonlight as it poured into pools that gathered around the roots of the trees, like fountains sculpted out of wood. This space with its trees felt like a holy place, even more hallowed than the Sanctuary. Helen walked into it with reverent steps. The light of the bugs caught in the pools, adding to the wonder of the scene.

Helen's eyes were drawn to the pool of the first tree, where its ripples created strange patterns that played with the light. Falling on her hands and knees, she stared into the pool. As she watched, the patterns became images, showing Helen a city—*her* city. She saw the people of Veren as they had been, before Mered's army came, before the other governors turned against her father. When she thought of him, the image changed to one of her father and mother, smiling… happy. They reached out as a reflection of Helen ran to them and the three of them embraced. It was Helen as she was here in the forest, a young woman, not a young girl. Not only was it as though their isolation had not happened yet, but as though it had never happened at all. *If I just put my hand in the water,* Helen thought, *this scene will become real. I will be with my parents again.* She didn't know where the thought came from, but it felt true. Reaching out her hand, the magnetism of the image pulled her toward it.

She stopped herself before her fingertips touched the surface of the water. Would it *really* be real? Was saving the kingdom as simple as plunging her hand in a pool of water? Or would she forget all that had passed, but still have the feeling in the back of her mind that something had been left undone? Something important. And what would happen to Neil?

Helen brought her hand back. The image of her family faded as she stood and stepped away.

As the light in the first pool dwindled, the second came to life with patterns of its own. She went to it and knelt again. An image formed of a city, but this time one Helen had never seen before. People worked, talked, and laughed as they went about their lives. The scene took her to a street where she saw herself walking with Neil, their hands entwined. Warmth rose in her cheeks. *This can't be real, either,* she told herself.

The image changed into one of a man's face looking up at her. It felt both unfamiliar and familiar at the same time. His dark blue eyes—full of the life of ageless lifetimes—held Helen's gaze, as though he were truly seeing her. His tanned, yet regal, face was creased by a kind, fatherly expression. Brown hair fell in waves around his ears. The details of his face were sharp, yet gentle. Helen knew, though she didn't know how, that this was Zaric. He held out a hand, beckoning to her.

She pushed herself back a few feet before getting up. The pull of this image was stronger than the first. Still, she was afraid that if she took his hand now, she would never know what she could see in the third pool.

When she looked to the last tree, the patterns in its pool danced, drawing her eye to it. Helen began to kneel, but stopped when she saw the face of Ian laughing up at her. Behind him, she saw a palace built in a desert oasis, formed from orange and yellow stone. Ian walked into the palace and the scene shifted to a large room with a throne on a dais against the opposite wall.

The man sitting on the throne watched as Ian knelt before him, fist resting over his heart and eyes cast on the floor in a show of fealty. The eyes of the enthroned man pierced the image with dark intensity, holding Helen motionless, as though he were pulling her into the scene with him. Short dark hair came to a point in the man's forehead, topped with an elaborate golden crown. His short beard accentuated the smirk on his lips. She knew it must be Mered.

Gripped with shock and fear, afraid of being seen by this evil man, Helen wanted to turn and run, but the scene shifted again. On the dais, to the left of the throne, a second throne began to appear, the hazy, shadowy image forming from the bottom. Helen couldn't pull her eyes away as the bottom of a dark dress appeared, growing to include the bend of the knees. Ornamented hands and wrists rested on the arms of the throne. Long, dark sleeves covered slender arms and led to delicate shoulders and a graceful, adorned neck. Helen gasped and brought her hands to her mouth when the face cleared. It was *her* face. She didn't recognize the hard, dark look in her eyes. Completing the shock, her piled and braided hair was encircled by a golden crown. The image of Mered reached across the space between them and grasped the hand of the image of Helen.

Without a second thought, Helen rushed back to the second tree and threw herself down at its pool. Zaric's image appeared again, holding out his hand. Helen thrust her hand into the water.

She was still in the forest. The setting around her remained the same. All that changed was the fading of the image of Zaric's face. The mud at the bottom of the pool enveloped Helen's fingers. Closing her fist, she felt something small and hard enclosed within her fist.

Bringing her hand up, she tried to look at it, but it was too caked with mud. She held it in the water, using her thumbs to clear away the dirt. When she brought it out again, she found herself holding a small, round, dark gem, twinkling like a star in the moonlight.

115

# Chapter 12

The sound of voices awoke Helen the next morning. Her eyes opened wide and she looked around, seized by uneasiness, forgetting for a few moments where she was and who she was with. The early sun peered through the trees, its brightness forcing Helen to blink until her eyes could bear the light. She listened until she realized the voices belonged to Neil and Siri, who were whispering a few feet away. Helen sighed inaudibly and allowed her mind to drift to what she had seen in the night. At first, she believed it was a dream, but when she looked down at her hands, she found that she was tightly holding the coin bag, where she had dropped the gem when she returned to camp. She hid it in the folds of her skirt, knowing that she couldn't hide the action of putting it in her bag without rousing suspicion.

"You're awake!" Neil exclaimed, cutting off his conversation. His manner was different from what Helen was used to, much more spirited and less acerbic.

"Yes," Helen answered with discomfort. She reached for her bag and slung it across her shoulder. "We should have left before the sun came up," she went on. "As soon as the sky lightened."

"I tried to wake you," Neil answered, taken aback. "You didn't even move."

"I didn't realize I was that tired."

Though Neil wasn't satisfied with this explanation—Helen was usually awake long before he was—he said nothing and tossed Helen a thick slice of bread. When she was sure he wasn't looking, she slipped the coin purse into her bag.

They soon started walking, Neil next to Helen while Siri hung back. He cast a glance over his shoulder, waiting to speak until he was sure that Siri was out of earshot and too distracted to be curious. Still, he spoke in a whisper.

"Where did you go last night?" he asked. He looked at her with so much concern and solemnity that Helen felt a little bit guilty. Staring back at Neil, she wondered how much she dared to tell him—how much he was willing to believe. She wanted to tell him everything. The words rose into her throat and she hoped that he would believe every word she said, but she couldn't help glancing at Siri. She still didn't trust the other woman or Neil's unusual attention toward her. It was too late to prevent Siri from learning about the keys, but Helen could at least keep this recent discovery from her.

"I went for a walk," she finally replied. "I couldn't sleep and I needed some air."

"We're surrounded by air, Helen. You don't need to wander off into the woods to get more. It was foolish to put yourself in such an exposed position. You might have been attacked."

"Did you see anyone else besides me?"

"No, but that's not the point," he said. "I'm glad I didn't see anyone. Do you realize what kind of danger you were putting yourself into, going off alone? You know we won't be safe until we reach Camelora."

"Yes, I know that, but do you?"

They stared at each other for a moment before Neil looked away.

"Anyway," Helen went on, "I was alone for three weeks before I reached you."

"But if I had known that—" Neil protested, but cut himself off.

"Please, Neil, don't start treating me differently just because there's someone to impress. We're in just as much danger together as we are apart. Neither of us has ever learned to fight, we really don't know how many people are trying to find us, and we aren't entirely sure what they're capable of. You need to trust me."

Neil's brow furrowed and his lips parted, but he only managed to slowly exhale. He slowed his pace to stroll alongside Siri. Helen watched him briefly, confused by her own behavior. She had accused Neil of not trusting her, while, at the same time, she was withholding information from him. But it would be pointless to call him back now—then she would have to tell Siri as well. She fingered the strap on her bag and took a few deep breaths.

Helen let Neil and Siri walk together, leading a few feet ahead of them. Although they walked close enough for her to hear every word of Neil and Siri's conversation, it was too trivial for Helen to pay any attention to it. Neil asked questions and Siri gave short answers which often sounded rehearsed. Helen stayed alert enough to catch anything Siri might say of interest, but otherwise allowed her mind to wander.

The next day began much like the one before. Helen began to feel the weight of isolation. Siri did her best to be friendly with Helen as she became more comfortable with Helen and Neil, and Helen tried to reciprocate the openness, but she couldn't manage much more than basic civility. There was an indifference under the surface of Siri's eyes, despite her prettiest smiles.

High walls of stone, dirt, and grass rose on either side of the path as they came to another hill, creating a safer sense of solitude that Helen found welcoming. There were no trees above them for anyone to hide in. It reminded her of the staircase they had found a few days before, though not so narrow. The decline was gradual, not steep. Helen wondered if anyone ever took this route. Knowing the people of the southern lands, no one was really interested in going north.

Travel between regions was left to merchants and governors. Every story she had ever been told as a girl—besides those told by Neil's grandfather—portrayed the northern lands as a barren waste, covered in broken stone, dead trees, and ghosts, the remainder of a lost and unwanted kingdom where no one dared to go, and even if they did, there was nothing there to tempt them. None of the people who told these stories had ever been there themselves, but they accepted the rumors as true. From what Siri had said before, the people of the western lands told the same tales.

After a few hours a small gap appeared not far ahead between the stone walls where the path opened onto the northern country, although it was too narrow to see anything more than sky. They increased their pace. As they moved forward, the gap grew wider, revealing the colors of the land ahead, bright green and grey and brown, with a hint of blue. A few yards farther ahead they emerged from the pass. They came to an abrupt stop and Helen realized for the first time just how small these towering cliffs were.

Before them lay the most beautiful, wide, and expansive land any of them had ever seen. The southern lands were dotted with green hills and trees and winding rivers, with dry desert-like land close to Veren, but nothing to equal this country's grandeur. Yet the scene ahead of them wasn't quite right. Helen's mind told her so, but she couldn't determine what was out of place. She wasn't surprised to see the swift-moving clouds in the sky cast shadows over the stony, rugged, imposing mountains that rose on the northernmost border of the valley. The pine and oak trees were tall and thick. The air was different from any Helen had ever breathed before, full of warmth and life, telling her that they were finally close to their destination. This, she realized, was only a tiny glimpse of a land even larger than she could imagine. But the few meandering rivers which emerged from the bottoms of these mountains made their way to a long and broad lake, which stretched across the valley and reached the grass at the bottom of the slope where Helen, Neil, and Siri stood. In this light the lake was a deep shade of rich blue, and its water looked inviting and cool. Rising from the lake was a small island, crested with a large cluster of pine trees.

She pulled out the book and opened it to the map, tracing their course over the crest of the hill and down to a wide valley. There wasn't supposed to be a lake here. A name was written in a faint hand: The Valley of Trier.

"Where do we go now?" Neil asked, looking out at the lake, not realizing the extent of the obstacle. "We need to try to go around."

"This shouldn't be here," Helen stated, nodding toward the lake. "This should be a valley."

"What do you mean?" Neil inquired.

Helen showed him the map, tapping the valley it indicated. "This should be a valley."

Neil's face fell, though he tried not to show it. He tried to shrug off the inconsistency by saying, "Landscapes change. One of the rivers must have closed off and flooded the valley. We'll have to find some way around."

"Should we try to scramble up the cliffs?" Helen wondered.

Siri laughed. "You would fall before you reached the top. Where would you go once you got to the top, anyway? You would probably find yourself faced with the lake farther on."

"I think you mean 'we,'" Helen pointed out, unable to hide the annoyance in her voice.

"You're the one following that map," Siri retorted, "not me. I'm willing to retrace my steps and go in a different direction entirely."

Helen wanted to snap at Siri in response but stopped herself. Suspecting Siri of being an enemy was no reason to turn her into one. Instead, Helen descended the hill to see the lake from a different vantage point. Neil followed, but Siri remained where she was.

"We aren't even following the written path anymore," Neil said, his tone gentle. "Whether we find a way across this lake or go back and take another route, it makes no difference."

"It could add days to our journey," Helen argued, matching Neil's gentle tone.

"Maybe it's meant to. There's nothing that says how long this journey should be."

"This valley would have been the closest route to get us back on track. These mountains and valleys aren't exactly connected well to each other."

"We're still chasing a fairy tale, Helen," he sighed. "Perhaps this whole journey is fruitless. All we've managed to do is back ourselves into a corner."

Helen turned her head away. She started to think that he was right, though part of her fought against that thought. She had imagined that this task would be easier the farther they went, but it was proving to be the opposite. It was harder to picture their destination, harder to see the path to take. If it weren't for the fact that she had no home to return to, Helen would have given up right then.

Through the folds of her skirt, she felt the coin purse that was still in her pocket. The keys. To Helen, they were the one thing that proved their journey wasn't pointless. They found these keys and they found them for a reason. No matter how impossible the way seemed, they needed to keep moving forward.

Looking down at the glassy, crystal water and the path of dazzling reflected sunlight that stretched over its surface, an idea came to her. The impossibility of it made her frown, but at the same time the past few weeks had taught her that she shouldn't really believe anything was impossible. She looked at Neil and forced a grin, and again asked, "Do you trust me?"

"Yes," he answered without hesitating. "I've already said that."

"You might have to save me if I'm wrong," she said. Then, taking a deep breath, she closed her eyes and began to walk forward. When she reached the edge of the water, she didn't stop.

A cold shock ran through her body, penetrating every nerve, and she gasped as the early-season water soaked her shoes. Helen jumped backward onto the shore, too embarrassed to turn around.

"What are you doing?" Neil exclaimed.

"Are you crazy?" Siri yelled, her words overlapping Neil's as she ran down to join him.

Trying to appear unconcerned, Helen bent down and removed her boots and stockings. Composing herself, she again moved forward.

The coldness of the water was stronger this time on her unprotected feet, but she was determined that her idea would work. Gathering all her confidence, she took a few more steps, but all she managed to do was get her skirt even more wet. Shivering, she again moved back to dry ground.

"You can't walk through it," Neil said, coming forward and catching her by the arm. "It's too deep."

"I'm not trying to walk through it," Helen rejoined.

Discouraged but not willing to admit it, she looked across to the island once again as she pulled her arm from Neil's grasp. It sat in the middle of the lake, mocking and untouchable, but she still felt drawn to it. Everything inside of her yearned to reach it. Still, she wished she were alone. It embarrassed her to know that Neil and Siri—especially Siri—were standing so close, watching her failed attempts.

Helen again closed her eyes, holding the image of the island in her mind. The path led them to this shore and the shore faced the island. Helen was determined to reach it. Behind her closed lids, she saw the shore, the lake, the island. The path of sunlight on the surface of the water became solid, as though Helen could walk across it. Straightening her back and shaking off her inhibitions, she walked forward.

She had gone a few feet before she noticed what she was doing. The water hadn't yet touched her feet, though she knew she should have passed the line of the shore by now. Deciding to look down, she opened her eyes and saw her feet resting on top of the water. This only lasted for a fraction of a second before natural disbelief told her that what she was seeing was impossible and couldn't be real. Her mind refused to believe in the solidity of the water beneath her feet. Her concentration broke and she fell through the surface of the lake, stumbling and falling forward, catching herself just as Neil's hands cuffed her arms.

Helen couldn't hold back the smile that grew across her face, turning her face up to Neil as she regained her balance. Then, she laughed. Neil's brows contracted in confusion.

"What did you do?" he asked quietly.

Helen had no words or explanation for him. Shaking her head, she went back to the shore. Neil waded behind her, then stood a few feet away with his eyes fixed on her face. Helen gazed out at the island and gathered her skirts in one hand, then stepped forward again, not needing to close her eyes as she walked. When she didn't fall through the surface of the lake, she broke into a run. For a moment Neil watched, then turned to Siri and held out his hand. "Come on, Siri," he said.

Siri shook her head. "It's impossible," she answered.

"If Helen can do it, so can we," Neil argued.

"Come back for me if you find a boat," she replied.

"And if we don't find a boat?"

Siri hesitated for a minute. "If you come back, then I'll believe we can make it. Either way, come back for me if you make it across."

On the lake, Helen was moving farther away. Neil looked from her to Siri, then back. He exhaled slowly. Without another word, he followed

Helen, forcing his mind not to wonder at the fact that his feet were moving over the water.

The water felt like soft earth under Helen's feet. She could feel its coolness around her ankles, but none of its wetness. After a few minutes, any uneasiness she might have felt dissipated. She grew accustomed to the gentle movement of the current and ran almost as though the water wasn't even there. Her thoughts and emotions began to swell inside of her until she wanted nothing more than to erupt into elated laughter. The scene around her was brighter and the sunlight glistened and danced on the surface of the water. For the first time, she didn't just know, but comprehended that she was in the northern land, farther than her imagination had ever taken her before. The land ahead opened, its details becoming more and more distinct. A tiny waterfall she hadn't seen from across the lake trickled down the cliff straight ahead, spilling into a lagoon.

Gradually, the water beneath her feet shallowed, the grass and rocks beneath becoming more visible. She slowed to a walk. The lapping of the water pushed her toward the shore, making her stomach tingle. As she stepped off the water and onto the grass, Helen had trouble finding her footing and swayed for a moment before falling forward, catching herself on her hands. She stayed this way until her head stopped spinning, then exhaled and got to her feet. The water bathed her ankles from the undulating lake and she turned to see the shore opposite. With surprise, she saw that Neil wasn't far behind her. She watched him as he came closer and waited for him to step onto the grass. Expecting him to fall as she had done, Helen stood ready to catch him.

"That was the most fantastic thing I've ever done," Neil exclaimed, though the words sounded inadequate. He leaned against Helen for support. They cracked into laughter at the impossibility of what they had managed to do.

Helen looked around, taking in the lake and the island with its trees and rocks and grassy slope, as well as the sky above with its swiftly moving clouds. She breathed deeply to calm her emotions, reminding herself that no matter how many wonderful, impossible things she did, there was still more to do.

It was easy to see now that the island wasn't really an island, but a hill too tall to be covered when the valley flooded. There was more to the story of this lake than they could tell simply by looking at it.

"Siri wouldn't come?" Helen asked, turning to Neil. He shook his head in reply and Helen decided not to press it. "I guess we should try to find some way to get her across."

She turned inland and started to walk up the hill, looking for any sign of a boat, though she didn't believe she would find one. Neil stood still, watching her. "When did you know there must be a key here?" he asked.

"When we realized there was no way across the lake," Helen said, pausing her half-hearted search. "This lake hasn't been here long. You can tell by the grass beneath it and on the shore. I felt it more than I thought it, though."

"You could have said something before we crossed."

Helen shaped her reply in her mind before speaking. "I wasn't sure then. I'm still not. Anyway, we don't know Siri very well. She stole something from Ian, so what would stop her from stealing something from us? She doesn't believe in Camelora or Zaric. She would probably only see the keys as valuable gems."

"You don't trust her," Neil stated in a flat tone.

"Do you?"

He hesitated. "I don't know," he finally said. "I don't trust anyone, besides you. But I do remember someone very much like Siri coming to my home not long ago, asking me to join her on a journey to a place neither of us had ever seen, in search of a man we can't be sure exists."

This statement stung Helen. If she couldn't bring herself to trust Siri, could she really expect anyone to trust her? She hated to think that they were so much alike. Worst of all, she sensed Neil's disappointment in her.

"I guess we don't really know each other," Neil continued, causing Helen's pain to sink deeper.

"We've known each other our whole lives," she contradicted.

"We knew each other as children. We aren't children anymore."

"I hope we haven't changed that much. And I don't think Siri trusts *us*."

"I'm beginning to think she shouldn't."

They stood in silence. She wished for a way to explain what she felt, but she wasn't even sure if her discomfort around Siri was because of Siri, or because of her own feelings of insignificance—or even envy. There was no way to answer Neil until she could answer that one question. "I'm sorry," she said, hoping her words communicated the sincerity she felt, although her sorrow came more from hurting Neil than Siri.

"Well, unless you expect the key to fall into our hands, we should probably start looking," Neil said. "Where do you think it would be?"

Helen indicated the lagoon, then followed Neil as he walked to it. If the water didn't belong there, neither did the lagoon. It made sense that it was meant to hide something. A magnetic pull had also taken hold of Helen's mind until all that occupied it was the water. They stepped into the pool at its base, the water softening the grass, dirt, and rocks beneath it. Some larger rocks and boulders littered the lagoon. Helen and Neil inspected them, looking for hidden slots on them or beneath them, but they were all solid and set firmly into place. As they got nearer to the waterfall, they found nothing but a cascade of clear water rolling down the cliff. Neil put his hands through the water and pushed against the rock, but it was solid. The cliff was flat and smooth. The water ran down the front of it in even sheets. It would be impossible to hide anything beneath this waterfall.

"Do you think your feeling might be wrong?" Neil questioned.

"This waterfall… this lagoon… they don't belong here. They must be hiding something."

"Helen, this waterfall is like glass. All I see under it is rock. And there's nothing else here. I think you might be overthinking."

Helen scrunched up her face. She stared at the waterfall for a minute, then asked, "Do you think it might have something to do with the water? Like the fire before." Cupping her hands, she put them in the running curtain and allowed the water to gather. She pulled her hands out again and peered into them, not sure what she was expecting to see. But the water only drained through her fingers.

Neil glanced down, too, and couldn't help saying, "There's nothing there."

Helen dropped her hands.

"You're not losing your patience, are you?" Neil asked her. "If you lose your patience, I think we'll all be lost."

"Can you try to take this seriously?" Helen snapped. "Or at least not be so skeptical."

Neil didn't know how to respond, surprised at Helen's outburst, so he said nothing. But his demeanor softened, which relieved Helen. She didn't like his coldness—it made her feel more alone than being alone ever could. Now, Neil stared at the water running in front of his face, a look of concentration replacing his previous air of annoyance. He contemplated the trees on top of the island, the grass on either side of them, and then the water itself, and Helen followed his intent gaze, trying to break into his thoughts. In the abbey and the garden, the space where the key was hidden was limited, but here, there were no boundaries. The key could be anywhere. Yet Helen felt it was right in front of them.

"Let's check the trees," Neil said, heading toward the path that would take them to the top of the hill. Helen followed, beginning to doubt as well. After a few feet, Neil stopped abruptly.

"What is it?" Helen asked.

"You feel drawn to the waterfall."

"I said that, yes."

"I have an idea."

He took up his place in front of the waterfall again and stared at it just as before. Helen returned to his side.

"In the abbey," Neil said, "I put my hand into the fire, but it didn't burn me."

"In the garden," Helen said, "I picked a flower."

"And we just crossed a lake with no boat, without drowning in it. Now, we're standing in front of a wall of solid rock. What do you think is the least obvious solution?"

There was a twinkle in Neil's eye as he said this. Not wanting to ask what he was thinking, Helen simply watched him. Without reservation, he stepped forward, into the cascade. Helen was startled, and yet, she could only look on in wonder. His face went through the water, then his entire head, his torso and arms, and finally his legs. In amazement, Helen stared at the place where Neil had been, but he had disappeared. Her nerves tingled through her whole body. She took a deep breath and followed.

The water tickled her nose, then her cheeks and eyelids. The fear of breathing the water in stopped her from gasping at its icy coldness. A shiver ran through her body as the water ran down her head and over her clothes. She felt herself growing heavier in the wetness. But instead of hitting a solid rock wall, she soon emerged from the waterfall into a cool, empty space. She opened her eyes.

Beyond the cascading curtain, where the cliff should have been, was a cave, lit so brightly, Helen almost believed it wasn't a cave at all, but an open alcove. The source of the light was the water on the floor, which came almost to Helen's knees. But, when she looked at the water, it didn't seem unusual at all. Still, its light bounced off the grey stone of the walls and filled the entire space. Neil stood in the middle of the cave, smiling though he was dripping wet, gesturing in his excitement—more excited than Helen had seen him since they were children.

"It's amazing!" he exclaimed. "Of all the wonders we've seen, this is the most wonderful."

"I wonder how many things I've missed in my life," Helen said, unable to hold back her own exhilaration, "because I wasn't looking in the right way."

Neil's face brightened—a look that still surprised Helen—then turned to face the other end of the enclosure. It wasn't hard to find what he was looking for because the cave was almost completely empty. The only thing in it was a basin, carved with intricate designs and cut into the opposite wall, as high as Neil's chest. The reflection of light on water danced above the basin and he stepped forward, peering inside the small pool. He turned to Helen and waved her over, though she was already stepping toward him.

They stood next to each other and gazed down. Resting at the bottom of the shallow pool, glittering with its own radiant light, was a bright orange gem, cut into a perfectly round sphere. Neil reached in without hesitation, pulled it out, and held it up. The brilliance of the jewel was more than they could have imagined.

Helen took the small purse from her pocket and handed it to Neil, not thinking twice until he held it. She tried to snatch it back, realizing that there was still something she hadn't told him. He gave her a curious look as he opened the bag, looked inside, and dropped the stone in, then froze. His gaze, she knew, was locked on the blue gem, resting along with the others. Neil's immobility only lasted a few seconds, then he closed the bag and weighed it in his hand.

"Where did that fourth stone come from?" Neil asked, trying to sound natural, but holding the bag in a tight grip.

"I found it a couple of nights ago," Helen answered, "when I went into the woods. I've been meaning to tell you—"

"Don't you trust me, Helen?" Neil interrupted. His expression blended anger, betrayal, and sadness.

"Yes, of course." She flinched under Neil's gaze, but still reached out and seized the purse from his hand. She looked down at it for a moment before slipping it into her bag. She debated whether she should say what she wanted to or not before looking at Neil. "I think I was afraid you wouldn't believe my story."

"How could that stop you from telling it? You tell me your stories all the time. If this has something to do with Siri, you could have found a way to tell me without her hearing."

"You don't know what I saw that night," Helen blurted out.

Neil stood staring at her, his face set like stone. "What did you see, Helen?" he inquired.

Helen opened her mouth to tell him—to explain about the lights and the trees and the pools and the images—but thought twice about it. Neil would only scoff and try to explain it away. "You wouldn't understand," she told him instead.

"Are you sure it's not a trap? It could be a false key and we'll be stuck when we reach the Gateway."

"It's a real key, Neil. I know it is."

"How can you know? It was a stupid thing to do, going off into the woods alone. You should have woken me up so we could go together. You could have been in danger, Helen. We all could have. So many things could have happened that you didn't even consider. How would you like it if I had wandered off on my own? And then to keep the most important part of it from me. How would you feel if I acted with so much disregard for everyone's safety?"

"You already are!" Helen shouted. She immediately regretted her words.

Neil looked more injured and confused than angry. He shook his head at Helen and turned away from her.

He hadn't walked far before the ground beneath them began to shake.

"What are you doing?" Neil accused, turning to Helen again.

"It isn't me," she argued. She reached for the wall to steady herself, but Neil grabbed her hand and pulled her with him as he ran back through the waterfall.

They didn't stop running until they reached the far end of the lagoon. Turning, they watched as the hill shook, loosening the boulders at the top of the cliff until they fell into the stream at the top of the waterfall, some of them falling into the lagoon below. Creating a dam, the boulders stopped the flow of the water. The waterfall disappeared, exposing the solid wall of rock beneath it. Faster than they expected, Helen and Neil looked on as the lagoon dried up, its water absorbed into the ground below. After the lagoon, the lake followed, dissolving into the grassy valley in a matter of minutes.

# Chapter 13

The sun was setting by the time they reached the northern edge of the valley. It was still cold enough to prevent Neil's and Helen's clothes from drying quickly. Although she had brought a change of clothes, Helen only had one pair of boots, and they were still wet from her first attempt to cross the lake. She sat curled up and wrapped in a blanket, trying to warm her feet as she read Neil's book in the flickering firelight. Neil and Siri sat across from her. They had lost time going back for Siri, though she did meet them halfway across the valley after the water receded. No one said anything—they were too tired to talk. The events of the day had been more taxing than any of them had realized. Helen read until her eyes were sore from trying to focus in the dim light, while Neil sat deep in thought and Siri looked bored and restless. With a hesitant glance across the fire, Helen put the book back into her bag, laid her head on it, and closed her eyes.

Siri sensed something wrong between Helen and Neil—a growing rift—though she hadn't asked what brought it on. She suspected it had something to do with her and had to stifle her pleasure at the thought to prevent Neil from seeing it. She watched Helen for a few minutes. When she was sure the other young woman was asleep, she moved closer to Neil.

"I get the feeling," Siri said in a low whisper, "that there's something you aren't telling me."

Neil weighed in his mind whether or not he wanted to tell her about the argument with Helen. It was personal and he knew Helen wouldn't want him to. The two women didn't trust each other, anyway, and he needed to be careful not to fuel that.

Siri gave him a bright, wide smile. He saw a dimple in her left cheek he hadn't noticed before—though it was true she had never really smiled before. "What I saw today was impossible," she continued.

"If it was impossible, we wouldn't have done it," Neil countered. This made Siri laugh, but she checked herself, glancing again at Helen. She was finally warming up to him, Neil thought, and he liked this side of her. "We've told you about as much as you've told us, Siri. I'm not unwilling to be open. Tell me what you would like to know and I'll answer the best I can."

"What did you find on the island?" Siri asked after a minute's contemplation. "What happened between you and Helen?"

Neil couldn't hide his surprise. Her fiery eyes twinkled with knowing expectation. She stifled a laugh by putting her delicate, slender fingers to her lips. "Did you find another key, Neil?" she went on.

He continued to stare, trying to think of what to say. Siri had never acted like this before and he felt like he was talking to a new person. He wasn't expecting such a direct question. His mind went back to the brief conversation with Helen as they watched the enemy camp. He knew that their mentioning the keys hadn't escaped Siri's notice, but she hadn't asked about them and he hadn't taken the time to explain them to her. He suspected that she knew more than she indicated.

"A key to what, Siri?" he finally said. It was impossible to laugh it off or deny it—Siri had already seen the expression on his face. "What do you know?"

"We don't have to play that game, Neil. You need the keys in order to get to this 'King Zaric' Helen talks about. When you and Helen went across the lake, you must have found a key."

"What do you know about the keys?"

"Helen forgot to put that book of hers away the other night when she fell asleep. I was curious, so I looked through it. She guards it so closely I thought it might be something interesting. There are a lot of stories in there that you never told me, Neil."

"They're children's stories. I didn't think you would be interested in children's stories. I have a hard time believing them and thought you might be the same way."

"If this man you're trying to find and the land he lives in are nothing but children's stories, what is your journey for? It seems like a silly reason to leave your home. Helen doesn't seem to believe that they're only children's stories."

"I couldn't convince Helen not to go," Neil replied. "I tried, but she wouldn't listen. In the end, I came with her to protect her. I was afraid she didn't know just how dangerous it was."

"Do you?"

"Probably not, but at least neither of us is alone."

"But you don't actually believe in Zaric," Siri stated.

Neil hesitated before replying. He couldn't fail to notice the allure of her eyes. She was a beautiful woman—three or four years older than him and Helen—and he hated for her to think he was childish. For the first time in his life, he had this strange feeling of wanting to impress a woman. But he had seen so much since coming with Helen and he also hated to lie. He chose the safest answer and said, "I don't know."

"Think about it, Neil. If Zaric is still alive, how old would he be? The stories about him have been around for a very long time—hundreds of years, probably, from what that book says. If you find your way to this 'Camelora,' you'll most likely find one of his descendants instead of the man himself, and then it will be a man who can't help you, because he's only a man and he doesn't care about the state of the world. He's perfectly content to stay in his little kingdom, away from all of the harm. Do you really think he would want to help you?"

Neil's soul knotted. Siri's words mirrored the thoughts he had when Helen first came to him. Now, he wasn't so sure. Considering the impossible things he and Helen had done, meeting a man who had lived for hundreds of years didn't seem as implausible. But Siri looked at him with eyes that made him doubt. His grandfather had often said he knew Zaric, but Neil couldn't remember him ever saying how old Zaric was. In the stories, he came across as a young man, but that fact was never actually stated. There was also the possibility that the stories his grandfather told were just stories to entertain a little boy and nothing more. In his last feverish days, perhaps his grandfather's mind had become so muddled and clouded, he started to believe his own stories. This didn't explain the fact that his parents—or Meira and Stephen—believed in Zaric, but Neil knew that his childhood perspective wasn't the same as his older perspective. The others could be wrong.

"May I see the keys, Neil?" Siri asked. Her voice was sweet, melodic—especially when she said his name.

Slowly, Neil shook his head. "I don't have them," he answered.

"Does Helen have them?" Siri's brow creased in worry and confusion.

"She keeps them, yes."

"Doesn't she trust you?"

"Yes, of course. She wouldn't have asked me to come along with her if she didn't. We can't both have them at the same time. Helen has always carried the keys."

"So why not let you carry them once in a while? Isn't it strange that she wants to have sole possession of them? I'm sure no one would think twice about you carrying some plain, ordinary keys."

"But they're not—" Neil began, then stopped. Inwardly he groaned, knowing he couldn't leave the sentence dangling in the air. "They're not like that," he stated unconvincingly.

"What are they like?"

Neil hated to show any distrust of Siri, but if he held back the truth, that was exactly what he would be doing. Yet if he told her, he risked earning Helen's distrust if she found out. He didn't doubt she would. He looked at Siri, hoping her expression would justify his trust. Her large dark eyes were like the depths of the night sky, especially in this light, and he felt himself falling into them. He was sure there was no harm in a woman like Siri. She was very much like Helen, simply trying to get away from Mered's men.

"They're jewels," Neil said. "Gems cut into perfect spheres, unlike anything I've ever seen before. They don't look like keys at all."

Siri thought for a moment, then spoke in a sympathetic voice. "I know you and Helen have known each other for a long time. I also know that she doesn't trust me. But I'm sorry to say, *I* don't trust *her*. She took you away from your home and has risked your life over and over again, all to search for a man who may not even be alive anymore—if he ever was alive. Perhaps what she really wanted you for was to find these rare, precious, and valuable stones. Imagine what a poor girl like Helen could do with something worth so much."

"She's a governor's daughter. Governors don't really need to search the world for precious stones."

"You don't have to accept this idea, Neil, but I'm afraid I must say I'm disappointed that you didn't think of this before. You don't seem to be the sort of man who is easily fooled. Could it be their power is used for a different purpose—one she isn't telling you?"

Siri's dark eyes were playful, laughing in the glow of the fire. "Why should Helen carry the stones, anyway?" she continued. "They would probably be safer if they were in your hands. Don't you agree?"

As he looked at Siri, Neil tried to think of some reason why he shouldn't believe what she said, but her theory was more plausible than the stories he had always been told. Even so, he couldn't quite accept that Helen was using him in order to get something for herself. She was much too innocent to do anything like that. But, there could be another reason, one that would prove that they had both been fooled. If Siri was right and Zaric was only a man interested in keeping himself away from the dangers of the world, he might also be using Helen and Neil to find the keys for himself. If this was true, it would be best for Neil to keep the keys safe, to save Helen from the disappointment of finding out that her hero was nothing but a greedy, selfish, ordinary man. He resolved that, for Helen's protection, he would need to take the keys.

* * *

Neil barely slept. He was sure he was right, but his mind was conflicted and muddled. He imagined too many scenarios, too many possibilities, all at once. He tried to convince himself that it was better to betray Helen before she could betray him, but it was still hard to believe that she actually intended to betray him at all. He had known her for so long—but he also hadn't seen her for so long. A person could change in unexpected ways, affected by life's most desperate circumstances. And Helen's attitude toward Siri was suspicious. Was it prompted by distrust or guilt? Siri's idea was logical, while Neil's own theory cleared Helen of all actual blame. Yet it felt like a cruel trick. Neil sat up and put his fingers to his temples, then pushed them through his hair and took a deep breath. He looked over to Helen, who was still sleeping, her face wearing a harmless expression. Not for the first time, she reminded him of the girl he once knew. Neil was surprised to see that the bag he had watched her place under her head the night before was now lying at her side. She must have moved it in her sleep because it was unlike her to leave her bag in such a vulnerable position, suspicious as she was.

As noiselessly as possible, Neil stood and walked to Helen, kneeling next to her. Opening her bag with care, he peered in. Inside he saw her book, crossbow, and telescope. He sifted through the contents of the bag and found a few other small things, but the small purse was gone. A little more frantically, he felt through everything again, but still came up with nothing.

"Do you really think I'm that stupid?"

The calm, whispering voice made Neil jump. Clenched with surprise, he turned his eyes to Helen. Her dark green eyes looked up at him with an expression of fear mingled with disappointment. Neil felt as though he had plunged into black emptiness.

"Where are the keys?" he asked, not wanting to reveal the hollowness that spread in his chest.

"They're safe," Helen answered as she sat up.

"But where?"

"I heard you last night, Neil. I thought you were beginning to see, but I guess you're just a coward. You couldn't even stand up to her."

"What do you know, Helen?" Neil said, turning on her without warning. "You think you're brave just because you've read a book and remembered some childish stories. You're chasing a man who may not even exist, and you call me a coward when I try to keep you from disappointment and embarrassment."

"Disappointment! I think you've managed that pretty well already. Just leave me alone, Neil. I'm sorry I came to you in the first place. Take Siri back south and I'll go the rest of the way by myself."

With that, she slung her bag over her shoulder, got to her feet, and started to walk into the woods. Neil called to her, but she ignored him.

He turned and saw Siri sitting up, her expressionless eyes following Helen. "We're leaving now," he said with more sharpness than he intended. "Get your things and come with me."

Helen could hear Neil and Siri whispering behind her, but she didn't turn around. She didn't expect to get away from them. She wasn't trying to. She didn't see the hill she was walking toward, or feel the ground rising beneath her feet. All she could think about was how to keep her emotions from erupting. It was difficult to fight the burning anger swelling inside of her, but she clenched her teeth and folded her arms across her body in an effort to contain it. The worst part was that she had no idea what she was going to do now. A deep loneliness penetrated her heart and she couldn't hold it back. She missed her mother and father, and now she felt the full weight of the burden of this task.

"Helen!" Neil called behind her, but she paid no attention and increased the speed of her steps. An idea came to her and she pulled the book from her bag, fumbling through its pages, tearing a few slightly in the process. "Will you listen to me, Helen?" Neil went on.

The words that formed in her mind would only bite and she didn't want to be that way. It was best to leave them unsaid.

"How can you know you're right?"

Helen stopped, blinked a few times to clear her eyes, and then turned to face Neil. He stood a few feet in front of her, with Siri standing silently behind him. Was that a look of triumph she tried to hide?

Neil's eyes dropped to the book, then raised again to Helen's face. "What arc you doing, Helen?"

"I'm trying to see if the map can point us to the nearest village," she answered. "You and Siri can stop there and I'll go the rest of the way alone."

"Just think for a minute, Helen," Siri said, her voice heavy with concern. "You're being rash."

"Trying to find Zaric is the only way to stop Mered's rise. I know you two don't believe that, but I do. This isn't your journey, Siri. We don't even know who you are. You don't have to come with me anymore—either of you."

Helen started to walk away again, and again heard whispering behind her.

"Aren't you afraid of what will happen if we separate?" Neil called out. "There could be another trap."

A flash of memory passed before Helen's eyes—a flash of violet light and falling rain—but she decided she didn't care. If it happened again, she would find a way out of it.

The ground sloped downward. After another minute Helen was out of the trees. Ahead of her lay another wide valley, which filled her with both a sense of awe and a feeling of dread. She tried not to think of how long it would take to cross this. It was obvious it would be a few more days before they found a village, when all she wanted was to be free to move by herself right now, without the weight of apprehension and betrayal. Even more depressing was the fact that there was no sign of the Gateway and no chance that this ordeal would soon end. To the west, the white clouds were turning grey. *Very fitting,* she thought. Helen kept her eyes on her feet and tried to force herself forward.

After what felt like an hour, Helen reached the bottom of the slope, fully aware that Neil and Siri were still a few yards behind her. She had made no attempt to shake them and they had made no attempt to catch up. But once they reached level ground, all three of them stopped suddenly. They looked at the sky and couldn't make sense of what they saw. Not only were the grey clouds in the west, but also to the north, south, and east, all rolling toward each other like boiling water. The grey color darkened until it was almost black. Neil and Siri drew close to Helen, their nervousness filling the air like a tangible fog. A cold wind began to blow.

"What is this?" Siri asked, her voice barely audible. The fear in her eyes was much more genuine than anything Helen had seen in Siri's face before. Looking at the sky again, Helen saw that the clouds weren't rolling straight across it, but down toward the valley.

"Do you see shelter anywhere?" Helen asked, assuming an air of calmness, though she was trying to suppress a deep feeling of panic.

"A bridge," Neil replied, pointing. "Up there."

"Come on," Helen commanded, running forward.

Without warning, almost before they realized what was happening, the rolling clouds accelerated, pushing downwards as well as forwards. Helen felt Neil grab her hand just before the force of the wind knocked them to the ground. Dazed, they looked up, but a thick mist had enveloped them, swirling in a roaring wind. They held their heads close together just to be able to see or hear each other. The force of the wind made it difficult to open their eyes.

"Where's Siri?" Helen asked.

Neil turned his head and called her name, but the sound didn't escape his lips. "I think she might be behind us," he said.

"But which way are we facing?" Helen asked in return. She spun around, trying to see something—anything. Fear ran like fire up and down her spine as it began to snow. Neil kept a tight hold on her hand.

"What's going on?" Neil asked, using all his effort to project his voice.

The chill of the wind and snow pelted Helen's body like chunks of ice. Her joints grew stiff with the sharp burning of the cold and she felt an uncomfortable and achy numbness growing in her fingers and toes. Neil's face was pale and his lips were turning purple as the temperature continued to drop.

"We need to move," she finally said.

"But which way should we go?"

"It doesn't matter. It's too cold and we need to move."

Helen stood and walked, fighting against the wind. Neil stayed close beside her, gripping her hand. She peered ahead, trying to make out the shape of anything that might give them a clue to where they were, but all she saw was mist and snow. The swirling whiteness that surrounded them made her dizzy. She took a deep breath to steady herself, but instead of a feeling of calm, she felt a burning, restricted sensation in her lungs. She gasped, but the suffocating feeling only grew stronger. Neil's grip on her hand slackened—though she couldn't be sure that it wasn't *her* grip on *his* that was slipping—and she turned her head to look at him as she tried to take his hand in both of hers, feeling a foreign and frantic panic. It was hard for her eyes to focus. She felt like her head was being held under water. She couldn't breathe and she was falling—or floating.

At last, her eyes closed.

* * *

Light and consciousness filled Helen's mind, but she didn't open her eyes. She was lying on something soft and warm, not cold like the snow-covered ground she expected. Everything around her was quiet. The light coming through her eyelids was bright and she rolled onto her face, burying her head in a pillow. She was covered with blankets. She blinked until her eyes stopped aching, then rolled onto her back again, wincing at the stiffness of her muscles. In this position, all she saw were the exposed wooden slats of the inside of a cabin roof.

It was then that she allowed herself to wonder where she was. Her mind went back to the fog in the valley and the feeling of suffocation. It didn't seem possible that they could have survived that. They... Neil!

Helen sat up too fast to look around the room. A feeling of weakness struck her, her head began to spin, and she fell back onto the pillow.

"Why do people always believe they're ready to get up as soon as they can open their eyes?" a voice said with playful annoyance. Helen turned her head and watched a man walk toward her from a far corner of the room. Her first reaction was one of panic—that she might somehow be in danger. She realized, though, that she wasn't in a position to run. "Lift your head slowly and you might have better luck," the man continued.

Helen did as she was told, raising herself gently, then rested against the wall behind the bed for support. The man sat on the edge of the bed, his entire being cheerful. "My name is Alan," he said. Helen hesitated, giving a single nod without taking her eyes off him. The man didn't seem threatening, but Neil hadn't seen Siri as threatening, either.

Cautiously, Helen looked around. It was a small, almost bare room. There was only one door, which either meant there was only one way to escape, or this man merely lived in a very modest one-room cabin. Sunlight poured through the windows. What comforted Helen, though, was the sight of a small cot a few feet away, and Neil lying upon it.

"He looks pale," she said, in part to Alan, but mostly to herself. She was surprised at the weakness of her own voice.

"You should see yourself," he replied.

"Is this Camelora?"

"No."

"How long have we been here?" Helen asked.

"About eight hours."

"We can't stay," she exclaimed, trying to throw the blankets off, but Alan put his hand on the edge of the mattress to hold them down. "Ian will catch up to us," Helen insisted. "We need to find the Gateway before he does."

"I don't want you to worry about Ian," Alan said. The gentle cadence in his voice had a calming effect. "Even if you leave two days from now, you'll reach the Gateway before he does. I don't think he can find it without you, and he doesn't know where you are. And he can't find this place."

Unable to grasp how he knew so much, Helen looked Alan in the eyes. There was a strange something about this man, something inside of him that she had never seen in anyone else before. It was an overwhelming, ancient, and complicated goodness.

"You understand every word I'm saying," Helen stated as the realization emerged.

"Of course. Everything you say makes sense."

Helen once more looked around the room. "Where's Siri?" she asked.

"Siri?"

"The girl who was with us. Didn't you bring her here, too? Is she alive?"

"The two of you were the only ones in the valley," he answered. "There was no one else with you."

"But she was there—" Helen began, then stopped. The confused look on Alan's face told her that he wouldn't be able to give her any useful information concerning Siri. "How did you find us, Alan? We've been running from Ian for days, and it seems strange that *you* found us instead of him."

"I've been watching for you," Alan answered with laughing patience. "Zaric asked me to stay here, years ago, to wait for you."

Helen stared in rare disbelief. And yet she couldn't help believing it. "You know Zaric?"

"Yes," he stated, looking directly into Helen's eyes, his own twinkling. "Of course I know Zaric."

# Chapter 14

"How did Zaric know we would be here?" Helen asked.

"Really, Helen," Alan said, "there's no point in asking questions you already know the answers to. You have been following the path Zaric created years ago."

"But we stopped following the path on the map," she argued. "We had to."

"The map," he countered, confused. "The map didn't show the path you were meant to follow. He arranged everything along the route he knew you would take. I'm not sure what path Neil's grandfather marked in that book, but as far as I know, he never wrote down the path to the keys. It would have been too dangerous. It's all in the book you carry with you, though—in the stories. Zaric placed me here so that I could look for you when I saw the storm pass. I went to the valley, found you and Neil—the two of you only—nearly dead, and I brought you back here. It's as simple as that. Now, you can either rest some more, or have something to eat. Which do you prefer?"

He stood as he finished this statement, then went back to the fire. Her body stiff, Helen slipped her legs out from under her blankets and sat on the edge of the bed, stretching her arms outwards and arching her back, trying to release the tightness in her muscles. She rolled her neck as she stood, then crossed the floor to the table, not far from where Alan crouched, stirring something in a pot.

"Is it far to Camelora?" she asked, lowering herself into a chair.

"No," Alan answered. "Not far at all. But you should actually ask how far we are from the Gateway. You can't reach Camelora until you reach the Gateway."

"All right," Helen said, smiling to herself. "How far is it to the Gateway?"

"Not far."

"I'm tired of walking," she continued after a lengthy pause. Alan stood and faced her, sympathy infused into his manner, but he didn't even pretend to have something to say in return. Instead, he set a bowl of soup in front of her, then sat to watch her eat. Helen didn't realize how cold and hungry she was until the hot soup was inside of her. The numbness that remained from the strange fog and snow dispelled.

"Will Neil be all right?" Helen asked when her bowl was empty.

Alan laughed. To Helen, his laugh was pleasant and just as warming as the soup she had eaten. "He isn't dead, there are no signs of fever, so I think it's safe to say he will be all right."

Alan stood up again and opened the windows of the cottage, letting the fresh air in. It was delicious to Helen—everything since waking up was. With a measure of guilt, she thought of how much she had needed that day's rest. She was ashamed to even think she could be so tired.

"Soon we'll be with Zaric," Helen observed out loud, "and soon we'll be safe."

Alan paused at the window, then turned to her with a serious expression. "Don't relax too soon, Helen. You still need to find the Gateway and get through it, and you don't know what else you may run into after that. It may be a long time before this kingdom or anyone in it is safe."

Helen nodded. She knew that this warning should cause some concern, but her emotions were too light and her anticipation prevented her from feeling the full weight of the words. She couldn't believe it would be any more difficult than what they had already passed through. And knowing now that even the dangers they faced had been expected by Zaric, he would easily see them through anything left to come.

* * *

Helen woke up the next morning before dawn broke through the windows. She blinked a few times, forcing the blurriness out of her eyes, then looked over at Neil's cot. It was empty. She jumped out of bed and looked around the room. No one else was there. Not even taking the time to put on her boots, she ran out of the cottage.

Just outside the door, Neil and Alan stood looking at the land ahead of them. They turned to smile at Helen when they heard her come out. She sighed with relief.

"Alan's been telling me about this land," Neil stated. "Apparently, it's the best farmland in all the regions, but no one knows about it. When this is all over, I might just settle here."

Helen didn't say anything, only nodded. A pang of guilt pierced her for the farm Neil no longer had. She couldn't help wondering if part of the land's appeal was how few neighbors Neil would have to avoid. The three of them stood in peaceful silence, looking at the land and hills, the distant jagged mountains, the blue sky that was progressively losing all traces of night, and the white clouds that displayed the wonderful tinge of vibrant golden sunlight that touched them before it touched the world. Distant birds chatted and sang with each other and the long grass rustled softly.

"Is this what Camelora's like?" Helen asked, her whole being filled with contentment.

"Oh, Camelora's much more magnificent," Alan answered with his now familiar smile. "Much more full of life and energy. I'll be glad when the Gateway is open. It's been so long since I saw Camelora. Sometimes I see it in my dreams, but dreams are nothing compared to reality."

"And Zaric," Neil said. "What's he like?"

"He's very hard to describe. Anyway, I don't want to waste your time in telling you. By this time tomorrow, you just might be seeing him for yourself."

"Tomorrow!" Helen exclaimed. "Is it really that close?"

"Of course. I'm sure you must have known you would reach it in the end. Isn't that why you came?"

Helen blushed, realizing that it was a ridiculous question. Neil flinched at Alan's words, offended.

"I think we need to forgive Alan for being so blunt," Helen said. "His honesty is relieving."

"But, what about Siri?" he asked, after a few moments of soaking in the silence.

"Helen was asking about her yesterday," Alan said thoughtfully. Neil turned to Helen with unmasked surprise. "Believe it or not, that storm was designed to protect you. If there were any dangers following you, they would be weeded out. I helped Zaric create it, years ago. The two of you were the only ones I found in that valley."

"But she must have been there," Neil argued. "Are you sure she wasn't buried under the snow?"

"Most of the snow was gone when I reached you. It would have been easy to see a third person. But I didn't, and I won't change my story."

"You don't seem very concerned," Neil went on. "Do you think we only imagined her?"

"I don't doubt what you say, but there's really nothing I can do. I never saw Siri, so I can't tell you where she's gone. All I can tell you is, if she was gone when I arrived, she was *not* an ally of Zaric. Would you like breakfast?"

The abrupt switch caught Neil unprepared and he couldn't find his voice or the words to argue before Alan went into his cabin, leaving Neil and Helen behind. The sun was on the horizon now, casting its light over this quiet land.

"Should we try to find her?" Neil finally asked.

"Where would we look?" Helen questioned in return, her words coming out with more of a bite than she intended.

"I don't know, but we promised to protect her. Maybe if we go back to the valley, we might find something to show us where she went."

"I don't think Alan took us from the valley just to have us go back. You heard what he said: if she wasn't with us, it's because we needed protection from her."

Neil set his mouth in a tight line, holding back the words he wanted to spit out. He felt that he knew Siri better than some man—a stranger to all of them—who had never met her.

"It would probably be best for us to go to the Gateway," Helen continued. "If we're as close as Alan says, it would be pointless to turn around now." Helen stole a glance at Neil, noted his look of uncertainty, and added, "If it's that important to you, Zaric should be able to help us find Siri."

Neil considered this for a moment, then nodded. "We'll go to the Gateway, then."

Helen expected him to turn and go into the cabin once he had said this, but instead he stood still, his arms folded, his eyes unfocused in contemplation.

"Thank you for staying with me," Helen said. "In the valley, when you took my hand, thank you for doing that."

"You're my only friend," Neil replied. "I couldn't lose you."

"Even though I haven't always been a good friend in return?"

"I haven't exactly been the best friend, either—getting angry, being irritable, not always listening."

"How can you listen when I don't speak? I didn't trust you like I should have, but I do now. Do you want to know how I found that third stone?"

For a short interval, Neil only looked at her. Helen was determined to hold his gaze. Then, he nodded.

She dove into her story. She told him about the lights, about the trees, and about the pools. Every scene, every image she could remember was explained. She shared what she had felt—what she still felt—leaving nothing out.

When she was done, Helen waited for some response. Neil only contemplated her. A wave of sadness came over her. "You don't believe me," she stated.

"I believe every word you said," Neil contradicted, his voice low. "Every single word."

They lapsed again into silence. A wave of uneasiness came over Helen, a feeling she had been able to avoid until this time, standing on the safest spot of ground she had stood on in weeks. "Sometimes," she began with a sigh, "I'm afraid."

"Afraid of Mered?" Neil asked.

"No," she answered, drawing the word out as she thought before the rest of her words came out in a rush. "I'm afraid of Zaric. I'm afraid we'll reach Camelora and he won't want us—that he'll send us back. I'm afraid we'll reach the end and I'll be disappointed by what I see. I want to keep moving, because if I stop, I might just realize how useless I am. If I stop moving, I think about my father and mother. I wonder if I've done enough or if I've done everything I was meant to do. And if I stop, the grief will catch up with me and I'll curl up and cry."

"Then why don't you?"

Helen couldn't find the words to answer. She could feel the fear and worry swelling inside of her. "There isn't enough time," she decisively replied, unwilling to speak above a whisper.

She took a deep breath to calm herself and stop the noisome emotion that threatened to overwhelm her. But her own emotions were forgotten when, suddenly, the atmosphere around them felt wrong. It was colder. Involuntarily, she shivered. Confused, she tried to find some change in the scenery surrounding them. It was all the same as before. And yet, by some instinct, she turned to face the cabin, sensing Alan's presence. He stood in the doorway.

"Helen! Neil!" he called. "Will you come inside?"

Helen and Neil did as they were told. At the doorway, Alan's manner was natural, calm; but once they were in the cabin, he moved around uneasily, trying to gather up Helen's and Neil's things with as much haste as he could. They both joined him, though they weren't sure why he was in such a hurry.

"You need to leave now," Alan stated. "I can't let you stay here any longer."

"What's wrong?" Neil asked, closing his bag and slinging it over his shoulder.

"Is Ian coming?" Helen enquired without waiting for Alan to answer Neil's question.

Alan nodded, his face more serious than Helen had seen it the whole time they had been with him. The usual twinkle in his eyes was nowhere to be seen. "I can tell the signs," he said. "Go as fast as you can for the next two hours, without stopping. Head northeast. If you need to stop, only rest for a few minutes. You aren't far from Camelora, but once the Gateway is opened, anyone can get through. Try not to get separated. You both need to make it to Zaric."

"Every time we think we might get a chance to rest..." Helen began, with no intention of finishing.

Alan threw open the door and stepped aside. Helen went out first, pressing Alan's hand as she passed. As Neil started to follow, Alan grabbed him by the arm and whispered in his ear, "Keep her safe, Neil.

She has the keys and that Gateway needs to be opened before Mered gets them. I hope I'll see you again soon. I trust you."

"At least one of us does," Neil replied, then followed Helen without another word. She had already walked around the cabin and started to ascend the hill behind it. He ran to catch up. They walked together as quickly as they dared.

"I wish I could feel what Alan is feeling," Neil said. "I haven't noticed anything different."

"I felt something, but I wouldn't have known what it was," Helen replied. "But I believe him. He knows much more about Mered than I ever want to. How will we know when it's been two hours?"

"Don't city people have much use for telling time, Helen?"

The terrain they covered was undulating and inconsistent, full of dips and rises, which they hoped would make it difficult for anyone following to keep them in sight. Helen glanced over her shoulder every time they reached the crest of a hill, but saw no one. They were utterly alone, a realization that was both frightening and comforting. Yet she didn't quite feel all alone and she found it hard to go forward without looking around every few seconds. She thought it was strange that, for the first time on this journey, no birds were singing. A wave of weakness spread over her as well, as though she hadn't quite caught her breath after the previous day's storm. It felt as though they had been walking all day, but the position of the sun in the sky said otherwise. Eventually, they walked down a hill and into another open valley.

The sound of leaves rustling drew her eyes and attention away from the ground ahead and she unconsciously collided with Neil, who had stopped in front of her.

"Is everything all right?" she asked.

"It's been two hours. But, I can't see anything special about this place. It's just a big open space."

"Maybe we need to go a little farther. Your timing might not be very exact. Mine usually isn't."

Neil considered this, then nodded in agreement. They walked forward again. They had only gone a few yards when the air ahead resisted them with a violence that knocked them off balance and threw them to the ground. They both sat motionless in surprise, then Helen got to her feet, groaning. She looked straight ahead to see what blocked their way, but all she could see was the empty valley and the large hill beyond. She stepped forward, holding her hand out in front of her. Once she reached the same point they had come to before, a tremendous, icy shock sprang through her arm and she gasped as though she had fallen into a frozen river. She pulled her arm back, shaking her hand.

"A barrier," Neil stated. "We're definitely close. Do you still have the telescope?"

Helen took it from her bag and handed it to Neil. He looked around, searching the hills and trees, while Helen looked with her own eyes.

"Helen!" Neil exclaimed excitedly, unable to hide his smile. He handed her the telescope, then pointed to the hill to their right. Helen looked through the telescope, following the line of his pointing arm. At the top of the trees, so small they were barely visible, were a row of white marble columns.

# Chapter 15

She lowered the telescope, wishing she could see more, but the trees grew too densely. Only those columns were visible. After a pause, she lifted the telescope again to convince herself that what she saw was real. Elation rose inside of her at the realization that this was truly the Gateway. It took great effort to suppress it. No roof covered the columns and they appeared worn and deteriorated. They weren't evenly spaced—she wondered how many had fallen over time. Others leaned noticeably. She wouldn't allow herself to become too excited until she knew for sure that nothing was wrong with the Gateway itself. It worried her that the Gateway might be damaged, that it wouldn't open, even with the keys. Helen studied the trees beneath the columns, trying to see a path. But there didn't seem to be any route at all. The forest was packed thickly and wildly. She no longer needed to suppress her elation, since the inaccessibility of the Gateway did that for her. It seemed more unreachable now than it did throughout their journey.

"How do you think it works?" Neil asked in a reverent tone, as though he was afraid of his own voice. Helen replied with a shrug. "We probably shouldn't stand around and wait," he went on. "It might take us a while to get through those trees."

They started forward, but only took a few steps before the faint sound of a horse's hooves stopped them. Fearing what she would see,

Helen's heart pounded with a sense of dread as she turned to see a horse and rider coming over the distant southern hill, riding faster than either of them had ever seen anyone ride.

"Is it too much to hope that it's just another traveler," Neil said, "who happens to be going in the same direction we are?"

"No one ever comes this far north," Helen replied, trying not to let her voice tremble. "We should run."

"He's coming too fast," he said, the sight of the horse keeping him from moving. He shook his head as he thought. Neil spoke with authority and commanded, "Take the keys to the Gateway, Helen. I'll hold him back."

"No, Neil, I can't go alone," Helen argued, not trying to disguise her panic. "We don't know what could be in those trees. Alan told us to stay together."

"If Ian happens to know a path to the Gateway, it would be better for me to keep him occupied down here. We have to at least try. Alan doesn't know Ian, or at least his plans. I'll find you after you open the Gateway. Now, go, Helen."

"What if something bad happens, Neil? Have you ever really used a sword before?"

Neil hesitated for a moment, watching the rider approach. The fact that it was Ian was unmistakable and in another moment he would be dangerously close to them. "Minor detail. Go, Helen."

Reluctant to argue anymore, Helen hesitated only a few more seconds before deciding to obey. She turned from Neil and broke into a run, trying not to stumble over the rough ground under the long and wild grass. Her greatest worry, though, was that the panic in her chest would compress her lungs. She made her way to the foot of the hill, below the point where the Gateway stood. The trees on the edge of the woods weren't difficult to pass through, but they thickened as she moved deeper, now walking instead of running and taking shallow breaths. She pushed her way past sharp, prickly limbs and twigs. The large trunks grew too close together for her to walk in a straight line. The ground was littered with fallen logs, roots, and rocks, and the shadows made it hard for her to see where to step. She cried out as her foot caught something and she fell to the ground, unable to stop herself. Finding her footing again, she placed her hand against the trunk of the nearest tree and took a deep breath before walking again. For the first time, she didn't try to hold back the tears of fear and frustration. Looking up, though, she saw that the trees were starting to thin out. Helen strained her ears, hoping to hear sounds from the valley below, but she could only hear her own heartbeat and footsteps, the effort of her breaths, the rustling of her clothes moving through the foliage, and the occasional breeze through the trees. With caution, she looked forward and slackened her pace. There was a clearing a few yards ahead and Helen could just make out the shape of the columns between the trees.

She reached the edge of the clearing and stopped. Her apprehension growing, she peered around, scanning the trees and land surrounding her. She wouldn't step into the open until she knew the way was clear. Her eyes found nothing, but she was frightened, doubting herself. Something strange was in the air, a feeling very much like the one she had felt when she first saw Ian. This place was too quiet, yet restless. Helen felt a heavy discomfort knowing that Neil was so far away. The precarious white columns, resting on a white stone platform, stood a few more yards ahead. She wanted to believe that she would be safe as soon as she reached them, but instead she had the urge to run back to the valley. Yet running back might be just as dangerous as running forward and the Gateway needed to be opened. She pushed her fears deeper inside her mind and ran to the pavilion.

The Gateway had once been an impressive and beautiful place, she could tell, but the platform was now littered with bits of crumbling marble and large stone slabs from the fallen roof and columns, creating a labyrinthine path across the weathered floor that she needed to pick her way over and around. A small table stood in the middle of the platform, by some miracle untouched by the collapsed grandeur surrounding it. Helen made her way to it with care. She brushed the debris and dust off its surface, hoping to find an inscription, but was disappointed to find only five small indentations, arranged in a circle. Confusion engulfed her. She counted them over and over again, placing her finger in each small hole, too weary to believe she had counted wrong. She took the small pouch out of her bag, opened it, and looked down at the four keys inside. One by one, she took them from the bag in the order she and Neil had found them and set them in the circle, beginning at the top. Tapping her fingers on the table, she stared at the empty depression.

Everything inside of her fell like the columns around her. Her thoughts whirled disjointedly, trying to understand where she had been mistaken. The book had told them to find four keys. Or at least that was what she thought she had read. The path they had taken led them to four keys. Helen tried to make sense of this new puzzle. They had believed they were done, that they had reached the end of the journey. Even Alan had believed it. But, he had never asked to see the keys. Perhaps he had assumed that they had found all five, not just four.

Would they have to go back and try to find the last key? If only they had thought to show Alan what they had already found. Would he have been able to tell them that they still needed one more? Helen hoped she wouldn't reach the valley and find Neil dead. She didn't know how she would stop Ian, but she had done it before and would find a way again.

As she was about to gather the keys and turn away from the table, a thought formed, though she didn't know where it came from. She put her hand to her throat and felt the small necklace her mother had given her. Unclasping the chain from her neck, Helen held the necklace in the palm of her hand, hoping her idea wasn't wrong, but not wanting to take the time to argue with herself. She wrapped her fingers around the tear-shaped trinket and squeezed. The delicate silver shattered readily, stinging her palm and fingers as it broke and cut into her skin. Helen opened her hand and saw a white pearl resting among the broken slivers of silver.

A twig snapped at the opposite edge of the pavilion. Helen realized that she had allowed her attention to falter, no longer alert to her surroundings. She looked up and saw Siri standing a few yards ahead of her, holding a long reed to her lips. Helen didn't have time to react before feeling a pinch in her neck. The sudden, sharp pain made her cry out. She reached up and felt a small, feathered dart. Looking at Siri, she felt a pity that surprised even herself, disappointed that her doubts were true. But instead of the expression of triumph Helen expected Siri to wear, she wore no expression at all, her face hard and inflexible. Numb weakness trickled through Helen's arms. She grasped the edges of the table to keep from falling as the sensation spread throughout her body. With unsteady fingers, she rolled the pearl across the table and slid it into the last empty place.

A ripple of pale blue light spread out from the table, washing over Helen like warm, refreshing water, invigorating her limbs for a brief moment. It moved out in every direction, through the clearing and then the trees, sweeping down the hill, accompanied by a soft ringing sound that crescendoed as it moved. The scene around Helen blurred. She closed her eyes and collapsed to the floor.

* * *

Neil held his sword clumsily with both hands as he watched Ian ride toward him. His hands trembled, but his feet, at least, were steady. As he stood in the middle of this field, so far from everything he had ever known before, he remembered that he was only a farmer and he felt less than confident. It had been years since his father took him to the yearly fairs and games in his village and he saw someone use a sword—and that was nothing like holding one himself. Helen was reluctant to leave him because she knew this as well as he did. Volunteering to hold Ian off had merely been an offer to die for her—and for Zaric. This last thought surprised Neil and did nothing to lessen his fear.

There was a slight smirk on Ian's face as he came closer. His speed didn't slacken. He swung his sword in a sweeping motion and, as Neil tried to raise his sword in defense, the broad side of Ian's hit him in the middle of the chest, knocking him onto his back and expelling all of the air from his lungs.

He took a minute to fill his lungs again, gasping and swallowing air before he scrambled to his feet and turned, grimacing at the pain. Ian sat lazily on his horse, laughing without warmth. "Do you think I really want to fight you?" he mocked. "I'm sorry, Neil, but you just aren't worth my time."

He steered his horse around and started to gallop toward the hill. A wave of panic went over Neil, overwhelming all the fear he felt for his own safety. He needed to hold Ian off long enough for Helen to open the Gateway, though he didn't know what would happen when she did. He wondered how much time had passed between Helen leaving and Ian reaching him. It didn't seem likely that she had reached the top of the hill yet. But there didn't appear to be any way to stop Ian.

"No!" Neil shouted, feeling stupid as he did. Yet when he spoke, a shiver went through the field. For a moment, he thought he had only imagined it, but with the shiver, Ian's horse startled and fidgeted, and nothing Ian said to coax him calmed him down. The horse became more and more agitated until, finally, Ian was thrown from the saddle.

He got to his feet and, walking in long strides, anger lining his face, crossed the yards that separated him from Neil. He swung with great force, but this time Neil was prepared to block the blow.

"I think I'll enjoy killing you both," Ian shot out, beating his sword against Neil's, causing a vibration that rang through the hilt and Neil's arm until it shook his core. "I've suffered so much for your mistakes. You should have joined me, Neil. It's better to live than to die for a worthless cause."

Neil didn't respond, focusing instead on warding off Ian's blows, hoping he could prevent Ian's sword from cutting into him just long enough for them to see a sign that the Gateway had opened. Each strike made his sword heavier in his hands and Neil was forced to step back as Ian stepped forward, applying a pressure along the blade of Neil's sword to disarm him. Soon Neil was on his knees, the weight of Ian's sword threatening to break the bones in his arms.

"It's almost inspiring," Ian said, "to realize that you honestly believe you're giving Helen time to open the Gateway. Have you ever considered I might not be working alone? When you die, it will be for nothing."

In a whip-like motion, Ian struck Neil's hand with the broad of his sword, forcing the sword out of his hand as he released an involuntary yell, crouching down and cradling his hand. Ian raised his sword again, his face taut and triumphant, but a sudden, bright flicker at the top of the hill pulled both men's eyes away. Within seconds, a wave of blue light rolled down the hill, through the trees, and into the valley. It washed over them like a gale of wind. Neil closed his eyes.

He expected the force of the wave to push him to the ground, but instead, he felt an odd sensation in his chest, as though the rush of light had revitalized him. This feeling was like nothing Neil had ever felt before, as though his soul had been stretched and cracked like the shell of an egg. With his eyes closed, he could see this valley in a green more vivid than when his eyes were open. The sun shone brighter and he thought that the world laughed. Excited voices filled the air, though he couldn't tell what they were saying or where they were coming from. And then it all stopped and the air fell silent.

Neil opened his eyes, expecting to find Ian standing over him with his sword swinging. Instead, he was lying on the ground a few feet away, pale and unconscious, but still breathing. He thought for a moment, stepping toward Ian with his sword held out in front of him, considering his position. It would be easy to prevent Ian from ever following them again. But Neil knew himself too well and didn't have to think too long before he sheathed his sword and ran to the hill.

The tangle of trees disoriented Neil. He found it difficult to make his way to the crest, wondering if he was even going the right way. He would see a glimpse of the Gateway's columns, but they disappeared again before he could think of how to reach them. He only hoped Helen had thought to stay at the Gateway and wait for him. When the trees began to clear and the pavilion was distinctly visible before him, he exhaled.

"Helen!" he called as he neared the hilltop. There was no answer. He listened intently as he walked forward, trying to keep his gaze steady as he searched the area. Seeing a figure lying on the ground a few feet away, he rushed forward and fell to the ground. He turned it, expecting to see Helen's face. Shock and confusion seized him as he realized it was Siri. For a minute, he couldn't move, or even think about moving. He was afraid he already knew why she was there as Ian's words rang through his head, but he didn't want to believe it. Neil's mind had already connected why Ian had been affected by the wave in a way Neil hadn't. Siri's face was just as pale as Ian's and a hollow reed lay on the ground only inches from her hand.

"Helen?" he called again, moving past Siri. He couldn't see his companion anywhere. He could almost hear his heart beating and his throat constricted as he walked across the platform, stepping over debris and fallen columns. He couldn't believe the wave would have harmed Helen. Unless, of course, being so close to the Gateway when it opened sent out a shock too strong for her to handle. Or she had gone back to the valley, looking for Neil. He now hoped she had. However, the ominous reed next to Siri tickled the back of his mind.

Neil came within a few feet of the small table and halted, then continued to move forward. Another bundle lay on the floor on the other side of the table, mostly obscured by it and the broken pieces of a column, and he knew it must be Helen. Walking around the table, the world froze when he saw the tiny feathered dart embedded in her neck. Tears burned his horror-stricken eyes as he fell to his knees next to her, touching her pale, cold face with gentle fingers. "Helen?" he whispered, wishing she would respond.

Dumbfounded, Neil sat down and pulled Helen's limp body onto his lap. He tried to convince himself that none of this was real, that his mind was confused. Perhaps the wave of light had knocked him to the ground after all, and he was lying unconscious, nightmarishly dreaming, in the field below. He had seen this as Helen's journey from the beginning. Neil didn't know how to move on without her.

He rested his forehead against Helen's and allowed his tears to fall, but he would *not* break down. In his mind, he repeated that thought over and over. He only needed a few minutes to fortify himself and prepare for the trek to Camelora. The map should show him the way.

He felt a brush of air against his cheek and froze. Helen's breath. Helen was still breathing. Although it was shallow and hard to detect, Helen's breath was still there. Neil breathed out his relief, holding Helen even closer.

But he didn't want to waste any time. Pulling his grandfather's book from Helen's bag, he turned to the map and found the dot marking Camelora. He traced back to where he knew he was, studying the route until it was committed to his memory. Taking Helen's bag from her shoulder, he slung it over his own. He found the small bag that had held the stones where it had fallen to the ground, plucked the dart from Helen's neck, and dropped it in. Then, he gathered Helen in his arms and got to his feet.

Like moving in a dream, Neil couldn't walk quickly enough. He wished for greater strength—and he felt strange. So many thoughts were going through his mind all at once, the primary one being whether he would be able to get Helen to Camelora in time for Zaric to help her. He remembered his parents. The thought crossed his mind that Helen wasn't meant to make it to the lost city. An uncomfortable nausea settled in his stomach. It took all of his energy to fight his fears and focus on getting away from this place. Repeatedly he tried to convince himself that Camelora couldn't be very far from the Gateway. But, the longer he walked—always higher and higher—the more his hope faded. His thoughts slipped into his memories as he thought of Helen's distrust of Siri. He even wished he had found some way to kill Ian before he had managed to get this far. Most of all, he wished he had gone with Helen. If only he had believed that they could reach the Gateway together before Ian reached them, he might have been able to protect her from Siri. Neil shook away fresh regret and tried to imagine his destination.

Soon, he realized he was climbing a hill without another one rising behind it. Neil tried to will his feet to move him with more speed. He couldn't fight his impatience. Camelora must be on the other side of this hill, he told himself, sprawling out in a valley below, waiting for him. He pushed himself harder and held Helen closer.

He reached the top of the hill and, for a minute, stood frozen. Then, he sat on the ground, leaned over Helen, unable to contain his frustrations and disappointment. The valley ahead of him was dull, greyish-green, and somewhat hazy—an empty, dead wasteland.

Though he wouldn't allow himself to admit it before, Neil believed that Camelora was real, and not simply because Helen believed it was real. He couldn't help believing his grandfather's stories, the things his grandfather had always believed himself, even if his confidence was shaken. His grandfather wove the stories into Neil's soul until there was no way to separate them from his own identity. Inside, he knew it was all true, he only held onto the possibility that it wasn't to save himself from disappointment. As long as Helen was with him, though, everything seemed possible. Zaric was real and he would take his kingdom back from Mered. When Helen spoke, her voice filled with hope, it was difficult not to see Camelora in his mind, beautiful and peaceful.

But, perhaps Zaric himself was dead and his city had crumbled into ruins long ago. Ian and Siri would wake up, follow Neil, and take him back to Mered. He knew now that he wouldn't go with them and he and Helen would both die, if she wasn't already dead. Or, if he tried, Neil might overcome Ian, as Helen had done more than once before. But he still wouldn't know where to go. Straight ahead was his only option.

Neil raised his head, feeling a little calmer now. He had seen too much the past few days to allow himself to think that it wasn't true. King Zaric was real and, in some way, he would save them. He was waiting for them in Camelora and Neil was willing to believe one last time that Zaric would prevent one of his supporters from dying. Helen and Neil had walked so many miles and pushed themselves farther than they would have for any other reason—they had even walked over a lake. He smiled as he remembered that impossible feat. Now that Helen was dying, it wasn't enough for her to believe; Neil had to believe for himself. And he did.

Before him, the valley began to change. The haze gradually melted away, leaving behind grass that was much less grey than before. As it turned greener, Neil realized that it had always been green, almost as vivid as the color he had seen just after the Gateway opened. And as he watched, stones appeared and took a more definite shape, filling the opposite end of the valley and creeping up the opposite hillside. A few small walls formed first, then clusters of stone houses, and finally, above it all, a modest stone palace. The city reminded Neil of Stephen and Meira's city, but much more vibrant and beautiful. The fields around the city were defined and cultivated, both charming and practical. Irregular movements revealed that people were working in these fields. Sunlight rested on the city, brightening it. The blue sky and white clouds above enhanced the brilliance of the land below, and the land magnified the beauty of the sky above. In the distance, the stony mountains were still deeply capped with snow. The entire picture was more majestic than anything Neil had seen before, each piece complementing the others.

A cleansing release filled Neil, like he was truly feeling life for the first time in years. He got to his feet again and started forward, but looked down at Helen's face and paused. He placed his hand above her nose and mouth until he felt her breath against it. She had come so far and now she couldn't see the end of the path. With hurried steps, he started his descent down the hill. If he could get Helen to the palace, there was still hope that she would see Camelora.

# Chapter 16

Neil's body ached by the time he reached the outskirts of the city. His legs and arms grew more and more weak. He worried his strength would run out before he reached the palace. More than just the physical exertion, he felt the strain of reaching Zaric before the last breath left Helen's body and the dread that he was already too late. But he forced himself to continue walking. His mind held tightly to the hope he felt of seeing Zaric. Without that hope, he was afraid the city might disappear again.

As he reached the fields bordering the city, he also reached the working people he had seen from the hill, men and women plowing and preparing the soil for seeds. They noticed Neil now, at first only stopping to stare as he walked by, some coming up to the low hedge that separated the road from the fields and shifting their glances to the bundle he held in his arms. Then, an indistinguishable shout rose up—first from one person, then from many. Only then did Neil realize how little strength he had left. His legs gave out and he stumbled, cradling Helen as close to his body as he could.

A wave of people descended upon him—along with a barrage of questions. "Please, help us," he managed to stammer, his voice weak.

"Find the king!" someone nearby yelled. A young man nodded and pushed through the crowd, then ran when he was clear of them.

A woman tried to take Helen, but Neil only tightened his grip. The commotion overwhelmed him. The one thing holding him together was his instinct to protect her. He locked eyes with the woman, who nodded in understanding before calling out, "Water! Someone bring water!"

"Is she still alive?" came a question, though Neil couldn't tell from whom it came.

"Yes," he replied. "I—I think so. If only just barely."

The voices gradually died down until only a handful of people whispered to each other, but the crowd remained. In fact, Neil could have sworn it grew.

A man broke through the gathering, carrying a large cup filled with water. He put it to Neil's lips and Neil drank, relief flooding him as the liquid drenched his dry throat. When he had drained the cup, he nodded his thanks to the man.

Looking at the wall of faces encircling him, bewildered by their attention, Neil asked, "Do you know who we are?"

"Of course," another man answered with wide eyes. "Everyone in Camelora knows about Helen and Neil."

Neil scanned the people again with different eyes, wondering at the same time exactly what they were thinking as they looked at him. "Is that a good thing or a bad thing?" he wondered aloud.

Then, without any other sound than the rustling of their feet, the crowd parted and a man rushed through. Neil felt a tug of recognition deep inside himself. The man had the kindest face he had ever seen—more kind than his father, or even his grandfather—roughened and tanned from exposure to the sun, yet appearing to be ageless. His deep blue eyes shone brightly, emitting comfort like warmth from a fire, although his mouth was set in a serious line. Repose filled Neil and his soul lightened as he realized that this was King Zaric. The stories had been true—everything Helen believed and said was real. Neil's emotions settled like a stone in his throat.

Zaric didn't say anything as he approached Neil and crouched down. The king held out his arms to take Helen. Neil opened his mouth, yet a few seconds went by before he could speak. "I'm so sorry," he whispered, his eyes filling with tears. He swallowed a few times before going on. "I didn't mean to let this happen. I didn't know."

With his arms still outstretched, Zaric looked Neil in the eye, his face filled with compassion. "You need to trust me, Neil," he said.

Neil nodded. He gently placed Helen in Zaric's arms, then sat still as the king got up and turned back to the city. Neil stared after him without really seeing and continued to stare long after he disappeared through the gates.

* * *

A few hours later, Neil sat in a quiet bedroom, next to an open window. The sun had just fallen below the western hills and lamps were being lit in the streets and houses below. From here, he could look out onto the entire city and valley and see the life moving within it, without feeling obligated to be a part of it. The solemnity that had engulfed the city when he entered had subsided. Now, it hummed with voices and noises. There was an air of peace mingled with excitement throughout the entire place and, although his head was full of worry, Neil didn't feel that he would want to be worried anywhere else. Camelora felt just as safe as Helen had always said. Neil's mind relaxed as he leaned his head against the wall, feeling the reprieve of his first night of no longer trying to reach his destination.

There was a soft knock on the door. Neil turned his head, not sure if he wanted to be left alone, or if he should answer it. Finally, he called out, "Come in."

The door opened and Zaric entered. Neil jumped to his feet but Zaric shook his head and waved for him to sit back down. He sat in a chair a few feet away from the young man. Now that his mind was more settled, Neil looked at the king with interest. He had seen great men before, and Zaric wasn't like any of them. Neil had expected to see a pampered and proud man who relied on an entourage of servants to open all his doors, carry anything he might need, catering to his every whim. That was the way the rumors about the regions' governors often ran. But the man who sat in front of Neil had the rough hands of a man who worked hard, the windswept face of a man who spent his days in the fields, and, although he held his head with confidence, his expression was gentle and caring. There was no reason for Neil to have known before, when Zaric came down the steps of the castle, that he was seeing the king—it was only something he knew inside of himself, like he had met Zaric before.

"Will she be all right?" Neil asked.

"We're doing what we can. It's a strange sort of poison. It paralyzed her rapidly, but it appears to be killing her slowly."

Neil flinched at the word "killing" and looked down at the floor, then his hands, then at the city outside the window. His voice dropping to a whisper, he said, "I failed, didn't I?"

Zaric shook his head. "No, you didn't fail. You did what was expected of you. You found the keys and opened the Gateway. You even brought Helen to me."

"But she wasn't supposed to get hurt," Neil argued. "We were supposed to stay together. Alan told us to stay together." The words struck pain in his chest and he wished he hadn't said them. The possibilities of what he might have done—should have done—to keep Helen safe flooded him again. If he had only gone to the Gateway with her instead of trying to hinder Ian. Or perhaps if he hadn't trusted Siri so much, wanting to believe that she was harmless, though he knew the whole time that it wasn't true. So many possibilities—chances to do something right—and he had made so many wrong choices.

"You brought her to me and I thank you for that."

"She would have been more useful to you than I am," Neil blurted. He hesitated before going on, but decided not to hold himself back. "She believed that you were here, that Camelora was here, even when there was no reason to believe it. Sometimes, she was so infuriatingly determined and stubborn—even impulsive—but she was honest, good, everything we all should be. So much better than me in every way. Sometimes she was so afraid—I could see it in her eyes—but she was determined. I was afraid to believe something so completely that might not be true."

Calm swept over him. For too long he had kept these thoughts and feelings inside, not willing to admit them to anyone—or even himself. They were a heavier weight on his arms than Helen had been.

"Neil," Zaric said after a momentary pause, "do you believe now?"

Neil let a few long moments go by, then answered, "Yes, I believe. I started to believe a long time ago—I always had a feeling all of this was true. I never would have found Camelora if I didn't allow myself to believe. Now, I honestly believe that you are King Zaric and you will stop Mered."

Zaric smiled at this. "Do you trust me, Neil?" he asked.

"Yes, I trust you."

"You must trust that reality isn't everything you see. What would be the fun in life, the joy of discovery, if that were true? How would we ever accomplish anything? Don't worry anymore, and stop thinking that you already know everything there is to know."

"I'm pretty sure I know nothing."

"Almost nothing," Zaric winked.

Neil hesitated, wanting to ask Zaric a question, but not sure how, despite the fact that it was the primary question in his mind since leaving his cottage. He turned the idea over in his mind a few times before finally asking, "Why didn't you save my parents? They believed in you, but you didn't come and heal them. They were too young to die. *I* was too young for them to die. I didn't want them to go. Why did the Eternal One take them from me?"

"You and I can't decide how old is too old and how young is too young. Every life is different. We each have different tasks to accomplish. Once we finish them, we move on. Death itself is only a different kind of life. Your parents were good people who never forgot about me. They worked hard and they finished what they needed to do."

"But I want them here with me, just as I want Helen here with me. There is still so much they could have done."

"Neil, you are capable of so many great things. Whether or not your parents and Helen are here, you can do so much. Perhaps instead of asking why they're gone, ask why you're still here. What you can do to honor them, to help them see that their son is willing to be the man they raised him to be. There are many people in this world who can help us defeat Mered if we can only find them. Don't forget that you'll die someday, too, and then you'll see your parents again. Until then, I need you here. Will you believe that, Neil? Will you trust me that much?"

Again, Neil turned to gaze out the window. He felt that Zaric could see past his eyes and into his thoughts and it was easier to think of what he wanted to say when he looked away. Grey clouds filled the sky now. An image flashed in Neil's mind, an image of Ian standing with a dagger drawn and Helen holding her crossbow, and rain falling in a small clearing. The clouds moving violently. Helen's face burned vividly in his mind, as he had seen it many times in the past few days, so often with a familiar brightness in her eyes.

"I want her to be all right," Neil said, in part to Zaric and in part only to himself. "She's all I have left."

The rain hit the window now in a steady rhythm, running down in small streams, making a soothing noise. His senses awoke with a new awareness. He felt the city around him, and the valley around the city. In his head, he heard the excited voices of Zaric's followers, knowing that now their lives were going to change and become better than they had ever been. He heard now what he had seen earlier—the wave of the Gateway opening.

"I trust you with my life," Neil stated, a new firmness settling in his voice as he looked without flinching at Zaric. "With my life, with my death, and everything in between."

Zaric nodded once, then stood up. "Stop referring to Helen as though she were dead," he said as he placed his hand on Neil's shoulder for a few seconds before leaving the room. Neil glanced around, not sure if he wanted to laugh or cry. All he knew for certain was that he felt safe and confident for the first time in four years.

*  *  *

Zaric walked resolutely down the hall, without hurry and careful not to make a sound. His palace had been built to be used and every room was occupied; he didn't want to wake anyone. He didn't even carry a candle. The moonlight came through a row of large windows along one wall and he knew this place too well to need any other light.

He came to a room at the end of the hallway and stopped. Everything was silent around him. He looked back down the corridor. It was still and lifeless. In a slow, deliberate motion, he opened the door, stepped into the room, and turned the knob as he closed it, preventing it from making a sound.

Unlike the hallway, this room was brightly lit. Candelabras were mounted to all four walls at regular intervals, casting an orange and yellow light onto every surface. The room was bare except for a long, plain wooden table standing in the middle of it. Helen lay on the table, covered with a thin blanket. A middle-aged woman sat next to her, staring at Helen's face with too much intensity to notice anything else as she pressed a damp cloth to Helen's forehead. Zaric stood for a minute, leaning against the door as he looked at the table. Taking a deep breath, he walked forward.

"You may wait outside," he said to the woman, who jumped a little at the sound of his voice, then nodded, stood with a soft rustle of fabric, and left the room without question.

Zaric went to the table and looked down at Helen's face, which was just as pale as it had been when Neil had handed her to Zaric. Her tattered and worn clothes were a sign of the length and roughness of her journey. The women Zaric had assigned to attend to her had washed the dirt from her skin and seen to the cuts and scrapes that adorned her body. The smell of the ointment they had used filled the air and the worst cuts were bandaged. These kind touches did nothing, though, to assuage the shock that went through him as Zaric rested his head above Helen's mouth and heard her shallow breathing. He placed two fingers on her wrist. Her pulse was barely detectable.

Zaric took both of Helen's hands in his. In a rush, a warm current of air began to circle through the room. The light from the candelabras became as bright as daylight, dancing off the walls and floor and ceiling, as if the light were alive. Smiling down at Helen as he channeled his energy through his hands into hers, Zaric lowered his head, placing his lips close to her ear. "Helen," he whispered. "Helen, wake up."

Nothing happened. Zaric straightened his back and watched Helen in patient expectation. Then, her breathing stopped. For half-a-minute, Zaric waited for the breathing to continue. It didn't. "Helen!" he called out in a commanding voice, sending a wave of energy throughout the room and reverberating against the walls.

It began with a slight movement under her eyelids. Her face lost its paleness, the color pulsing from her cheeks and soon spreading to her forehead and neck, then over her entire body. Helen gasped and opened her eyes wide, as though she had emerged from deep water. She blinked rapidly, her whole body tense, then her eyes locked on Zaric. With a laugh, he raised her hands to his lips and kissed them. Gently, with one hand under her back, he lifted her to a sitting position. She looked at him, confused, then glanced around the room. But her eyes were drawn again to the king. She put her hands on his face, not quite sure that either she or he were real. Tears welled in her eyes. "It's *you*," she half-exclaimed, half-whispered. "It's *you*."

Tears filled Zaric's eyes as well. Helen put her arms around his neck and placed her head on his shoulder. "I knew we would find you," she said.

"You're safe now," Zaric told her. "And I'm glad you came. But I'm sorry I had to wake you. We haven't finished needing you yet. I know you've done quite a lot, but I'm afraid there's still more work to do."

Helen pulled away and nodded. Then, filled with sudden concern, she exclaimed, "Neil! Is he all right? Where is he?"

"Neil's fine," Zaric assured her. "He's the one who brought you here."

"May I see him?"

"In the morning. But now, I need you to tell me how you feel."

Helen put her hand to her neck, her memory reconstructing all that had happened before being awoken by Zaric. She felt nothing that could make her believe she had been shot with a dart—not even a trace of the tingling she so well remembered in her arms. Yet she keenly remembered standing at the Gateway and seeing Siri in front of her, holding a reed. Her body felt no pain now, but her mind still knew the sharpness of the sting of the dart's point and the fear the poison created as it coursed through her body.

"Was I dead?" she asked.

"Not quite, but nearly."

The thought was strange and unreal, paralyzing Helen's understanding. "For how long?"

"Less than a day," Zaric answered.

Helen looked at his face, so full of peace and goodness beyond anything she had ever imagined. Although she didn't understand, she knew by looking at Zaric that it wasn't necessary to understand. "I feel hungry," she stated. "Very hungry."

"Well, then, let's find you something to eat."

# Chapter 17

Helen rested on the bed in her room, her eyes fixed on the single flickering candle on the table next to her. She wasn't tired and couldn't sleep, She didn't want to. Now that she had reached her destination, there was nothing to propel her forwards and draw her mind away from thoughts of her parents and the fear she felt for them. The thought of what awaited her in her dreams terrified her.

Sitting up against the headboard, Helen brought her knees under her chin as she studied the room. Zaric had brought her here after her late supper, telling her it would be hers as long as she chose to stay in Camelora. It was a modest bedroom—very small and tidy—but it was everything Helen could want. After weeks of sleeping on the cold ground, she was glad to have a comfortable room that she wouldn't be forced to leave. Pale moonlight drifted through the window, reassuring Helen with its easy glow. Its softness was protective in a way she couldn't explain. Yet she was restless as she rose from the bed and walked to the window. For a while, she sat on the wide windowsill with her arms wrapped around her knees, her head resting against the glass, looking up at the sky, with its bright moon and countless stars, taking in the new world around her. The ground was damp from the earlier storm and some lingering clouds intermittently blocked out the moonlight. Helen had never been in a place where the air felt so alive, as if it were breathing just as she was.

Feeling the need for a walk, she took the candle and opened the door, stepping into the hall. Like all the hallways overlooking the palace courtyard, this one was lit by the moon, the light bouncing serenely off the floor and walls. Helen studied her surroundings, trying to memorize the corridor so that she would be able to find her way back again later. On the door-side of the hallway, oil lamps were mounted to the wall in the spaces between the closed doors. None of them were lit. Helen didn't remember seeing any light but the candle and the moon as she and Zaric walked to this room. Taking the cover off the lamp next to her door, she held the flame of her candle to its wick until it caught. Replacing the cover, she hoped no one would extinguish the flame before she found her room again.

As she explored the corridors of the palace, Helen was reminded of the abbey she and Neil had found, as well as Stephen and Meira's city. This palace was just as still and quiet as those places had been, but she felt the added comfort of knowing that, behind the closed doors, other people were sleeping, breathing, alive. The loneliness and uncertainty of her journey had disappeared. She walked without haste down hallways and up staircases, never moving downward, basking in the comfort of not being alone. Helen soon found herself climbing a winding staircase in a tower at the corner of the building, surrounded by windows looking out in every direction. There was a door near the top of the tower and she went through it, coming out on the wide, empty roof.

It was cool outside and Helen shivered as a chilling sensation ran down her spine. She wished she had thrown on her cloak. Going to the parapet, she looked out over the city. Helen was glad to be seeing Camelora for the first time in the early morning. It was mostly still, with only a few lights scattered throughout it. Illuminated by the moon, it was more ethereal and enchanting than any place she had seen before.

There was comfort in its peacefulness, like a lullaby. The sounds of night—birds and crickets and wind in the trees—filled the air. Helen leaned against the wall and breathed Camelora in. The reality that she had reached her destination hit her at last. She was in Camelora, feeling the stones of its palace beneath her bare feet as she stood under the deep indigo sky, white moon, and diamond stars. It was real. As the awareness of her position became more unquestionable, so did the knowledge that she had found Zaric and that he would be able to help her save Veren—and her parents. This hope steadily seeped into her soul.

As she stood in thought, her ears picked out the sound of the roof door creaking on its hinges. Instinct took control and her heart beat faster as she looked around for a place to hide, but the rooftop was wide, open, and exposed. But her alarm subsided and Helen wanted to laugh at herself as she watched the door open, feeling her cheeks burn. She was safe here. The laughter truly did come when Neil stepped onto the roof. Helen rushed forward, but stopped when Neil took a step back. He stared with wide, disbelieving eyes and his body became tense. He blinked like he was trying to blink away a dream, then simply stared. In the silence, Helen felt like the ghost she was sure Neil believed he saw. A light spread over his face.

"Helen," he said softly. "Are you real?"

Helen nodded. Neil relaxed again and took a couple of steps forward. Helen completed the distance and embraced him.

"You came back," he whispered. "I was sure you were gone. How did you come back?"

"Zaric brought me back," she answered.

"You're real and you're all right."

"Yes."

"I was afraid you wouldn't make it. You were so pale and nothing I did could wake you up."

"You brought me here," Helen corrected. "You brought me to Zaric."

"I'm sorry, Helen. If I hadn't told you to go alone, I would have been able to protect you. If only I hadn't trusted Siri in the first place. If you had died—"

Helen winced at this word and Neil cut off the rest of his statement.

"How could you really have known she wasn't telling the truth?" Helen stated. "I know I didn't trust Siri, but I was never really sure if that was just out of envy or something else. To be honest, I was jealous of the attention you gave her. And I would have been in danger even if you hadn't trusted her. You did what you thought was right."

"You sound like Zaric."

"I doubt that."

Neil placed his hand on Helen's cheek as though he was still trying to convince himself that she was real. She tried not to look surprised and didn't pull away, but he soon grew abashed and lowered his hand.

"Has he told you what happens next?" Neil asked to dispel his embarrassment.

Helen shook her head. "You?"

"No. I haven't spoken to him too much since I came. He had other things to worry about. But I get the feeling that opening the Gateway was a minor accomplishment compared to what Zaric expects from us. The people in this place know who we are, and I don't mean some vague story about a man and a woman finding the keys to open the Gateway. They know us by name."

This idea mortified Helen. At times she wasn't sure who she was herself. She wondered what the Camelorans expected of them, and she wondered if she and Neil could stand the burden of those expectations.

"But we aren't alone this time," she said, finishing her thought out loud. "We have Zaric."

"And Mered knows it. That might make him hesitate to come after us anytime soon."

For the first time Neil had spoken about Mered as though he believed in him and Helen couldn't help her sharp reaction, turning to look at his face. They had been in Camelora for less than a day and there was already a visible difference in Neil that made Helen feel more confident and secure than she had ever felt. With Neil's wholehearted help, she finally felt that anything else Zaric required would be possible.

***

Ten people—six men and four women—sat around the large, oval table that occupied the room where Zaric ushered Helen and Neil. Zaric had pulled the two of them away just as they were finishing dinner in the dining hall, where all the palace's inhabitants—palace workers, advisers, as well as those who had no family and nowhere else to go—ate together. He beckoned for them to follow him, then led them down the corridor to this inconspicuous room. The people already there talked in quick whispers. Zaric motioned toward two unoccupied chairs and Neil and Helen sat dutifully, while he sat at the head of the table. As he moved his chair closer into position, the whispers abruptly stopped.

"I'm sorry to pull you all away from your normal evening activities," Zaric said, "when it isn't our usual time to meet. But I'm afraid this isn't a usual circumstance."

Some of the people around the table nodded in acquiescence, while some muttered a few indistinguishable words in reply. No one looked annoyed by the interruption of their daily routine, which alleviated some of Helen's worries. She found the general civility of the Camelorans a little bit disconcerting. Even at its best times Veren was nothing like this.

"I should start with introductions," Zaric went on, glancing at Helen and Neil before pointing to each person in turn, beginning at his left, and slowly saying their names. "Zelene, Garrick, Arron, Cynthia, Trevelyan, Genevieve, Flecher, Arlen, Phyllida, and Gowon. These men and women form the King's Council. They assist with the everyday government of Camelora. You will work more closely with them than with anyone else in the city." He then addressed the entire table. "You have all heard by now that our guests are Helen and Neil. If you haven't, I must be working you too hard. Their arrival here will change the present and future of Camelora, which is why I found it necessary to ask you all to come here this evening. Life will soon change for everyone."

Besides turning their eyes to their two guests, this statement brought out no other reaction from the council. As a little girl, Helen had often sat in a secret alcove above her father's council room when he met with his Governor's Council. This same statement spoken to that group would have caused a rush of whispers. But this council had already anticipated this disruption in their lives. The difference was startling. Helen felt her face grow warm with Zaric's words. She felt uncomfortable at the thought of their arrival changing anything, as well as at the thought that it didn't surprise these men and women at all. Hopefully, she would soon get used to how different Camelora was from the rest of the land.

"If you wouldn't mind, Helen and Neil, I would like you to tell the council about your journey here. It will help us to see what we are facing, and what needs to be done."

"Should we question them separately?" Phyllida interjected, as though she had just remembered an important piece of protocol.

"I don't think that will be necessary," Zaric said with a wave of his hand. "There is no doubt in my mind that they are who they say they are. But thank you for the suggestion." He made an encouraging motion, looking at his guests.

Neil and Helen glanced at each other and Neil nudged her lightly.

It was clear he had no intention of beginning the story. Helen began, nervousness resting in her throat, starting with the day Mered's men entered her city. She traced her journey in as much detail as she dared to give, without saying more than she was comfortable to. When she reached the part where she came to Neil's cottage, she touched Neil's hand with her fingertips and he took the cue to join in, supplying information when Helen paused or couldn't give it, like the day in the abbey, or his conversations with Siri. Helen noticed a faint redness in his cheeks when he came to this last part. Sometimes their voices overlapped, and many times they had to go back and fill in scenes they had missed. They spoke about Ian and the other soldiers they had seen, and Stephen and Meira and Alan. At times someone in the council would ask them to elaborate on an element they themselves hadn't considered very important, forcing them to remember details they had almost forgotten. When they finished, the room was silent for a few moments.

"Stephen and Meira have evacuated their city," Trevelyan stated. "Wasn't that our last stronghold in the outer kingdom?"

"But you never saw Mered's army," Arron directed toward Neil.

"No. We never saw more than a handful of men. Well, *I* never saw more than a handful."

"And most of those I saw were occupying Veren," Helen put in.

"You managed to stay ahead of them at least," Cynthia said.

"Most of them," Helen corrected. "We aren't sure how many he has mobilized, anyway."

"How much time do you think we have?" Zelene asked Zaric, her voice soft and betraying only a hint of concern.

"I'm not sure," Zaric answered, shaking his head. "We don't know how large Mered's army is or what he plans to do. He has always been unpredictable. The important thing is for us to come up with a plan of our own."

"The stories have always said—" Arlen began, but Zaric cut him off.

"The stories deal in generalities," he said. "They only tell us what we need to do and what *might* happen. It's up to us to decide how."

"Stephen and Meira said that the people of their city would scatter across the western settlements," Neil stated. "Are there others like them, others who are willing to fight Mered?"

"The wave of light that you both saw when the Gateway opened," Zaric said, "was a call going out to the kingdom. Everyone will have felt it, and some people will even understand it. Those men and women who still support me know that the Gateway has been opened—that the people of Camelora will be preparing to fight Mered—and now they should be preparing themselves. Many will come to Camelora on their own, without having to be gathered, following the direction of the call. But I'm afraid that won't be enough."

"We need to go out and find those who are loyal to Zaric," Genevieve said. "And we need to find those who will be loyal, even if they've never heard his name before. Our problem is, Mered has had years to build support for himself. We don't have quite so much time. Did you observe the people's attitudes in any of the settlements between Camdor and Camelora?"

"I'm afraid not," Neil answered. "Our path didn't take us anywhere near the northern cities and villages."

"But Zaric said that we don't know Mered's plan," Helen argued. "Maybe he isn't as ready as we think. We could have a few years."

"That will depend on the support Mered has gained," Gowon answered. "We at least know he has swayed most of the governors. It's true that we might have a couple of years—if we're lucky. A few months if we're not. But you're right: as Zaric said, we don't know what Mered is planning. He's occupying Veren and has made himself visible in Camdor. He has resources most of us could never imagine."

"We will need to go out into the kingdom, Zaric," Phyllida said with resignation. "Organize us into groups so that we can find your existing supporters and also try to convince as many people as we can to join us. Stephen and Meira have no doubt started this process already."

"Only as long as you don't plan for too many of us to go at once," Trevelyan said in reply. "Mered will notice if we go with too much force. He may be capable of crushing us before we get far. And we can't leave Camelora unprotected. These people are the strongest you have."

"I agree with you both," Zaric stated, though Helen suspected Zaric had already thought of these ideas himself. "We will take a few small groups—no more than two or three dozen people in all—outside of Camelora. If we start in the north, we should find more willing supporters. We will make our way southward as far as we can go without drawing too much attention to ourselves. As Trevelyan said, some of you will need to stay in Camelora. It is the strongest point in the kingdom, but at the same time it is the most vulnerable. Whatever happens, Mered must be kept out of the city. I will take a few days to decide how I want to divide you up and who will stay to protect Camelora. In the meantime, we need to train Helen and Neil to defend themselves. Garrick, I will leave that task to you."

Garrick nodded in assent. Helen sat without responding, her hands resting in a knot in her lap as she listened to every word, not sure what she could say, or if she wanted to say anything. It was foolish, she knew, to think that the part she played was over. She hadn't thought beyond opening the Gateway and asking Zaric to help her save her parents. Now, she wondered what Zaric had in mind for her to do and how she could be trained to defend herself against something Zaric himself wasn't even sure of. A few more words were spoken by Zaric and some of the members of the council, then they were dismissed. The men and women around the table drifted away until Helen and Neil were left alone with Zaric.

"Is something wrong?" Zaric asked Helen with unforced patience.

It embarrassed Helen that her emotions were written so clearly on her face. "I'm afraid my reason for coming to Camelora wasn't *just* to fulfill the stories and open the Gateway. I *do* care about saving the people of the kingdom. But when Mered's men came to my city, they arrested my father. I don't know where he is or if he's still alive. After I left, I think they took my mother, too. One of my reasons for coming to you was to ask you to help me free them."

"That's nothing to be ashamed of, Helen," Zaric responded. "If you will trust me, I will find a way to discover what happened to your father and how we can help him. Leave it to me and don't trouble yourself about it."

In that instant, Helen's mind cleared of all doubt. Her trust in Zaric was complete; she knew that he would do what he promised. The embarrassment was still there, though. She hated to admit her selfishness. Zaric's assurances did nothing to erase that. The things she had just heard in this room made her think of so many things at once, it was hard for her mind to grasp a hold on any of it. She wanted her father to be all right and for the people of the kingdom to be safe, but she wasn't sure she could really have both. She wasn't prepared for her entire world to change. With a feeble smile, she stood up. Zaric reached out and pressed her hand gently. She returned the gesture before leaving the room.

When the sound of her steps faded down the hallway, Zaric looked at Neil, then beckoned for the young man to follow as he crossed to the opposite side of the room, through a large wooden door that led to a terrace. This terrace faced the western horizon, where the glow of sunlight still reached above the line of the mountains. They stood silently for a few minutes, watching the after-sunset sky glow in varying shades of orange and blue, dotted with a few early stars. The air was cooler in Camelora than in Neil's own village at this time of year. He tried to keep himself from shivering.

"I'm sure Helen figured out a long time ago that finding you wouldn't be the end of our problems," Neil said, folding his arms in an attempt to stay warm, "even if she doesn't realize it."

"Yes," Zaric answered, "but you knew it all along."

"My perspective was different. I didn't think finding you would solve *any* of our problems."

"Very true. But whether you see it or not, your actions have shown me what you're willing to do for me and these people, and just how much I can trust you. Perhaps we can say, at least, that your perspective was slightly more realistic. I can only do so much. The rest of you will have to play a part."

"Helen and I aren't fighters. We came here for protection and I'm not sure how much we can really help. I'm just a farmer, she's a governor's daughter. Everything we did on our way to Camelora—all of the things you think were brave—we only did because we were too afraid to die."

Zaric chuckled, turning to Neil for the first time since their conversation began. At first, Neil wasn't sure what to think of this. He didn't like being laughed at. But, there was a constant kindness in Zaric's eyes that made it impossible for him to think that Zaric could be disrespectful toward anyone.

"I could turn philosopher on you," Zaric said, "but I won't. I'm a farmer, too, along with many other people in this city. Others are shepherds, some are craftsmen or launderers or physicians. We have people with every skill necessary for a city of this size to function. Still, we all need to know how to defend ourselves. The time will come when the soldiers we do have won't be enough to stop Mered's army."

"So, all of the people in this city know how to fight," Neil stated.

"All who are able, anyway. We have rules to ensure our survival, both through defense and preservation. Children begin to learn at the age of ten, boys *and* girls. Those who are too old or physically unable would never be expected to fight, though they do know how. I wouldn't put it past them to try. And even though women and older children learn, we won't allow them to fight until every other option is exhausted. Whatever happens, our society *must* survive."

"So Helen's safe, then," Neil sighed.   But this relief was only momentary. Zaric waited too long to respond.

"Helen has a unique role," was his simple declaration.

"What unique role?" Neil questioned, trying to hide his concern.

"That's something I must discuss with Helen and Helen alone. She will have her choice, of course. There is always a choice."

"There's nothing special about us, Zaric.  Helen and I are just two people who came a very long way from home to find someone who may not have been real."

"Yes, but now you know that I *am* real.  It shouldn't be impossible to believe everything else after you discovered that, should it? You've done more than I think you can possibly understand, or at least more than you'll allow yourself to understand.  You opened the Gateway. Because of you, a call went out to the people.  Some of them might even understand its meaning. I am very pleased with all you've done. It will take some time, though, for us to gather our supporters. Until then the people must be protected."

Neil looked up at the few stars that had appeared in the sky and tried to imagine himself standing next to his cottage, so far away. He almost wished he could see these people the way he had always seen people before: nameless, faceless beings whom he didn't have to care about, because they cared nothing about him. If only Helen hadn't come to him with her memories and stories, and a confidence that he envied and wanted desperately to absorb, he might be enjoying the solitude of his own home and he wouldn't feel so afraid. Yet it was impossible to look at his life before without feeling what he had learned since then. He had been changed over the past few weeks and the person he had become would never fit into the life he had once lived.

"I still trust you," Neil said. "I just feel—overwhelmed."

Zaric nodded but said nothing. Neil appreciated the king's wisdom. His silence was more comforting than any words could have been.

# Chapter 18

Ian sat at a small, square table in an almost-bare room. Long, narrow windows were set into two of the walls, allowing light to come in from outside, forming distorted shadows at irregular intervals. Siri paced along one of these walls, stopping every half-minute at one of the windows, watching the grey clouds overhead glide and gather in a smooth motion. A slight breeze rustled the leaves of the few trees surrounding the castle. The shrubs and dirt of the desert landscape created a sense of isolation and desolation that made her shiver. The world was eerily quiet. Even the birds that flew in and out of the trees were afraid to sing. Siri and Ian didn't speak to each other—or even look at each other—both feigning disinterest in the other's presence. Still, they both jumped and tensed as a door slammed down the outside corridor. The sound of heavy footsteps echoed, moving closer.

The door opened and crashed against the wall. Ian sprang to his feet and Siri spun around. They stood with backs straight, arms clasped behind their backs. Mered stood, fierce and threatening, in the doorway. His dark eyes glared with cold, stinging intensity, forcing Ian and Siri to look away. In his best moods, Mered was a handsome man, with well-formed features and an uncommon olive complexion. He spoke persuasively, knowing how to tell people exactly what they wanted to hear. But in his anger, he became terrible and grotesque, impossible to stand up to, approach, or even look at.

"What did I ask you to do, Ian?" he bellowed. Automatically, Ian opened his mouth, but couldn't think of the right words to use. Mered cocked his head expectantly.

"You told us to stop them," Ian finally blurted, trying to sound more confident than he felt, knowing very well that he was failing, "no matter what we had to do."

"Yes, Ian, no matter what you had to do. Stop Neil and Helen, and bring Neil to me. Even if it meant you had to die. But you didn't do that, did you? You weren't able to even do that much."

For the first time, Siri and Ian looked at each other briefly. He had expected her to sneer, but was surprised to see that she was more frightened than he had ever seen her before. She turned her eyes again to the window.  Ian was disappointed in, but not surprised by, her weakness.

"But I was!" Ian argued. "It just didn't work out that way. Siri's still alive, too."

"At least Sirena did what I told her to do. Didn't you, Sirena?" Siri didn't respond, or even react, to the statement. Mered stepped across the room and cupped her face with his hands, turning it toward him. Siri covered her fear with indifference, a trick she had learned long ago. "Sirena killed the girl. That should affect Zaric's plans significantly. I believe he had great prospects for Helen."

"But she didn't stop Helen from opening the Gateway," Ian insisted. He couldn't understand why Siri should be praised while he was berated. He had no intention of letting that happen. All along, he was sure, his job had been much more difficult than Siri's. There had never been much hope that Helen would join them, although there was a glimmer that Neil might be turned. Mered himself had underestimated Helen's strength and sent Ian out with less preparation than he needed. "And she didn't convince Neil to join you," he added.

"No," Mered said, his eyes lingering on Siri's face. She cocked her head, just as he had done before, and Mered smiled. "But neither did you, Ian. I sent you first. You didn't succeed in convincing Helen *or* Neil."

"It was Helen. She was too strong for me."

"Too strong for you? Ian, you are the strongest man in my employ. At least, that's what you like to tell everyone. Are you telling me you couldn't stop one little girl? Are none of my men capable of that? Sirena stopped her and she's only a weakling herself. Look at all the influence we've gained, all of the lands we've conquered, and hardly anyone realizes we've done it. So many people have chosen to work with me. Helen is only one girl. We could have upset Zaric's designs considerably, but you failed."

"If we failed so miserably," Ian said bitterly, "why didn't you just do it yourself?"

In long strides, Mered crossed the room and struck Ian across the face with the back of his hand, the force of the blow causing Ian to stagger. Siri jumped at the sound and squeezed her eyes shut. "Never question my methods!" Mered screamed.

"Please, sir," Siri exclaimed.

Mered stared at her, then back at Ian. "Is there something wrong, Sirena?" he asked icily, deliberately. "Are you trying to show your weakness?"

"No," Siri said with a cold laugh. "It's just that you're using so much of your strength on Ian and he isn't worth it. He isn't worth *any* of it. You know how the anger drains you."

Taking shorter, slower steps than before, Mered crossed back to Siri. She folded her arms to hide her trembling but managed to keep her back straight. She wasn't sure which frightened her more: Mered's swift action against Ian or his slow movement toward her. He forced her to look at him again. "Do you feel guilty, Sirena?" His whisper pierced her chest. She winced. "I see through your 'concern.' You can't blame me for your decisions. You chose to kill the girl."

"You ordered me to," Siri said after a brief pause. Mered raised his hand as he had before and Siri flinched, but he didn't hit her. She forced herself to hold his gaze until he lowered his hand.

"You chose to obey me, Sirena. Haven't I always treated you well? I've told you I'm very proud of you. And you wouldn't want to disappoint your parents, would you? They have always been among my best supporters. Wouldn't you want them to be proud of you?"

Siri nodded, but she was afraid her eyes revealed the lie. Those who were found to be lying to Mered in order to please him were punished as though they had told a truth he didn't like. At this moment, Siri didn't care what her parents thought of her or her service to Mered. She only wanted time alone, to rid her mind of the image of Helen's face, wracked with pain, after being struck by the dart.

"Sir," Ian said, taking a couple of steps toward Mered and Siri, "let me fix my mistake."

Irritation written across his features, Mered turned to Ian.

"Let me take some men," Ian said, "and we'll attack Camelora. The call might have gone out for the people to arm themselves, but they won't be ready for us yet. They might not even believe it. If we can surprise them and get to Zaric himself. . . The people won't want to follow a dead king. The land will be yours and no one can take it from you."

"Have you ever tried to attack Camelora, Ian?" Mered asked mockingly. "No? Have you ever fought Zaric? Do you really believe he would be weak enough for you to attack him and win? Zaric is always ready for an attack and even if you took all of our forces it wouldn't be enough. We need more men. And how would it look to the rest of the land if we attack a city without provocation? Not all the governors and regions are in my hands yet. We would lose all the ground we've gained. Don't waste my time, Ian. We have to come up with a new plan."

"But I'm sure I can do this."

"That's what you said when I sent you to stop Neil and Helen. Your rashness will be the death of you, Ian. The only reason I haven't killed you myself is because this is the first time you have ever failed me, and even that reason is a thin thread. I have other followers who grow stronger by the day. We will develop a new plan, a new strategy—one that won't fail."

With this, Mered pushed Ian aside and stalked out of the room without another word. Siri hesitated for a few seconds, then started to leave as well, her arms still folded protectively, her face colorless and blank.

"Will you help me, Siri?" Ian asked, reaching out a hand to stop her.

"Do I look like a fool, Ian?" she asked in return, brushing his hand away. "I've already given more than I wanted. I'm not going to kill myself for your lost cause."

She glared at him as she left the room, rubbing her cheeks in an effort to bring warmth back into them. Ian watched her go, rapping his fingers on the tabletop. Then, with determination, he swept out of the room and walked out the front doors of the castle.

* * *

"I would never have imagined a city could be like this," Neil said as he and Helen walked down the wide main street of Camelora one afternoon. "It's almost scary."

They were becoming more accustomed to life in this city, feeling very much like they belonged there. Neil spent the first half of each day working in the fields, glad to be doing familiar work, while Helen chose to learn weaving. The second half of the day was devoted to learning defense—sometimes with Zaric, but most of the time with Garrick. Neil caught on quicker than he expected, while Helen made as much progress as she dared. She was afraid to become too good, a fact they all recognized but never mentioned. When their daily training concluded, they were given time to themselves, to do whatever they pleased. They sometimes chose to spend this time together and sometimes chose to explore the castle or Camelora alone. Neil often found himself wandering into the library—a habit Helen teased him about—while she climbed to the roof to look over the city, the fields, and the hills and mountains. They both liked to leave the palace gates and go into the city, to see its people and houses and shops—lives so different from anything either of them had ever seen before. While the rest of the land and regions changed their way of life over the centuries, Camelora remained the same, preserving the customs of a millennium earlier. The streets were clean and orderly, each one very much like all the others until they became more familiar with their dissimilarities. None of the Camelorans were rich and none were poor, but this didn't negate the uniqueness of everyone they met. Helen and Neil rarely saw money exchanged in the shops or the marketplace. Instead, the people bartered the items they made for those they needed. Children ran and played through the streets while the adults chatted. It was a place where no one was uncomfortable. Even the largest arguments were settled quickly, both parties pleased with the outcome. It was almost idyllic enough for Helen to forget that it would soon have to change. Still, though, the thought of impending difficulties and conflicts crowded the back of her mind.

"When all of this is over," Helen said, "do you think the city will be this way again? There is so much they don't know about the world outside."

"I doubt it," Neil said, after a moment of thought. "It will probably be better. They will *choose* to live this way, not just because it's the only way they know."

"Can it get better than this?"

"These people have been preparing their whole lives—probably for generations—to fight Mered. I'm pretty sure their lives will have more meaning once they realize exactly what they're capable of."

"How long do you think it will take, before everything begins?"

"Are you getting impatient, Helen?"

She stayed quiet for a minute. In many ways, she *was* getting impatient. Being comfortable in Camelora made her feel guilty, knowing that she was enjoying peace her parents and thousands of others weren't feeling. The thought that her father was in danger was gradually replaced by the thought that she would be too late by the time she reached him. Her mind was running faster than the movement of life in Camelora.

"This place is too perfect," she sighed.

"Just perfect enough," Neil corrected.

"Helen! Neil!" a voice called to them from a few feet away. They turned to see Genevieve standing next to a stall, waving to them. A young woman stood behind the stall, about as old as they were, a nervous awe crossing her face and she smoothed her skirt with her hands. Helen and Neil stepped over and the girl grew more agitated, nodding briefly at Helen before focusing her attention on Neil. Stifling a giggle, Helen studied the ribbons and buttons of all shapes, sizes, and colors that covered the stall.

"This is my friend Minna," Genevieve said. "She's been dying to meet the two of you since you came."

The girl curtsied as though she faced a king and queen. Helen felt her cheeks grow warmer.

"Helen, have you finished that length of cloth you've been working on?" Genevieve asked.

"Not yet," Helen answered, then added apologetically, "I'm afraid it isn't very good."

"Don't be silly. I've seen it and I think it's just perfect. Much better than anything I've seen any other beginner make. I think it would be just right for a dress Minna wants to make for her sister."

"She's outgrown most of her clothes," Minna said, taking up Genevieve's line of conversation. "I want to make her something new. She's only five so the quality of the cloth doesn't matter too much. If you're willing to trade, you can have anything you like from my stall."

Helen looked down at the buttons and ribbons and tried to ignore the feeling of Neil's own stifled smile—an expression she had learned to recognize even when she wasn't looking at him. There was nothing in front of her that Helen felt she needed. Weaving was a more foreign skill than any she had tried to gain. She was intimidated by the thought of any activity that would require buttons or ribbons. But she managed a grin when she raised her eyes to Minna's face, which stared back at her with a hopeful expression. "I'll bring you the cloth as soon as it's finished," Helen told her. "I won't expect anything in return. We will consider it payment for the hospitality the people of your city have shown me."

"Are you sure?" Minna asked. "I have some buttons here that were given to me by my great-grandmother. . ."

"Perfectly sure. I couldn't take something as special as your great-grandmother's buttons."

Minna smiled in gratitude and bowed her head. Helen and Neil stepped away as Genevieve said good-bye to her friend, then, with quick strides, came up beside them.

"That was kind of you, Helen," she said in a low tone. "You acted just as I would. Buttons can be very useful, but I have no need for ribbons myself. How are the two of you settling into Camelora?"

"It's easier than I thought it would be," Helen replied. "It's almost like being at home. But everyone seems to have high expectations for us and that's overwhelming."

"You have all had years to prepare for what's coming," Neil added. "We don't feel very adequate."

Genevieve thought for a few seconds before answering. "The people of Camelora lack experience," she stated. "We have been prepared in theory, but I'm afraid reality will test us beyond anything we have imagined. Our life is too privileged. In the end, we will probably find that some of us just aren't strong enough."

A sudden sound halted their conversation, though Helen wasn't sure she could say she had really heard anything. It was an inaudible vibration that rattled through her, making her feel uneasy. Thinking she had only imagined it, she turned to look at Neil, perplexed. Helen looked up and down the street herself. Everyone within her line of vision stood frozen in place, confused and uncertain. Silence rippled as all the people on this street—and, it seemed, in the city—remained in this motionless state, in anticipation.

Then it came again, just as indescribable as before, but now Helen could tell that it wasn't a sound carried through the air, but one planted in her own head—and the heads of all the people of Camelora. The only way she knew to describe it was as a discordant clanging, a rusty warning signal accompanied by the thought of something being in the land that didn't belong there.

The wind began to blow, winding down the street. A murmur of voices rose as the people moved again, gathering up everything they could and taking it inside their shops and dwellings. Wooden wheels scraped across the cobbles and shutters and doors banged shut. Helen looked up at the sky and saw the clouds rolling in a familiar way. "Let's go back to the palace," Genevieve said, her eyes on the sky as well. She started forward as Neil took Helen's hand and pulled her attention away from the people.

Rain started to fall before they reached the end of the street, forcing them to run the rest of the way. Stronger gusts of wind pushed them forward and drove the rain even harder into their bodies. All around them doors and shutters banged closed and the swell of voices died down. Only occasional shouts reached their ears now. They had seen this procedure once or twice in drills since coming, but it was nerve-wracking now that it was no longer a practice.

A crowd had gathered at the entryway of the palace and Genevieve, Helen, and Neil had to push their way through. At first the people glared at them with annoyance, but annoyance turned to excitement once they realized who they were. They threw questions at them—but they were questions Helen and Neil wanted to ask as well, so they remained silent. Genevieve did her best to make apologies, admitting that she didn't know the answers herself. They managed to reach the large receiving room, where they could see Zaric standing in the middle of another large, disordered throng. Trevelyan stood inside the doorway. He was visibly relieved when he saw the three of them walking toward him.

"Finally, three people who don't look terrified," he stated, casting his eyes with meaning around the room. "A little confused or nervous, maybe, but not terrified. We've tried to tell them not to worry, but no one wants to listen."

"Did Zaric cause this?" Helen asked. "The last time we saw a storm like this, he had."

Trevelyan shook his head. "Camelora caused this. The land is reacting to something, we just don't know what."

"How can the land react to something?" Neil questioned with a laugh.

Trevelyan opened his mouth to answer, but was stopped by the appearance of Zaric, slipping in next to Helen. "Arm yourselves," he commanded, "and meet me in the council room. Tell anyone from the council who you see along the way."

The four didn't hesitate as they pushed through the people and back into the main hall, then headed to the armory. Most people in Camelora kept their weapons there, though Helen suspected that would soon need to change. She still felt uncomfortable carrying a sword. She envied Neil's ability to handle his with calm confidence. Her own bag with her crossbow was also in the room; one weapon, at least, that she had no qualms using. She picked up the bag with satisfaction.

When they reached the council room, most of the council was already there. Only Cynthia and Gowon were missing. Zaric stood in quiet patience at his usual place until they came through the door, Gowon holding a box as well as his own sword. Looking around the room, Zaric scanned each face, then nodded to himself as though he was satisfied.

"As most of you can tell from the warning signs we've seen," he began, "Camelora has been invaded. I can't tell how many people have entered, but from Camelora's reaction, the intruder or intruders are dangerous. We need to arm the people and separate you all into groups, then go out and search for the invaders. Please, don't fight unless you are provoked. Use every tactic you can to surround and capture anyone you find. But be cautious. If there are too many, keep yourselves hidden until help can come. Gowon, do you have the stones?"

Gowon nodded and held up the box.

"Each group will take calling stones," Zaric continued. "If you get into trouble, use them, and help will come to you. Now, go to your quarters of the city and gather the people. Even if the threat is small, it won't hurt for us to practice. I'm afraid this is only the first of many threats and they will only increase in severity."

He went around the room, quietly giving directions to pairs of council members on where to search. As he did this, Gowon walked around the room, handing each person two small, grey stones. The room began to hum as the members of the council whispered to each other, but Neil and Helen stood nervously aside, unable to say a word. Helen wondered who the intruders were—if it was only one or a larger army. The occupation of Veren came to the front of her mind in violent images, reawakening her fears. Men marching down the street outside the government house, their armor clanking, swinging their swords at anyone who tried to stand in their way. Children screaming. Men and women shouting as they ran to get out of the way, unprepared to stand against the armed men.

Helen considered the possibility that it might be Ian and Siri again, though she wondered why the two of them alone would attack in Camelora. Maybe it was Mered himself. She wasn't ready to meet any of them and she doubted that the people of Camelora were ready, either. A sharp pang rattled in her chest.

As though he were seeing inside her mind, Neil took Helen's hand and grasped it. She turned to him in surprise. "Don't go weak on me now, Helen," he said. "I need your strength. You were the only reason I managed to escape Ian before."

"You'll soon realize just how insignificant I am, Neil," she replied. Still, her doubts subsided.

Gowon walked up to them and held out the box of stones. Helen took one in each hand as she had seen others do and Neil did the same. "Put them in separate pockets," Gowon instructed. "If you run into trouble, rub the stones together counter-clockwise. Don't let them touch before then to avoid sending out an accidental call."

"How do they work?" Neil asked.

"Vibrations," Gowon replied, with a small measure of surprise, as if he expected them to already know. He walked on to the next person.

"Why do they always seem surprised when we don't know the answer?" Neil said in a tone that only Helen could hear.

When they had been given their instructions, the members of the council gradually left the room, until only Zaric, Helen, and Neil were left. "I want the two of you to go to the woods southwest of the city," Zaric told them, "through the passage in the large stone. Go into the trees and search that area."

"Just the two of us?" As he said this, Neil seemed more frightened than Helen had ever seen him before.

Zaric shook his head. "Of all the groups I'm sending out, you're the only one to question me. Yes, just the two of you. I trust you." He placed a hand on Neil's shoulder and took Helen's hand with the other. Then, without another word, he left the room.

"I'm more afraid we'll get lost than anything else," Neil stated, nervous and unsure. Helen knew her feelings mirrored Neil's.

Once outside of the city, the rain pounded down, driven with more force by the wind, drenching them within a minute. A thick fog gathered. Helen saw a few of the other groups before this fog appeared, heading in other directions, walking in orderly lines, each person an arm's length away from the person next to him or her. No other group contained less than ten people. They walked as though they had done this a hundred times before—Zaric had prepared his people for every possible situation. Now, though, Helen could see no one else. She stayed as close to Neil as she could to avoid losing sight of him. With the rest of the land swallowed by the greyness, Helen felt like she and Neil were once again facing the threat alone.

They soon reached the gap in the stone—an opening between two long, jagged walls too narrow for them to walk straight through. The stone wall with its gap, like the remains of a fortress, was the only element of Camelora that appeared to belong to a forgotten age, the only piece of the city's architecture that had not been maintained and used with each generation. No one knew what it had once surrounded or what its purpose had been. Its purpose now was as a convenient gateway to the forest. Once through, Helen wished they had brought a torch. The trees surrounding them were thick and tall, blocking out most of the dim light above. It would be difficult to see anyone coming toward them. Helen found herself doubting Zaric's decision to send them this way alone. Attentive to every sight and sound, they moved on. At least they were sheltered from the storm.

About half a mile into the woods, they reached a small glade—only a few yards wide—and were glad for the dim light it afforded them. Every sound came with sharpness and the rain still came down in thick drops. Their eyes scanned the edges of the clearing as they walked forward. Reaching the middle, Helen stopped as though an anchor had fallen in her stomach. She placed her hand on Neil's arm. There was a feeling in the air that she recognized—a sudden, slight, uncomfortable feeling that made her grow cold. In a mechanical motion, she pulled her crossbow from her bag and shot an arrow into the trees.

A man screamed in pain. He stumbled out of the trees, his fingers grasped around his arm, an arrow protruding between them. Helen gasped at the sight of him and Neil threw his arm protectively in front of her.

A cold, familiar voice asked, "Can you really *know* we mean you harm, Helen? You wouldn't hurt someone without knowing that."

Ian stepped out of the trees, a mocking grin dominating his face. There was a slight hesitation in his movements and a questioning expression in his eyes—questioning mingled with disbelief and tinged with fear. "Your instincts *are* getting better, Helen," he commented. "I will give you credit for that. Though perhaps I should take the credit myself. I would like to think I'm the one who made you what you are."

"What's wrong, Ian?" Helen asked, ignoring this comment. "You seem more nervous than usual. Did you expect to find me dead?"

"I'm glad to see you're not," he answered with mock relief. Standing next to the man who knelt on the ground, he pulled his sword from its scabbard and drove it into the man's chest, without taking his eyes off Helen. She screamed and took a step back. Her body trembled as the man groaned and fell to the ground. He didn't move again.

"You see," Ian resumed, "right now, Mered is praising Siri for killing you. If I bring you to him alive, her favor will slip—perhaps slip into a cold, dark abyss. No one should receive undue credit. Wouldn't you agree? He might enjoy having the chance to kill you himself."

"Why would Mered send you with only one companion?" Neil asked, beginning to understand what Ian wasn't saying. "I'm sure he knows that Zaric is prepared to fight him. It seems strange that he would send so few men to find us. Well, me, I guess, since he thinks Helen is dead. Or does he even know you're here? I can't imagine Mered would be pleased with anyone acting without his orders."

Ian's face twisted with anger and he threw his arm out at Neil. A shadowy force flew from his fingers, knocking Neil to the ground. He scrambled to his feet, pulling out his sword just as Helen pulled her own.

"Get out here, you fools," Ian sneered. Confusion filled Helen's mind until three more men came out of the trees, hesitating as they stared at their fallen comrade. One look at Ian was all it took to erase the panic from their faces.

"If I can help it," Neil stated, "We aren't going with you."

"I don't mean to take *you*, Neil." Ian held out his arm again, but this time Helen brought the broad side of her sword down upon it. With a cry of anger and frustration, he turned to her instead, holding out his other hand. The shadow from his fingers hit Helen in the chest with greater force than the blow that knocked down Neil, lifting her off the ground. She dropped down, the air knocked from her lungs. Neil lunged forward, swinging his sword at Ian and stepping to the side. Ian deflected the blow.

"Grab the girl," Ian instructed. "I'll take care of the boy."

Helen scrambled to her feet and ran into the forest, trying to get as far away from the men as she could. Pulling the stones from her pockets, she rubbed them together with numb fingers. A dull hum arose, which no one else noticed. Too late she realized she had forgotten to pick up her sword and crossbow. They lay on the ground a few yards away—and the three advancing men stood between her and her weapons.

"What did Ian promise you?" Helen asked. The men didn't answer but continued to come toward her, communicating with each other with nods and eye movements. "If Neil is right and Mered doesn't know you're here, he can't actually fulfill any promise he has made. It's not in his power."

The men only sneered, continuing their advance. Helen's eyes darted around her, trying to find anything she could use as a weapon. All she saw were twigs and leaves and small bushes. The deeper she went into the trees, the harder it was to walk backwards without snagging her clothes and falling into tree trunks. At the first opportunity, she took hold of a low branch and snapped it from where it grew, holding it out in front of her in place of her sword.

The man in the center lunged for her. Seeing the move coming, she was able to step aside. A memory flashed before Helen's eyes of fog gathering around her feet. The first time she met Ian. Scuttling backward, she bought herself some distance, holding out her hand with the palm down. Wispy mist wound through the trees, encircling her before spreading to the attackers, rising past their knees, their hips, their chests. It obscured Helen's vision of the men, but didn't hide them completely. She knew that it did the same for them. She rushed backward even more.

With a nod from the man in the center, the three attackers spread out. Helen knew she needed to come up with a plan before they surrounded her and struck. A different memory flashed, this time of violet walls and gathering storm clouds. There were already storm clouds here in Camelora, high above the trees. Reaching out again, this time with her palm facing up, Helen used her will to tug the clouds, bringing them down into the trees. Rain fell. The intensity of the drops increased until they were mixed with hail. The clouds mingled with the mist, further obscuring Helen's vision. But she didn't want to lose sight of the men. She backed farther into the trees, trying to keep the three of them in sight.

The clouds slowed the men down but didn't stop them. Now, one man stood in front of her while the other two were almost even with her on her left and right. Soon, not even looking from the corners of her eyes would allow her to see all of them at once. Fear crept up inside Helen's chest, holding her throat like stone fingers. Tears burned the backs of her eyes. She had come so far. She still wanted to accomplish so much. Zaric had plans for her. This fight was unequal—unfair—but she didn't want to give into the thought that she would lose.

Helen screamed, allowing the tears to push forward and fall, indistinguishable from the rain that ran down her hair to her face. Pushing past her fear, she dropped the branch and held her hands out to the side, fingers spread wide. Bright lightning flashed and she closed her eyes against the white light. The buzz of energy nearly masked the sound of the attackers screaming.

When Helen opened her eyes, she saw the men to her left and right lying on the ground, motionless, their clothes charred and smoldering. The man a few yards in front of her stood still, disbelief causing his mouth to hang open, dread emanating from his eyes.

Before he could regain his senses, Helen took up the piece of wood and rushed forward. She pulled back the branch and swung as hard as she could, shouting in her effort. The branch contacted the man's head, sounding with a crack. With a cry the man fell on his face, hitting his head against a rock. He didn't move.

Helen only spared a few seconds to watch. Blinded by her fear, she hadn't paid attention to how far the men were driving her into the forest. When she was sure none of them would come after her, she abandoned them, hoping to find Neil and Ian again before it was too late.

* * *

Neil and Ian faced each other. Worry enveloped Neil's mind, telling him that he hadn't learned enough yet to take on this fight. He was not much better than he had been on the day the Gateway opened—a young man trying to remember the lessons taught by a father to his young son. What he had learned in the days since slipped out of his mind.

In contrast to what Neil felt, Ian stood before him with more self-assurance than Neil had ever seen—self-assurance bursting with arrogance. More than once as they stood, each waiting for the other to make a move, Ian laughed at the younger man, as though he saw something funny that Neil couldn't see. Neil knew it was a tactic to anger, intimidate, and frustrate him. He didn't want to show any hint that it worked. Instead, he tried to adopt a challenging air of his own, not removing his eyes from his enemy.

Ian jumped at Neil, swinging his sword at the young man's arm in a playful fashion. Neil took a wide step to the side. Overreacting to the feint, he was unable to regain his balance quickly, leaving himself in a vulnerable position and taking a blow on the opposite side as Ian whipped him with his blade. Neil flinched and suppressed a cry, though his arm stung. He locked his eyes with Ian's, not letting go of the challenge. He allowed Ian to circle around him, never losing eye contact. The fierceness in Ian's eyes awoke all his fears, conjuring images of everything that had happened since leaving his cottage, mingled with a sense of hopelessness. Every failing was magnified. Neil now understood what Helen felt when she was in Ian's presence.

Ian lunged. Raising his sword at his opponent's first step, Neil held off the blow. The smile disappeared from Ian's face and only hatred remained. He pushed down, straining Neil's arms. Pressing with all his might, Neil moved to the side. Ian's blade hit the ground, pinned down by Neil's.

But Neil didn't know what to do next. Ian pulled his sword free and again lunged at Neil, who was forced to run back to avoid the attack.

The strikes didn't let up. Wherever Neil went in the glade, Ian followed. Neil defended himself with every move he had learned, pushing back the thought that he might not remember all that he should. He wondered how Zaric could send him out, as unprepared for battle as he was. As he blocked himself from another blow, an image of his cottage burning flashed through his mind. He swung at Ian, but the swing was deflected. The image of Ian coming toward him with a knife filled his eyes and Neil attacked again. His mind was crowded now with thoughts of every threat he had faced, making it hard to think clearly or strike with purpose. Exhaustion seeped through his body and he was losing the composure he desperately needed. He felt the strength and motivation being drawn away.

Knowing that Ian was again getting into his head, he shook the thoughts out, took a few steps, and prepared himself for the next assault.

"You know you can't beat me," Ian spat, a sneer returning to his face. "What's the point in fighting?"

"You're only one man," Neil returned, panting. "How do you expect to take on an entire city?"

"I don't need to fight the whole city. I only need to kill their king. Then Mered will see just how valuable I am. He will give me everything I want then. But you, Neil... what's the point in fighting me? You can still join me."

"No," Neil retorted without a second thought. "I won't stand by and let you hurt these people."

Ian attacked again and the two men matched blow for blow. No matter what he did, though, Neil couldn't get a good hit. Again, the fear crept into his mind, this time showing him what could be. An army descending on Camelora with Ian at its head. People running, trying to protect their families. Fighters cut down faster than they could run. Ian approaching Zaric, driving his blade through the king's chest.

"No!" Neil shouted, pushing forward. As it had done the day at the Gateway, the force of Neil's word pushed Ian back, knocking him off-balance.

He regained his footing before he fell to the ground, advancing on Neil with a roar. Thrusting too fast for Neil to block, he pierced the young man's shoulder. Neil cried in pain, but caught himself before he fell to his knees.

"I will protect these people with every particle of my strength," Neil cried, hoping his promise carried power. He swung at Ian from below, aiming for the man's chest. Ian caught the swing, his blade ringing against Neil's as he stepped forward, applying pressure to the cross-guard of his sword.

Neil held on too long. Ian pushed. There was an audible snap and pain shot through his arm. With a scream, Neil fell to his knees and his sword fell to the ground. He held his wrist, every thought filled with the pain.

With a look of triumph, Ian raised his sword. For Neil, this second stretched out, as if this second became minutes. His whirring thoughts straightened themselves like a rope tightening. The faces of the people who had befriended him and Helen came to his mind one by one. Next, he saw the faces of people in his own village, the people he had spent so many years distancing himself from. They didn't deserve a life of servitude to Mered. None of them deserved a life of fear and tyranny.

He knew that there were more battles to come before Mered himself would be beaten, but this one battle now, and the decisions he made in it, would be a deciding factor in the future. It was a future he was willing to give his life for.

Movement in the trees caught his eye. He turned his head to see Helen run up to the clearing and stop, her eyes fixed on him. He smiled weakly at her as Ian brought his sword down across Neil's chest in a deep cut. Its force caused Neil to fall forward, catching himself with his good hand. Everything, for a fraction of a second, was silent. Helen let out a strangled scream.

The pain of the blow didn't come. Neil opened his eyes, wondering if death had come that quickly, but instead found that he was still in the clearing. Casting his eyes up, he looked to Ian, standing in front of him. The satisfaction on the man's face twisted into a distorted look of pain and surprise. For once, Ian looked vulnerable and pitiful in a way Neil could never have imagined. Neil's eyes were drawn to Ian's chest. His shirt was sliced open and covered in blood. A deep gash appeared across his body—the wound that should have been in Neil's own chest.

Scrambling away from his enemy—yet unable to take his eyes off him—Neil felt for blood or a cut on his own chest. He was untouched. His sword lay on the ground a few feet away and Helen's still rested where it had dropped before. It was the tip of Ian's sword which bore the bloody evidence of the slash.

The fatal injury Ian inflicted had, by some power, reflected back upon himself.

Neil's eyes welled up in remorse as Ian fell to his knees and dropped his sword. His face lost its color as he tried to breathe, but the breath didn't come. Then, he crumpled to the ground.

# Chapter 19

Neil stared down at Ian, but he didn't see the body in front of him. He couldn't move. He didn't want to. His mind couldn't comprehend what he was seeing or what had happened. It crossed his mind that death was playing a strange trick, or that this was what death was really like—jumbled moments of confusion. The sound of Helen moving behind him and the throbbing pain in his wrist helped him to shake this thought and see reality. As she walked up, her eyes were fixed on the body, twisted unnaturally on the ground. His senses returning, Neil looked down at his sword. It was still clean. Again, he looked at Ian's sword, still surprised to see it stained with blood—Ian's own blood. The sight made Neil feel sick. He sheathed his own sword, then took Ian's and wiped it on the grass.

Beginning from the clearing where they stood, Camelora's atmosphere calmed down. The rain and wind stopped and the clouds in the sky parted with the brightness of afternoon sunlight. The usual intensity and vibrancy of the colors of the land glowed, from the grass and the trees to the dirt and stones.

A noise came from the trees. Helen and Neil spun, expecting to see the men who had come with Ian, but instead they saw Zaric coming toward them, followed by Theren and a small band of men. Among them were the three men Helen had fought, bound and captive. They walked with some difficulty, groaning in pain from the wounds she had inflicted. The Camelorans held their swords defensively, but their hard expressions soon turned to surprise at the sight of Ian lying on the ground. Zaric's face showed a pity that Helen and Neil hadn't expected.

Seeing Zaric, Helen found it impossible to suppress her emotions. The mixed feelings of relieved fear and unexpected sympathy overwhelmed her. Neil wrapped his arm around her, pressing her gently. He opened his mouth to say something—though he didn't know what—but Helen turned at that moment, as if she sensed his intention, and shook her head. Slipping out of Neil's grasp, she smiled faintly, then turned the smile toward Zaric, who nodded in understanding. Her shoulders weighed down by all she felt, she walked out of the clearing and disappeared into the trees.

Neil started to follow, but Zaric stepped forward and put a hand on his shoulder. "Will you take care of Ian, please?" he asked Theren. Theren stooped down without hesitation and picked Ian up, then left in the same direction Helen had gone. Another man took up the body of the attacker Ian had struck down as the rest of the men followed. Neil and Zaric stood still.

"Will Helen be all right?" Neil asked.

"Helen is much stronger than she thinks," Zaric replied, "but this isn't the sort of thing anyone wants to see. Are you all right, Neil?"

Hesitantly, Neil answered, "I don't know. My wrist..."

"Let's get that taken care of," Zaric said. "On the way back, if you think you can, I'd like you to tell me what happened."

* * *

Zaric found Helen standing at the top of the tallest tower of the palace, looking over the city and the land beyond it. She knew it hadn't taken him long to realize where to find her. He often found Helen in this

211

place.

The streets were filled with Camelora's citizens, coming back from the afternoon's expedition, recounting over and over again their stories of the day's events. Their voices drifted like musical notes, filled with varying degrees of emotion. The warm, late afternoon sun shone in calm rays, hanging reassuringly in the sky—or at least that was how Helen wished to feel. A few light orange clouds drifted over the land, and some dipped below the horizon, hinting at something farther on that couldn't be seen. This view tended to lift Helen's spirits, but right now there was a dullness inside of her that nothing could shake. In his familiar way, Zaric stood beside her for a few minutes without saying a word.

"Why do you never just start talking?" Helen asked, feigning annoyance.

"If we could see just a little bit farther," he stated, instead of answering the question, "we could see the sea."

"I've never seen the sea. With all of the traveling I've done in my life, that's one thing I've never seen."

Zaric turned his eyes to Helen. "Are you sorry Ian is dead, Helen?" he asked gently.

"Yes," she replied, after a short pause. "I know it's strange, because he wanted to kill me, but I still hated to see it. No one should have to die that way. It's odd that anyone *can* die that way. I never wanted any of this to happen. But I suppose no one does. I didn't really want to leave my home, to come all this way—to know that I would still have to go so much farther."

"Do you know why you were chosen for this task? You care deeply about people. Probably more deeply than they care about themselves, in most cases. I admire that in you. I never want you to stop caring about the people you meet, good or evil. And you're right. No one should have to die that way, but how many more people would die if Ian wasn't stopped? In the end, he destroyed himself. He wanted power, while Neil wanted to protect the people of Camelora. Neil's choice was more powerful than Ian's desire."

"I didn't know Neil had that ability."

"Neither did I. I doubt Neil did, either, for that matter."

Helen thought for a minute before asking, "Will I see more of what I saw today?"

"It's hard to know what we will see, but I'm afraid our situation won't get better. There is a probability you will see more death—sometimes the deaths of those you love the most and sometimes the deaths of those who fight against you. But if we're afraid of what we might see, how can we ever make this land better?"

Helen nodded. Zaric wrapped an arm around her shoulders and held her tightly. For a few long minutes, Helen rested her face against his shoulder, glad that he was there.

"I have a proposal for you," Zaric said when Helen pulled back a little.

"A proposal?"

"Next week, I will do what we discussed with the council and send out small groups of men and women to assess the damage Mered has done in the kingdom, to see what he is planning to do, and to gather as many supporters as we can. I'm afraid we have wasted some valuable time already. I have a feeling that things are much worse than any of us realized. I have chosen a special task for myself, Helen, and I would like you to come with me."

Helen's heart and breath stopped and she couldn't think how to reply. The request wasn't unanticipated, but after weeks of wandering, she didn't know if she could wander anymore. Camelora was a quiet place and she didn't feel she had to worry about anything here. Without realizing it, she had allowed herself to get used to the quiet pace of life in this city. Yet, as Zaric had said, she couldn't help thinking about all the people. Many of them had no idea of the real danger they were in.

Having seen even just a small glimpse of what Mered could do made Helen feel an obligation toward those who couldn't see it.

"We will be going farther than you've ever been before," Zaric went on. "We'll even see the sea."

Helen looked out at the horizon, at the clouds that went just beyond reach. She wanted very much to see where they led.

"And what about my father?" she asked.

"We will try to find out where he's been taken and how to bring him back with us. It's already part of the plan and I promise to do everything I can to accomplish it."

She reflected for a little bit longer, although this promise was enough to make up her mind. "Yes, then," Helen said, nodding. "I will go with you."

* * *

The council once again sat around the table in the council room with Zaric standing at its head. The excitement of the previous day was still winding its way through the city, going back and forth repeatedly, causing mixed sensations of hopeful anticipation and fearful unease. The people knew that something was beginning. The council felt the same excitements, but experience had taught them to control their feelings. They had the advantage of working with Zaric more closely than the other citizens of Camelora. Helen wondered how many of them knew as much as she did. This was also the first time Helen had seen Neil since Ian's attack the day before. After speaking to Zaric on the tower she had gone straight to her room and ignored every knock that came to her door. Now, they sat together—Neil with his wrist bandaged and arm in a sling. Helen didn't know if Neil had been invited by Zaric to make this new journey as well. Nothing he had said so far gave her any clue and she hadn't been sure how to ask.

214

"Thank you all for being willing to come," Zaric said, casting his eyes over the curious faces before him, "and so soon. I know we have met much more often lately than we are used to, but it might be some time before we are all able to meet again. The events of yesterday only prove just how vital it is that we put a halt to Mered's movements before he makes his way to Camelora himself. Our forces alone won't do much to stop him.

"Mered is also gaining more control throughout the rest of the kingdom, taking power by deceit and by force. This is not what the people chose when they elected to break into regions centuries ago. It is now time for us to implement the plan we have made and go out into the kingdom to find those who are willing to support us. We also need to see what progress Mered has made. I have selected a small number of people to join me in the search. I hope that, even with what we have seen in the past two days, you will be willing to help me. We don't know how far Mered has reached or where he might have planted his spies. As we gain cooperation, we will ask our new allies to spread the word as well. And I intend for us to find Meira and Stephen."

The faces around the table brightened at this statement, as though the very mention of these two names had shined a light inside each of them.

"I have spoken with Helen already," Zaric continued, "and she has agreed to go. Genevieve, Phyllida, Trevelyan, Arron, and Flecher, I would like for you to consider taking on this task as well. We will invite a few others from the city. Do you agree with this plan?"

He looked at each council member in turn, and each member answered—some readily and some after a slight hesitation—with a "yes."

"What about the people of Camelora?" Gowon asked. "What will they do while you're gone?"

"I've already thought of them," Zaric said, "but, thank you, Gowon.

Last night I asked Garrick to govern the land in my absence and he has agreed. Neil will act as his assistant, as someone who has lived outside of the city. We need his experience. He has proven himself and I can't think of anyone better suited for the job."

The men and women around the table fixed their eyes on Neil but said nothing. Helen sat very still, not sure what to think. She had assumed Neil would be going with them—she *wanted* him to go with them. She didn't know if she could be comfortable traveling without him. But another part of her thought of the man she had approached just a few weeks before, the farmer who was satisfied with his life and unwilling to change it, unwilling to admit there was anything wrong in the world, unwilling to help Helen find Zaric. That man was not the man sitting next to her, who had agreed to help govern a city he had once doubted the existence of. Now the farmer had become a governor, and the governor's daughter had become—someone she couldn't describe.

"But we will need all of you to support this plan if it's going to work," Zaric continued. "Garrick and Neil will need the support of this entire council, even those who will be leaving Camelora with me. Those of you who remain will still be responsible to help the people of Camelora prepare for an invasion, leading them if one occurs before we return. We also need you to prepare for the men and women we bring back with us and those who may choose to come on their own. This task will be much larger than any we have ever undertaken before, but I am confident we will succeed if we all support each other.

"Tonight, I will make the announcement and send out a proclamation after dinner. Those I have asked to go out into the kingdom will leave in two days' time. We can waste no more time and I am anxious to get started. Are we all in agreement?"

The council members nodding in thoughtful silence. Nervous energy hummed through the room. It was strange that, even though they knew this day would come, the anticipation of it differed so greatly from the reality. They began to doubt their own preparations for these tasks, a fact that was evident on each man and woman's face.

"Now," said Zaric, sitting in his chair, "let's discuss the details."

* * *

The horizon promised to produce another beautiful sunrise as Helen left the walls of the city behind and started across the fields. She wouldn't leave with Zaric until tomorrow, but she had so little to pack that there was nothing left to do. More than once she had placed the necessary things into her bag, taken them out again, and then packed them once more. It was hard to tell if the discomfort she felt was due to her bag or the general feeling of not knowing what lay ahead. Her tension, mingled with her jumbled thoughts, made it hard to sleep. Wanting to relieve some of her anxiety, she had decided to take this early morning walk. She also wanted to see a familiar face and knew that she would find the one she was looking for in the fields.

Neil sat on a low stone wall with his back to Helen, facing the coming sunrise. He didn't move and she wondered if her footsteps blended too well with the wind to be heard or if he was too lost in thought to notice her, but, without turning around, he said, "I'm not really sure what Zaric's thinking." It was then that he turned his face toward her, allowing a rare grin to break his lips. "But *I* think he chose the wrong man."

"Does Zaric even make mistakes?" Helen stated, sitting down and pivoting her legs to face the east. "Anyway, he chose Garrick, not you."

"He's still given me more responsibility than I like."

"He trusts you. And so do I."

"I wish I could go with you."

"I wish you could, too. That's the one thing that scares me the most.

I went all that way to convince you to come with me, and now I feel like I'm abandoning you. I trust no one the way I trust you. But they need you here."

"Why do they need *me?* There are men and women on the council who are being left behind—and they would be much more capable than I am to act as Garrick's second. I know hardly anything about Camelora."

"But you know the world *outside* Camelora. No one else here does."

"But do I, really? You're forgetting that I've spent my whole life on a farm, and the past few years trying to live unnoticed."

"Well, when you put it that way, what is Zaric thinking?"

"'Keep to yourselves, everyone,'" Neil boomed to the empty field, holding out his arms to emphasize his mock-speech. "'Pretend that nothing in the kingdom can touch you and all of this will blow over.'"

For once, Helen saw the remnants of the boy she once knew. Looking at Neil's smiling face, his smiling eyes—she felt a foreign and confusing spark in her chest. "You weren't really like that, though," she said, pulling her eyes away and trying to focus on the horizon.

"No, not really. I still read Grandfather's stories. Deep down, I knew that, eventually, the stories would find me."

"You don't feel ready," Helen stated.

"No," Neil answered frankly, without hesitation.

"Good. A great leader is willing to admit his weaknesses. I've met too many who don't. Perhaps you're the one with the most to learn. But you don't want to go home, do you?"

Neil considered the question, then shook his head. "No," he answered. "There's nothing there for me now. This is where I belong. It has all the feelings of home that my real home lost when my parents died, if that makes sense. Anyway, I've done too much to run away now. Knowing what I know, how could I ever go back to that life? I would feel too guilty."

"Are you scared?" Helen asked.

"Yes."

"I don't envy you. I hate to be leaving so soon, but I don't think I could take on such an important role."

"And this is coming from the daughter of a governor," Neil teased. "They're famous for being bred to please, marry governors, and influence their husbands. In fact, I wouldn't have been surprised if you had become a governor in your own right—the first woman to govern a region of the land. I haven't forgotten how you took charge of everything when we were children, or how you took charge of everything when you came to my cottage a few weeks ago."

"Very funny. But it was the map that was in charge. The map and the stories."

"The map that turned out to be wrong and the stories filled with mistakes."

"How was I supposed to know that?" Helen retorted defensively. She cast a glare at Neil but couldn't hide the playfulness of her tone.

They sat without words for a few minutes before Neil continued with a serious thread. "You will be careful, won't you?"

"I've nearly died once. I don't plan to do that again anytime soon."

"Yes, but you didn't intend for it to happen before. At least I trust Zaric to take care of you. There *is* comfort in that."

Another lapse followed, but it was a comfortable lapse. Helen wondered at what point in the journey to Camelora she had stopped feeling apprehensive about the times when they had nothing to say. She didn't feel the need to talk. They simply watched together as the colors of the sky and landscape became richer. In the distant trees, birds sang, leaves swished, and Helen picked out the sound of running water, which she had never heard before. She had explored so little of Camelora and craved the chance to explore it more.

"What will happen afterwards, Helen?" Neil asked. "When the supporters are gathered and you come back and we defeat Mered—what happens then?"

"I don't know," Helen sighed. "When I try to think that far ahead, I get a headache. Too many things right now are uncertain."

"I don't think you understand. You're all I have left in this world. No matter what happens, promise me you'll do everything you can to come back."

Helen looked down to where Neil's hand rested on the wall and placed her own on top of it. "You mean more to me than you know, Neil. I wouldn't go if I didn't believe—know—I would see you again."

Their eyes locked and thoughts were shared in that look—thoughts without words. Inhaling slowly, Helen rested her head on Neil's shoulder. She did her best to memorize this moment, holding onto every detail so she could pull it up again when she needed its strength. Sitting with Neil, washed by the morning light as the sun rose amidst a mass of golden-rimmed clouds, every fear melted away. Together, they were strength and vitality.

Together, they were home.

# About the Author

Like P.G. Wodehouse, Vibeke Hiatt has been writing since the age of 5. By the 8th grade, she knew she would one day major in English. She graduated with an AA and BS in English from Utah Valley University. After graduation, she worked as a phone book editor, then a data analyst, before leaving the corporate world behind to become a full-time mom. *The Forgotten King* is her first novel. She lives in Utah's Salt Lake Valley with her husband and 4 children.

To learn more, visit moonriseonjupiter.com.

**You can connect with me on:**

- http://moonriseonjupiter.com
- https://twitter.com/VibekeHiatt
- https://www.facebook.com/vibekehiatt

www.ingramcontent.com/pod-product-compliance
Lightning Source LLC
Chambersburg PA
CBHW050258110726
47898CB00007B/2464